I0670146

Anthologies
Night of the Senses: Carnal Caresses
Christmas Goes Camo: Melting the Ice
Treble: Trouble at the Treble T
Subspace: Head Games
Bound to the Billionaire: Made for Him

Corporate Heat

DOUBLE DECEPTION

DESIREE HOLT

Double Deception
ISBN # 978-1-78686-372-0
©Copyright Desiree Holt 2018
Cover Art by Cherith Vaughn ©Copyright August 2018
Interior text design by Claire Siemaszkiewicz
Totally Bound Publishing

This is a work of fiction. All characters, places and events are from the author's imagination and should not be confused with fact. Any resemblance to persons, living or dead, events or places is purely coincidental.

All rights reserved. No part of this publication may be reproduced in any material form, whether by printing, photocopying, scanning or otherwise without the written permission of the publisher, Totally Bound Publishing.

Applications should be addressed in the first instance, in writing, to Totally Bound Publishing. Unauthorised or restricted acts in relation to this publication may result in civil proceedings and/or criminal prosecution.

The author and illustrator have asserted their respective rights under the Copyright Designs and Patents Acts 1988 (as amended) to be identified as the author of this book and illustrator of the artwork.

Published in 2018 by Totally Bound Publishing, United Kingdom.

No part of this book may be reproduced, scanned, or distributed in any printed or electronic form without permission. Please do not participate in or encourage piracy of copyrighted materials in violation of the authors' rights. Purchase only authorised copies.

Totally Bound Publishing is an imprint of Totally Entwined Group Limited.

If you purchased this book without a cover you should be aware that this book is stolen property. It was reported as "unsold and destroyed" to the publisher and neither the author nor the publisher has received any payment for this "stripped book".

DOUBLE DECEPTION

Dedication

First and foremost, this book is dedicated to Sydney Alfrido, an incredible individual and outstanding friend. She was the inspiration for Sydney Alfiore. My friend, I hope I did you justice.

To George, who needs to be named, for all the information on coding and writing programs and the ways it can be manipulated. Any mistakes are mine.

To some very special people, without whom none of this would ever happen: Margie Hager, Joseph Patrick Trainor, Janet Rodman, Shirley Long. And to this group add Misty Dawn, Mary McCoy, Denise Chapman-Hendrickson and of course all my wonderful readers out there. We take this journey together. I love you all.

Prologue

"You understand if you fail we will have no choice but to erase you. We cannot leave any loose ends."

Eightball — or Eight, for short, a nickname chosen in recognition of expertise with a pool cue, although lately it also seemed to reflect the reality of what was happening — took a slow sip of water, swallowed back a surge of fear and studied the person across the table. Fingers tightening on the glass were the only outward reaction to the frightening statement. It didn't take an interpreter to know what "erase" meant.

This situation had become a chokehold. Working for Software By Design had been the best job ever. Liam Benedict was one of the best in the business and chose his programmers very carefully. Even though Eight had worked with him at Winters and Pryce, Liam had spared nothing in the intense vetting process. It was a damn good thing Eight's dirty little secret had somehow not shown up. The gambling problem was under control, out of necessity. But then a discreet invitation to a private poker game came from one of the players at the casino. Who knew that such an invitation would create such havoc?

"I do not intend to fail. I will not fail. I keep telling you that."

Shan leaned forward slightly. "Just so you understand the price of failure."

"Just so *you* understand that if this is some kind of trap, you won't like the outcome."

God! If only gambling hadn't grabbed hold like a leech, refusing to let go. If only she was better at it instead of losing again and again. Even a fat salary didn't cover the losses now. If only the people holding the markers offered more than two choices — payment or death. This had seemed so simple to Eight after that first contact. Obvious now that they'd sniffed the situation out, offering sympathy at first. Then the carrot on the stick.

The risks were significant but the money! That much money would make it all go away. And with it a vow never to gamble again. Ever.

Their conversation paused when a waiter stopped at their booth, bringing them a fresh pot of tea. Meeting in a restaurant hadn't been Eight's first choice of location, but Shan always insisted. Probably because the place was owned by either a friend or a relative and they had a small room with absolute privacy. Even so, prior to beginning conversation, Eight always used a tiny little gizmo to sweep the room for bugs of any kind, audio or visual.

"So suspicious." Shan's mouth curved in a slight condescending grin.

"Because it's my ass on the line," Eight said, emphasizing each word.

"Perhaps we should not proceed with our arrangements." Shan lit a cigarette and deliberately blew the smoke at Eight, knowing how annoying it would be. "But then, of course, you would still have that obnoxious debt hanging over your head."

Eight gripped the tiny cup that held the steaming tea, determined not to give any sign that Shan's little games and tricks had any effect. This was the source of the money — a great deal of money — so there was a logical reason for putting up with it. Enjoying the sparring, though? Not so much. Just the price to pay for the money Eight would be receiving.

Dirty money.

But at once Eight shoved the thought aside.

"Well?" Shan prompted.

Eight forced a calm that was necessary and blew out a slow breath. There was only one way to play this.

"If you are pulling out of this, just let me know." Eight stared across the table. "There are other customers equally as willing to pay the price, you know."

"But would they dissolve your unmanageable debt as well as give you money to hide away someplace?" Shan laughed, an unpleasant sound. "I do not think you want to fuck with me and my friends." Narrowed eyes telegraphed a warning. "We would not take kindly to it."

Eight leaned forward. "And I would not take kindly to being jerked around. Liam is planning to run three final tests on the program. Then I can insert the altered code and make sure it works without leaving a trace."

Shan blew another stream of smoke. "And how soon will that be?"

"Soon. Possibly next week."

"You guarantee it?"

Eight shrugged. "Nothing is guaranteed and you know it. Just be assured that before the software is delivered to the client, the hidden codes will be inserted and you will receive a thumb drive with them."

"Tell me again why you can't just give us the program itself on a thumb drive?"

"I told her." Eight bit back another surge of anger. "I already explained this. When Liam runs the final test, he inserts what are called duress words that will signal him if anything is being copied. He's paranoid about it. I have one shot to insert the back door and, trust me, I will get it taken care of."

"You'd better. If you yank our chains, you could stop breathing without warning."

And that was no lie. She knew it. But they were in this too deep to back out now. The image of all that money overrode everything else.

"No problem."

"And what if your boss finds out?" Shan persisted. "How will you handle that?"

"He will never find out." Eight made a face. "I'm smarter than he gives me credit for. Anyway, right now he's too busy with a proposed offer from a big conglomerate to buy an interest in Software By Design and fold him into the corporate structure."

"An offer? From who?" Shan's eyes narrowed, body tensing. "You did not tell me that. What if the dynamics of the company change? What if he wants to bring in more people? How will you handle things? This could make things difficult."

Eight glared across the table. "I don't see how. I'll be doing this the same way if there are two people or ten there. It won't disrupt our business at all. In fact, it might even make it better. He'll be too busy to pay a lot of attention to me. Besides, I've been with him from the beginning. He has no reason to suspect anything."

"I still say this could be a problem." Shan leaned forward. "What is the name of the corporation? Do you even know? That could make a difference, too."

"Yes. Wait." Eight thought for a minute. "It's some company out of Texas. Arroyo, I think."

"What?" Shan's anger was almost visible, the controlled rage vibrating in waves. "And you didn't think to inform us of this before?"

Eight frowned. "Why would I? What difference would it make? Big companies acquire smaller ones all the time. Then they let them operate independently. Big fucking deal."

"You idiot." Shan's voice had a lethal edge to it. "Arroyo is one of the biggest conglomerates in the world. The woman who owns it sticks her nose into everything. This could put a serious dent in our process. How could you not mention this before?"

Eight made a rude noise. "I just told you. Because it didn't seem like such a big deal to me, except for the possibility of a fat raise in salary. Why are you so worried about them, anyway? They aren't even in this state."

The look in Shan's eyes was enough to shrivel the hardiest person. "They will want to change things at Software By Design. Alter the process of everything. Perhaps even want to bring in their own people as supervisors."

Eight's stomach clenched at the words. "I don't think that will happen."

"But you can't guarantee it. If I had known about it sooner, I could have sabotaged the situation."

"And ruined everything?" Eight slapped a hand on the table. "Trust me to handle this. No one will ever know about our arrangement or be able to trace what I will do."

"Perhaps we should consider removing you from Software By Design altogether. Isolate you to work on your own." Shan took a sip of tea, staring at Eight over the rim of the little cup. "We are about to have too many cooks in the kitchen."

Eight just glared, beginning to get pissed off. "I need to stay there until the beta testing is finished. Only then can I alter the code. I cannot do that unless I am there. I have to be able to do it after all the testing and before they're locked down. There's a small window of opportunity I cannot lose. Besides, if I leave, I might as well send an email saying *I did this*. No, I can handle my boss and Arroyo."

"Overconfidence can be one's downfall," Shan said. "Don't sell Arroyo short. Taylor Cantrell has an international reputation for being sharp, intelligent and very aware of everything going on. And your boss will be on edge making sure nothing goes wrong with any of the current projects. Who knows what he might stumble over?"

"I'm clever enough to do this without ringing any warning bells." Eight was ready to smack the other person. Only the knowledge of the big payoff prevented it. "We design software that theoretically prevents hacking into the buyer's computer system and stealing files. Protects the highly sensitive files on their computers. Liam creates the original software, at least right now. But then he assigns it to two of us to tweak for the specific client."

"Why two?" Shan interrupted.

"So there's always backup. If I can write that kind of code, don't you think I can incorporate a back door into it without tipping anyone off?"

Shan released a deep sigh. "Fine. As long as there are no traces that would track back to you – to us – there will be no problem. We will still be keeping an eye on things to make sure nothing interferes with our plan. So. Shall we say one week from tonight? For the next report and update?"

Eight's jaw tightened. "Yes. One week from tonight will work."

"Then we will meet here again. Same time."

Eight really did not like the choice of meeting place. This was Shan's territory and anything could happen. However, they were close to delivery of the software. No more than a couple of weeks away. Once the code was delivered, the first payment would change hands. A thrill of excitement danced in the air.

So, Eight nodded. "Same time, same place."

The meeting was over. As always, Eight left first, knowing Shan had people watching every move from the restaurant to the car. If Shan decided to counterattack the Arroyo connection in some way…

No. Victory was on the horizon! *Keep that in mind.* Victory and untold wealth by the time this was finished. That was enough to banish any and all reservations and leave a smile on Eight's face.

Chapter One

"Son of a bitch!"

Liam Benedict leapt out of the way to avoid the car barreling down on him in the parking garage. At the last minute, it appeared to swerve, passing so close it almost touched him. And would have if he hadn't been quick on his feet.

"Asshole!" he shouted after them.

What was wrong with the people in this city? Didn't they know how to drive? He sprinted for the elevator before whoever it was decided to take another run at him.

Come on, Liam. Take another run? This isn't some spy movie, for god's sake.

Well, maybe not, but it was certainly something. This was the third time in two days he'd had a close call like that. Three near misses, three different cars. If he were given to paranoia, he'd think someone or several someones had it in for him. But what the hell would anyone want with him? He hadn't had time to piss anyone off. He was too busy trying to deal with the sudden explosive growth of his young software company and the huge opportunity that would make him a major player in the business. And while it was exciting, it was certainly nothing to make anyone try to run him down.

He'd been living, breathing, eating and sleeping this company for the past two years. A sudden avalanche of new clients had created the need for more software engineers. Right now, he needed at least six more hours in each day just to keep up. With the programs his company created, there was no such thing as totally satisfied with their work. He could not afford for one piece of software to leave unless he put his own stamp of approval on it.

But tonight, all that could change. Tonight's meeting could take Software By Design to a much higher level. Give him the capital to hire more people, expand to larger office space, add more equipment. And have a less insane schedule for everyone.

His assistant nagged him about it, his overworked software designers bitched about it and he was just lucky clients were so anxious to get his product they put up with it. He supposed that was what happened when a little startup company suddenly exploded. The boss was needed everywhere at once, including at his own computers to work on software.

These days, it seemed he was always running late for everything. Today, he'd even set his watch ahead ten minutes, but that hadn't helped. As usual, he got involved at the office, then didn't adjust for evening traffic. Now he was running late for the meeting that could change his life.

So what else is new?

At first, he'd thought the letter from Taylor Cantrell, CEO of Arroyo Conglomerate, was a joke. He'd been sure someone was punking him. He had a nice little software company growing at a rapid rate, mostly because of the unique way they designed cyber security software. But he had no illusions about its place in the universe. Why would a multinational conglomerate even be interested in him?

But a Skype meeting convinced him this was, in fact, a serious offer. That, yes, the CEO herself did want to talk to him was the biggest shock of his life. Then came the negotiations and the Skype meetings with all the attorneys. Then two days ago, with the meeting all set, Taylor Cantrell herself called him. And asked him to have dinner with them.

The first thing he did when he received the invitation was call his attorney, Hank Freemen, a man he trusted implicitly.

"What do you think is up her sleeve? I mean, the woman runs this gigantic conglomerate, yet she wants to spend an evening with what's only a small cog in the wheel?"

"Do it," Hank Freeman advised. "Taylor Cantrell is a unique individual — sharp, savvy, smart. Her attorneys tell me she gets briefed every day and knows at any given time what is going on with all the Arroyo subsidiaries. I've gone over the contracts with a fine-toothed comb. We're good to go there."

"Any reason you know of why they'd want this private dinner with me before all the paperwork gets signed tomorrow?"

Hank nodded. "I asked around. The Cantrells always set up a lunch or dinner before the final meeting when the docs are signed. It's not a problem or I'd advise against it."

"I keep thinking this might be some kind of trap," Liam said.

"Not at all. She just doesn't like the first live face-to-face to be at the meeting where we do the deed. I hear this is where she makes her decisions on how involved Arroyo will be in your business and how high your profile will be in Arroyo."

Liam was stunned. "You're shitting me."

"Not even a little. Trust me, Liam. It's all good, really."

"Not bad for a nerd with a degree in computer engineering from the University of Michigan," he joked.

"Liam, you were never a nerd," Hank told him. "Maybe a little obsessed with getting your degree— probably the reason you ignored all those hot chicks who did everything but take off their panties to get you to notice them."

"Yeah, right," he snorted.

"No shit." Hank chuckled. "But when you wouldn't get your head out of your computer they were happy to turn their attention to me. Liam, my boy, you made my college career very successful on that front."

He wondered if there was more truth than poetry in that. What he did know was he'd devoted every waking minute to becoming the best in his profession. Now it looked as if it was all paying off in spades. Tomorrow he'd become part of Arroyo International and tonight he'd be having dinner with the Cantrells.

They had flown into Tampa late today on their private plane and Noah Cantrell had texted him when their plane landed. Liam had offered to pick them up, but they assured him they had transportation covered. He should just meet them at the hotel for dinner. In their suite.

Eight o'clock too late for dinner? Taylor texted. *Sorry we can't make it earlier.*

He didn't care if they wanted to eat dinner at midnight. *No problem.*

You a steak person?

Yes. Love a good piece of beef.

Steak for dinner okay then? We fly it in with us from the ranch.

They flew it in from their ranch? He might be way out of his league here, although in their Skype calls both Cantrells had seemed like down-to-earth people. And opportunities like this didn't come along very often. Sometimes never.

His reputation for designing security systems that were virtually hack-proof had his customer base exploding. In fact, at the moment, the company was working on software for two engineering firms with defense contracts, plus the aviation construction company that would use one of the designs to construct drones for the military. They were his most lucrative contracts to date and he was obsessed with making sure nothing went wrong.

His designers were great, but he needed more of them. He was so overloaded himself he barely had time to look for them. What he really wanted was someone who could ramrod the software development while working on projects of his own. Or *her* own, he thought. *Better not be sexist here.* Someone who could double and triple check the work of his software designers. That would leave him free to deal with clients and handle a few special projects.

This could be the biggest thing for his company since he opened the doors.

It hardly seemed possible that less than five years ago he'd been working for a major software company and Software By Design had been nothing but a dream. Now, he was poised to enter the global stage, take a big leap forward. He ate, slept and breathed SBD. One of these days he'd have to think about getting a life. Maybe after tomorrow's meeting he could move ahead with leasing new offices in Tampa's ever-growing West Shore district and do a better job of juggling a list of clients that was growing every day.

At the staff meeting where he'd given everyone the news, the reaction had been about what he expected. Mixed. Everything from enthusiastic to skeptical to "I-don't-care-unless-it-means-more-money-can-I-get-back-to-work-now." After this deal was finalized, he'd sit and talk to each of them individually. Discuss the new clients and split the jobs so everyone would be invested in the change. Tomorrow, at this time, the deal would be inked and he could begin implementing his plans.

If I don't somehow screw it up.

He was beyond pissed at himself for running late. He was pretty damn sure the Cantrells weren't late for meetings. He just hoped his fucking tardiness didn't blow the best opportunity ever to come his way.

At the garage elevator, he tapped his foot impatiently and checked the time on his watch, then caught a glimpse of himself in the reflecting doors of the elevator. The effect of the custom suit that fit his six-foot-plus frame was only slightly diminished by the fact that his thick brown hair was in need of a cut. Of course, the frown creasing his forehead didn't help, either.

He forced himself to take a breath and soften the tension gripping him.

Fine. I look fine. Like a well-dressed executive.

At least he'd been smart enough not to show up in the jeans and T-shirt he usually lived in.

When the elevator arrived, he squeezed into a car already crowded and gnashed his teeth in frustration until they reached the ground floor. The moment the doors opened, he rushed from the parking garage into the lobby of the uber-luxurious Hotel DaCosta Waterside and Marina.

Always running. Always in a hurry.

He dashed through the lobby, already formulating what he hoped would be a passable excuse. Of course, all the damn elevators were busy. When the doors to one finally slid open, he started to barrel inside, practically knocking over the woman about to step out.

"Excuse me," he mumbled, barely avoiding knocking her over.

"You should watch — Liam? Is that you?"

As anxious as he was to push the button for the tenth floor, he looked at the woman he'd nearly knocked over, stunned.

"Sydney?"

She laughed. "Unless I changed my name since the last time we saw each other."

Liam stood there, just staring. Sydney Alfiore. Powerhouse criminal defense attorney. The woman of his dreams in all her striking reality. Her eyes were a startling shade of blue, almost violet, that with her ebony hair made a mesmerizing sight. A woman who, from the moment they'd met at a cocktail party, made him hard just looking at her. No other woman had ever affected him that way, certainly not that fast, and they hadn't even been out on a date!

He never lacked for female companionship when he wanted it, but he had yet to meet one who could compete with his dedication to building Software By Design. That night he'd merely been doing his obligatory duty, attending a party hosted by one of his clients. He sure hadn't been looking for a woman. Since SBD had ballooned in a few short months, the only figures he'd paid attention to were his bottom line and the ones he used to write code.

Until the moment he laid eyes on Sydney, who flat-out knocked him on his ass. She was the first woman he'd met who made him want things he hadn't even thought about. A woman who could change his mind about a lot of things. His cock had hardened in an instant, enough so he'd had to drink iced water not to embarrass himself. The air around them had sparked with a sizzle so strong it was almost visible. And that was just at that first contact.

She was a striking figure in any crowd, tall, with rich silky hair that fell to her shoulders in rippling waves and framed a heart-shaped face. Other women in the room faded into the background.

Her name wasn't unfamiliar to him. The media seemed to love her and gave her plenty of coverage. A criminal defense attorney acknowledged as one of the best in the southeast, she was usually tied up with some big-ticket client who sucked up all her time.

But that night when they'd met, he'd discovered she was also bright, funny and had a sense of humor that meshed with his. Sydney Alfiore was an enticing combination of authority and femininity, brains and sensuality. A woman who turned heads. She'd certainly turned his.

"Have dinner with me?" he'd asked when the party broke up.

"I'm so sorry," she'd told him in a warm, sultry voice. He'd heard real regret in her words. "I'm tied up with a complicated trial. But I hope you'll call me again."

He'd wanted to. Every time he thought of her, both his brain and his cock sent him urgent messages. He'd watched the progress of her latest trial, watching for the right time to call and ask her out. But then his own schedule had begun to suffer from overload. Arroyo had come into the picture, two new contracts had dropped into his lap and he'd barely had time to sleep, never mind spend time with Sydney.

Of course, that didn't stop his sleep from being disturbed by intensely erotic dreams, all of them starring Sydney. The two of them seemed caught in a cycle of conflicting career obligations. He was immersed in meetings and projects, and the few times he'd had a little break and managed to call her, she hadn't been free.

"But please keep asking," she'd always told him. "This isn't a brush-off by any means. It's just my crazy schedule."

"Listen, if anyone understands, it's me," he'd assured her. "So don't worry, I will."

How had he not pushed things aside to make time for her when she was free?

Now here she was, and he wondered if fate had placed them together at this moment in his life. He'd love to tell her all about Arroyo and have a drink to celebrate. Maybe even…

He held the door open, wondering if they could make something happen tonight.

"You here with your latest client?"

"In a manner of speaking." She sighed. "Two witnesses flew into town and I was just getting them settled upstairs. They're turning out to be a real pain in the ass. What about you? What brings you to this hotel?"

"Business. Something really big has come my way, Syd. We're inking the deal tomorrow. Tonight is sort of an informal meeting before the final details." He snuck a look at his watch. "I'd love to tell you about it, except I'm already late meeting these people for dinner in their suite. I don't know how long I'll be, but…"

Hell. Why did these things always happen when he was tied up six ways from Sunday? Damn, damn, damn.

"We always seem to be in a hurry for something, don't we?" A corner of her mouth kicked up in a rueful grin.

"Yes." He shook his head. "That's the damn truth. Life's a bitch sometimes," he groaned. "One of these days we'll find a few hours when neither of us is busy and maybe we can get to know each other."

Her lips curved in a warm smile. "I'd like that." Then she snapped her fingers. "Listen. My witnesses are meeting me down here for dinner in a bit. If you and I are both finished at the same time, maybe we can at least have a drink."

"I'm all for that."

"Me too. Now go. Don't keep your people waiting. And good luck with whatever this is."

"Thanks." He punched the button. "Later." *I hope.*

By now the elevator car was crowded and he drummed his fingers against his thigh as it stopped on two different floors to let people out. At last he was at the Cantrell suite, knocking on the door. With a supreme effort of will, he put Sydney Alfiore out of his mind. For now.

"Liam!" Taylor Cantrell's smile was warm and friendly. "Come in. Please. Dinner will be up shortly."

"Sorry I'm late," he apologized. "I try to make it a point to be on time."

"Of course." She took a step back. "Come in. Please."

"How many times have I told you not to just open the door like that?" a deep male voice asked behind her. Then Noah Cantrell was there, one arm around her waist, the other hand extended in greeting.

"Great to meet you in person," Liam said, shaking the man's hand. "Again, sorry I'm late."

"Not to worry." Taylor waved a hand. "We're well aware how life gets in the way, no matter what we do. Come on in. We'll have some drinks and chat. The food should be here any minute."

He was trying to adjust his brain to the kind of wealth where you brought your own steaks on your private plane and the hotel prepared them for you. Of course, if you owned the hotel you were staying at, anything was possible. And Software By Design would soon be part of their world.

"Relax." Noah seemed to sense his tension. "How about a drink? I always like a shot of bourbon before dinner."

"Sure. Sounds good. Thanks."

As he sipped the whiskey, Liam took the opportunity to really look at the couple. Noah's Native American heritage was evident in his darker skin, black eyes and coal-black hair, which he wore tied back with a leather thong. Even in an expensive silk shirt and custom-tailored slacks, there was still the air of a savage about him. His official title was vice president of security for the entire conglomerate and Liam would bet money no one ever gave him trouble.

Taylor was as light as Noah was dark, with auburn hair and emerald-green eyes. Her smile was easy, the smile of a woman comfortable with herself and her life. Not many people looking at her would guess she was the chairman and CEO of a multinational, multi-billion-dollar corporation. But in their two Skype calls, Liam had learned her mind was sharp as a razor and nothing got past her.

Looking at them, at their relaxed attitude and their ease with each other, a person would be hard-pressed to realize they controlled an obscene amount of money and a company with divisions all over the world.

At that moment, a knock sounded on the door and Noah went to open it.

"Dinner's here," he called over his shoulder and stood aside so the waiter could roll in the cart.

"I don't know about you men," Taylor said when the food had been set out on the dining table, "but I'm famished. My brain works much better when I'm well fed. Noah's, too. I think I've spoiled him. He loves a good thick steak and you can't beat Texas beef, especially from our ranch."

"It looks fantastic," he assured her

"Come sit, then. Bring your drink with you."

Liam ended up with Noah on one side and Taylor on the other. Very neat, he thought.

"I wanted to meet with you tonight in an informal setting," Taylor said. "Tomorrow you'll become part of the Arroyo family. Despite the size of the corporation, I like to think of it as a large family and maintain personal contact with all the executives."

"I'm sure that keeps you very busy."

"It does. But I also like to get a personal read on who we're bringing into the family. Just a quirk of mine."

"She pretty much knows what she wants." Noah grinned. "She probably knew your balance sheets and statistics better than you do before she made that first contact."

Liam was sure it was a hell of a lot more than a quirk. It took a steel-trap mind and an innate sense of what worked and what didn't to run a company the size of Arroyo. He didn't think there were too many people in the world, male or female, who could take the reins of a giant conglomerate like Arroyo and not only run it efficiently but grow it in a smart manner.

He set his glass down carefully and looked from one to the other. "I have to say, I'm excited at the offer to make Software By Design a part of Arroyo."

"I see it as a good fit for us," Taylor explained. "A software company that creates high-profile, sophisticated security software will be a great asset to a lot of our other divisions. And I like the idea that you are already designing security software for defense contractors."

Liam nodded, well aware Taylor was probably right. "I'll tell you this. We're growing so fast I can hardly keep up with myself." His mouth curved in a rueful smile. "Hence the tardiness."

Taylor flipped a hand at hm. "No big deal. In a successful business, adhering to a clock is often hard. And Noah's right. I did study everything about your company before I contacted you. But tonight, what I'm most interested in is your vision for SBD. Discuss the ways we can integrate it into Arroyo. Cyber security has become a necessity in this age of hackers, especially for firms with extremely sensitive material to protect."

"So." Noah lifted his glass. "I think we should start with a toast to John, who set this ball rolling."

John Martino was a top-notch forensic accountant who lived in Tampa and had done some work for a couple of Liam's clients, most notably a financial research firm, Optimus.

"I agree." Liam raised his glass and touched it to each of the others. Then he took a sip of the smooth, aged bourbon Noah had poured for him.

"To the future," Taylor toasted.

Liam replaced his glass on the table. One drink, he'd told himself. This wasn't the time to get sloppy drunk. He'd need all his wits about him with this power couple.

"I'm fascinated with what you do," Taylor told hm. "Creating original security software that can be tailored for specific clients. And you also create simulations, right?"

She might have phrased it as a question, but Liam knew she'd had every detail of SBD memorized before making the offer to him.

"I can see a wide market out there for this."

So could Liam, but until now he'd had neither the money nor the resources to make that happen.

"SBD is still just a small software company," he reminded her. "Not on anyone's radar."

"Not *yet*," Taylor agreed. "But it was something that we were looking for. Had been looking for." She took a sip of her drink then set her glass down. "Reed Molloy, the owner of Optimus, was pretty impressed with your firm. John brought it up to us during a meeting last month. Suggested you could be an important part of the Arroyo structure and we should reach out to you."

Liam swallowed a laugh. *Like they said, it isn't what you know, it's who.* He could have busted his butt for the next ten years and still not had this opportunity.

"They were pretty happy with the program we wrote for them."

Noah chuckled. "I'll say. Molloy told John he had four of his best hackers trying to crack it and they couldn't get in. There are several companies in Arroyo's structure I'd like to see you write software for. Companies that have extensive sensitive financial information, especially those that are in sales of any kind. Not to mention defense contractors. We have divisions that contract a lot of government work."

"And we'd love to write specific programs for them. We have several clients in that line of work. Truth to tell, when I created Software By Design that was my main focus."

"Then we're both on the same page."

As they ate dinner, Taylor skillfully led him through the details of the creation of his idea, how he'd gone about developing the company and what he planned now. The personal things that didn't show up in any report or analysis. By the time they reached dessert, she knew as much about SBD as he did.

"So, there you have it," he said, doing his best to look calm and relaxed. He filled his coffee cup again from the carafe on the table and took a swallow.

"Well, I'm looking forward to working with you to grow the firm. Your attorney assured us you're happy with the arrangement?"

Hell, yes, he wanted to say. He retained fifty-one percent of the company and had access to all the Arroyo resources.

"Absolutely."

"I like to get to know people personally before I sign the final papers," she told him. "I've had businessmen tell me I'm crazy to do that while trying to manage a company the size of Arroyo."

"Not many people would become that personally involved," Liam agreed.

Taylor took a sip of water and set her glass carefully on the table. "My father was killed by someone who wanted to use Arroyo for their own illegal ends. He was a smart man who built the company from nothing. And I mean nothing. But he trusted people to be as honest as he was and he was deceived by some people very close to him. I won't make that mistake, no matter how good someone or something looks on paper. I've trusted my gut all my life and it hasn't let me down yet."

Liam studied her face, looking for some clue as to what she was thinking. "I hope I passed the test."

"And then some." She smiled at him. "I'm looking forward to bringing you into the Arroyo family, Liam. Welcome aboard."

She held out her hand and Liam shook it, still in somewhat of a daze.

"This is as good as a signature," she told him. "You never have to doubt my word."

"I looked over the list you sent us of possible sites for a move," Noah said. "You might as well use the Arroyo cloud to get you the best deal and also add in all the goodies you want. I'd like to check them out with you tomorrow?"

"Of course." He'd make time. This was important.

"Great. Let's meet in the lobby around ten in the morning. That work for you?"

"It does."

Taylor and Noah both rose, a signal the meeting was over.

Liam tried to think of something to say that didn't sound too stupid. "I'm looking forward to this collaboration."

"As are we," Taylor agreed.

"By the way," Noah jumped in, "we're having the annual corporate barbecue at our ranch next month. We'd love it if you would attend. Your attorney, too, and any of your employees you think should be included."

Okay, at thirty-five years old he shouldn't be swallowing his tongue in astonishment, so he just nodded.

"That would be nice. Thanks. If you give me the specifics, I'll make plane reservations."

Taylor shook her head. "We'll be sending the plane for you. Your attorney, too. There are executives he should meet. And as I said, if you think there is anyone else that should be included, just add them to the list."

"Looking forward to moving ahead with this." Noah shook his hand at the door. "Taylor has felt for a long time Arroyo should have its own software division. Welcome aboard."

Then Liam was out in the corridor, heading for the elevator, slightly dazed.

Chapter Two

With everything rattling around in his head, Liam almost forgot to get off the elevator when it reached the main floor. Only when the doors began to close automatically did he give himself a mental shake, push them open and step out.

He got as far as the lobby before he stopped and looked at his watch. Ten o'clock. Too early to go to bed, especially when he was riding such a high on what was happening. Sydney had said she might still be around, and maybe finished with her legal duties for the night. They were having dinner in the restaurant. Surely they'd be finished by now, right?

He was about to turn and head in that direction to check, when someone called his name. He turned to see the woman herself walking toward him. His body responded at once.

Cock, behave yourself.

Thank the lord he was wearing a dark suit where the bulge in his fly wouldn't be quite as obvious.

"Oh, good." She hurried over to hm. "You're still here."

The warm, familiar female voice wrapped itself around him like melting chocolate. She smiled at him, looking sexier than ever. He looked around but didn't see anyone with her.

"I was just about to come looking for you. What did you do with your dinner companions?"

"Sent them off to bed. They've got a big day tomorrow, doing trial prep. They need all the rest they can get."

Liam hitched an eyebrow. "Should I ask what your client did to need your excellent services?"

Sydney laughed. "I'm his attorney. He didn't do anything."

"Oh, right." Liam winked. "Of course not. Well, do you have time for a drink, then? I imagine you'll be up early tomorrow, too."

Say yes.

"I will, but we have such a hard time getting together, let's take advantage of it."

"I agree." His mouth twisted in a wry smile. "Yeah, our schedules aren't exactly the kind that make for any kind of relationship. We should probably consider what's left of this evening a gift and make use of it."

Sydney nodded. "Absolutely. Besides, you look to be bursting at the seams about something, so let me buy tonight. Come on."

The bar in the hotel was designed for intimacy. No bright lights, just soft coach lamps on the walls and at each booth. The carpeting on the floor was thick enough to absorb sound, so the conversations were muted. It was a place to entice a woman to bed or put together a secret business deal. And perfect for intimate conversation.

Liam followed Sydney into the bar, nudging her toward a booth in the far corner that a couple was just vacating. Conversation around them was little more than a low hum, people engrossed in each other, some serious, some smiling. A low-key, nonthreatening situation. So why, Liam asked himself, did a tiny chill suddenly skitter its way down his spine?

As casually as he could, he glanced around, trying to spot anyone who might be fixated on him. Watching him. But no one seemed to be paying him attention. Still, the feeling was there and he could not seem to get rid of it. When they reached the booth, he slid into the bench seat that backed up to the wall.

Sydney stared at him, one eyebrow lifted.

"Are you okay? Would you rather not do this now?"

He shook his head. "No. Not at all. I mean, I'm fine and I want to do this." He was determined not to waste this unexpected opportunity. "Have a drink with you."

"Okay." She studied him for a moment. "If you're sure."

Liam forced himself to relax. Having a drink with Sydney was the perfect ending to a day when his life had taken an extraordinary turn. Who better to share it with than the woman he couldn't get out of his head? The woman he wanted to strip naked and tumble in his bed so he could do all sorts of wild things with her. If he weren't aware of how crass it would sound, he'd ask her to have that drink with him at his townhouse in South Tampa.

No. Not this way. At least let her think you have some class.

"This is nice." He studied Sydney for a moment. "It seems as though life keeps conspiring to keep us apart, so this is an unexpected pleasure."

She nodded. "For me, too. Sometimes I wish…"

"Wish what?" *That we could get together more often, like now, as I do?*

"Maybe that there were more than twenty-four hours in a day." She shrugged. "No matter. Here we are."

"Yes." He winked. "A very unexpected pleasure. It's great that we both ended up in the same place tonight, even if it's just for a short while."

"I agree. Tell me how your dinner went tonight? I want to hear all about what's going on with you. Whatever it is sounds very exciting."

"I'm not sure I have any personal business to mention, if you want to know the truth," he joked.

Even as he spoke, he was scanning the room for anything that might be the source of his uneasiness.

Sydney reached across the table and touched his hand. "Liam, are you okay? Is something wrong?"

He gave himself a mental shake and did his best to knock it out of his mind and into a corner. He was probably just being paranoid, anyway, and for what reason? Damn it, he wasn't going to waste this unexpected opportunity worrying about some figment of his imagination.

"I'm fine." He grinned at her. "This has been an exciting few days for me, Syd. I'm probably still just wound up about everything."

"Must be something big. Did your dinner go well? Can I ask who it was with?"

He nodded, then waited until the waitress served their drinks before answering.

"Are you familiar with the Arroyo Corporation?"

Sydney gave a ladylike snort. "Of course. Who isn't? I think they own the world."

He leaned forward a little, blocking out the rest of the bar. "As of tomorrow, Software By Design will be part of the Arroyo family."

"Liam!" Sydney reached for his hands and gave them a squeeze. "But that's fantastic. Truly. A major step forward for you. Think of all the doors it will open. The type of clients you'll attract."

"No kidding. I can hardly believe it myself." He took a swallow of his bourbon, savoring its taste. "I'm thirty-five years old and I feel like a kid at Christmas."

"As well you should." She smiled at him. "That's quite a coup. How did you pull it off?"

He chuckled. "In the most unlikely way. Someone knew someone who knew someone."

He told her about John Martino and Optimus and Martino's dinner with the Cantrells.

Sydney cocked an eyebrow. "Yes, John certainly knows all the right people."

"That is just the damn truth," Liam agreed. He touched his glass to Sydney's. "A toast to people who know people."

"Amen to that." She took a long sip of her wine. "I'm excited for you, Liam."

"Yeah, I'm excited for me, too. I'm not sure if when I left Winters and Pryce I ever thought Software By Design would take off the way it has."

"You have an incredible brain," she told him, "and you put that master's in computer engineering to good use. You always have. I'm glad this is happening for you."

"Thanks."

"So, give with the details? When is all this happening? Will you have to move from Tampa? How is it going to work?"

By the time he was through sharing everything with her, they had finished their drinks and another round besides. Sydney told him about her current high-profile client, a hedge fund partner accused of stealing millions from his equally high-profile clients.

"I just wish he wasn't such a jackass." She sighed and raked her hair back from her face.

He noticed she was wearing a pink silicone bracelet that she was idly rubbing as they talked. He wondered what that was all about and if it would be rude to ask her. Maybe next time. If there was a next time. He swallowed a sigh.

"Why take him on as a client, then?"

She gave a delicate shrug of her shoulders. "Doing a favor for a friend. Let's leave it at that."

Silence sat like a third person in the booth while Liam tried to figure out what kind of friend would get her to do this kind of favor. He was trying to decide what to say next, unwilling to let the evening end on such an impersonal note, when that same chilly feeling from before did its dance up and down his spine. As casually as he could manage, he shifted enough to let his gaze roam the entire bar. Of course, in the dim lighting it would be hard to recognize someone he knew, never mind identify a stranger.

"Liam? Is there a problem?"

"No. Yes. I don't know." He raked his fingers through his hair. "It's probably just me on edge because of everything that's happening."

"Are you sure?" She reached across the table and touched his hand. "Sometimes our instincts send us messages before our brain gets them."

"Maybe." He raised his hand to signal for the check. "Let's get out of here, okay?"

"Yes, but I'm buying, remember? My gift for the celebration."

In the lobby he looked around, trying to be as casual about it as possible. He checked off the clerks behind registration. A group of people near the entrance were chattering about something. A handful of people were lined up at the lobby coffee bar that stayed open until midnight. A man about his age, in jeans and a sweater, sitting in one of the armchairs in a conversation grouping, reading something on a tablet. A couple stood in a corner of the lobby, the woman tapping something on her cell phone. Three more couples passed him, chatting as they headed for the entrance.

That was it. No one who looked suspicious, or gave him an evil eye.

I'm probably making something out of nothing. Too little sleep.

Still, that weird feeling crawling over him would not go away.

"Liam?"

He shifted his gaze to Sydney, who was looking at him with a worried expression.

"I'm good. It's…nothing."

"It's not nothing when you've been figuratively and sometimes for real looking over your shoulder since we got together tonight. Please tell me what the deal is? Maybe I can offer some suggestions."

He blew out a breath. "This is going to sound really stupid."

"Nothing is stupid if it causes you distress. Come on." She tugged on his jacket sleeve. "Let's go sit at that little table way over there in that corner. No one's hanging around there and we won't be disturbed."

She settled them at the table then fetched two coffees from the coffee bar.

"We both probably need sleep more than the caffeine," she said, as she took the chair across from him. "But if something's bothering you, it won't help if the liquor takes the edge off your awareness."

He lifted an eyebrow. "You think two drinks will put me under?"

Sydney laughed. "No, but it can make you or anyone less alert. Come on." She lifted her cup. "Drink up."

Liam took a grateful sip of the hot liquid. It seemed to do more for him than the two drinks he'd had.

"Okay, give," she told him.

"I keep thinking I'm paranoid," he began and took another swallow. "Three times in the last couple of days I've been nearly sideswiped by a car when I was walking. Or running, like when I was heading for the garage elevator."

"Are you sure it wasn't just some crazy drivers being careless? I know, I know." She held up a hand and again the hot-pink bracelet caught his eye. "I don't think you have an overactive imagination, but I have to ask. And what else? What happened tonight?"

"I had another near miss in the garage. I could swear a car tried to run me down, but I got out of the way fast enough. Then I wondered if I was just being paranoid. But ever since I came out of the meeting tonight, I've had the weirdest feeling someone is watching me."

"In the bar? In the lobby?" He gave her credit. She kept her eyes on him and didn't swivel around to look at everyone the way he might have expected. Instead she looked directly across the table at him, leaning in slightly, as if they were lovers having a hot drink before...before doing whatever came next.

And damn it! He wished at that moment they *were* lovers. Then he realized she was staring at him and he hadn't answered her question.

"Yes. To both places. I tried not to be obvious checking out the bar, and I kind of skimmed a glance over the lobby when we entered it." He took another hit of the coffee. "The thing is, Syd, I can't think who would want to hurt me."

"What about any of your projects? Would they be adversely affecting anyone?"

He chuffed a laugh. "Only if they wanted to steal information and our programs prevented that." He shook his head. "Our primary purpose is creating client-specific security software. In other words, rather than writing a program that can be mass marketed, we design one for each individual client. That way there is no duplication of programs."

"And that means?"

"That even if, god forbid, someone found a way to hack into the software at company A, they couldn't use the same Internet tools to hack into company B."

He saw the moment the realization of it clicked for her.

"So, some hacker couldn't, for example, find a way into the software and use it to hack a bunch of different businesses."

Liam nodded. "Right. They'd have to be able to diagnose the codes for each program and find a back door."

"You must charge the earth for them. Not that they aren't worth it, by any means."

"We charge fairly," he told her. "But a lot of work goes into each one. We have to analyze the company's needs and decide what type of code to write that will do the best job."

She frowned. "Do you think you could have a disgruntled client? Or a business you turned away?"

He shook his head. "I hand carry my clients like they're God in person. I spend a long time in meetings with them before we write the first line of code, so we know exactly what we need to protect against. We have defense contractors, international banks, you name it. So, we can't use a one size fits all. That's how we made our name."

"And why Arroyo wanted you in their fold," she pointed out. "Do you think whatever is happening has anything to do with the Arroyo deal?"

He shrugged. "Who knows? But I'd have to say no. There's no one who'd profit by killing this deal."

"Maybe by getting rid of you, another computer engineer could step in and steal your clients. Or grab your Arroyo deal."

He wanted to laugh at the absurdity of it.

"I don't think so. If someone is that good, they could just go in and pitch their own firm. Sydney, computer engineering isn't usually a violent profession."

"Then there's something going on you don't realize and you'd better figure out what it is. Best-case scenario? It will turn out to be your overactive imagination. But I've been doing what I do for a long time, Liam, and I've learned to never discount someone's intuition over imagination."

They were silent for a long moment as Liam let her words sink in. He was probably out of his mind on this, the result of too little sleep and too much adrenaline. But he promised himself he'd be a lot more alert from here on in, and double and triple check everything at work.

"I hate to do this." Sydney's warm voice broke into his thoughts. "But I've got an eight o'clock meeting in the morning and I have to show up with all parts of my brain functioning."

"Of course you do." He could have kicked himself for wasting her time with his craziness. "My bad."

"No, no." She reached across and touched his hand. When she looked at him, he could see the same swirl of heat in her eyes he himself was feeling. Would they ever get a chance to take it for a test drive? "I've enjoyed this as much as you, Liam."

He chuffed a laugh. "Even with my craziness?"

She nodded. "Even with."

Her hand still rested on his, and the feel of her soft fingers sent heat charging through him. Great. He'd either have to drink iced water before he could stand up or walk through the lobby with a raging hard-on.

"Put this in your electronic memo," he told her. "Once your trial is over, we're going to have dinner — a nice long romantic meal in an appropriately conducive place — and see if whatever this thing is circling around us that we're both ignoring is more than just wishful thinking."

Sydney burst out laughing.

"Why, Liam. How could I resist such a romantic offer?"

He managed a lopsided grin. "Yeah. My bad. I seem to be out of practice here."

"No worries. I think I'm in the same boat." He lips tilted up in a sly grin. "But it was fun, right? A nice little break?"

"More than," he agreed. "And yes. I'd love it if, when we get past the craziness we're both in right now, we could get together."

Liam picked up both empty paper cups and tossed them in a nearby discreet trashcan.

"Where are you parked?" he asked.

"In the garage. You too?"

He nodded. "Come on. We'll walk together."

That itch between his shoulder blades picked up as they crossed the lobby, but no one approached him and no one followed him, at least as much as he could tell. They rode up in the garage elevator together, Sydney getting off one floor below him.

They were the only two in the elevator and when she stepped off, Liam pressed the door to stay open.

"You'll be okay walking to your car?" he asked.

"No problem." Sydney winked at him. "I always keep my trusty pepper spray handy."

Pressing the door open with one leg, he reached out for Sydney's arm.

"Wait. Do you have to use it very often? That pepper spray?"

"No. Don't worry. It's more to make me feel better." She smiled. "Really, Liam. My car is right over there. I'll be fine." She started to walk away, stopped, turned back and stood on tiptoe to brush a soft kiss on his mouth. "Luck tomorrow."

Stunned, Liam just stood there, holding the elevator door propped open, until she was safely inside her car and the motor had turned over. He waved as she backed out of her space and headed toward the down ramp. He did his best to put the shock of that kiss out of his mind so he was hitting on all cylinders, but it was damn hard. What he really wanted was to go after her, drag her to his townhouse and spend the rest of the night losing himself in her.

But that would have to wait until this deal was settled and he wasn't looking over his shoulder. Another few minutes and he was at his own car. He moved with caution as two cars took the ramp up to his floor from the one below. He relaxed a fraction when they sought out parking spaces and didn't come near him. No one else appeared while he jogged from the elevator.

Only when he was in his own vehicle and heading down toward the exit did he allow himself to breathe normally. And wasn't this fucking ridiculous. He was a thirty-five-year-old computer engineer. Could he get more boring? Who would waste their time coming after him, anyway?

He tried to check on his way home to see if someone might be on his tail, but there were too many cars coming out of the downtown area to where he lived. Either they were good at losing themselves in traffic or no one was following him. Or maybe he was just becoming neurotic.

Chalk it up to too little sleep and too much coffee, he told himself. Maybe if he got more than three hours' sleep tonight, it would help. But there were no cars behind him when he pulled into the lane behind his townhouse and into his garage, with nobody on his tail.

Still, he breathed a lot easier when, after checking to make sure no one was parked just outside in either direction, he closed the garage door and was safely inside his townhouse. Before turning on any of the lights, he stood beside the living room window and peered outside through the tiny slits in the closed window blinds. He'd bought this place because it gave him the feeling he was living in a house but without the upkeep, and it was located conveniently for everything he needed. For the first time since he'd moved in, he wondered if he would have been better with a condo in a secure building? The row of townhouses fronted right on the sidewalk. Anyone could walk by and casually look into his living room.

Crap. Paranoid much, Benedict?

At last, sure that no one was going to come pounding on his door, he forced himself to take a few deep breaths and settle his crazy nerves. Then he flipped on the light in the foyer, climbed the stairs and dumped his briefcase on a chair in his bedroom. In seconds he had stripped off his clothes and fallen into bed.

When he closed his eyes, he prayed for a dreamless sleep. Instead, what he got was an image of Sydney Alfiore dancing almost naked, and a hard-on that threatened any possibility of sleep.

Chapter Three

Sydney closed the door to her condo and let out a long sigh. Today had been long and tomorrow promised to be even longer. Prepping witnesses for trial was never an easy task. For this case, it seemed to be even harder, considering the fact she had grave doubts about her client's claimed innocence. The smart thing would have been to walk away and not accept the case. Unfortunately, the request for representation had come from a former mentor and she was hard-pressed to refuse.

The two witnesses she'd met today were going to be as difficult as her client. She just hoped they could testify convincingly and not look like they were covering up a secret, as they had tonight at dinner. She hated clients like this and once again cursed her old mentor for saddling her with the case. Oh, well. She'd do what she always did, fight fiercely for the win. And after she'd won, she'd tell her former professor she didn't owe him another thing.

She had a brief flashback to a moment in her final year of law school, moot court, an exercise every senior law student went through. She'd been playing the role of the defense attorney, and she'd thought she'd presented such a passionate defense. A freshman had been drafted to play the part of the eighteen-year-old defendant. Sydney had been so full of herself and misplaced self-confidence. She had been shattered when the mock jury found him guilty and the mock trial judge sentenced him to twenty-five years in prison.

Even worse, her professor whom she idolized had flayed her with his words, criticizing her entire defense and telling her if she didn't get her act together she'd end up in a third-rate law firm, one where beggars couldn't be choosers. She'd since learned to don her invisible cloak of armor, one where only the very tough Sydney was seen by the public. Certainly not the uncertain senior law student who still lurked beneath the surface.

It had started right after the disastrous mock trial when she'd bought the silicone bracelet with the date of the jury verdict on it. She put it on at the onset of every new case and never took it off until the trial was concluded, not even to shower. It reminded her what happened when a person was overconfident and ill-prepared.

The one bright spot in today's very long day had been running into Liam Benedict in the hotel lobby. God! The man was a walking sex dream and she'd bet money he didn't even know it. Not that he wasn't seen with his share of women. But, from what she knew, he was as driven in his career as she was in hers. She was passionately in love with the law. He was equally immersed in his firm that created specialized security software. She wondered if his relationships were as brief and shallow as hers.

Now, half-undressed, wearing only her panties, half-slip and bra, she leaned against the bathroom door and closed her eyes, calling up the image of the man. He was well over six feet, a comfortable height to match hers when she wore heels. He had the same thick black hair she remembered, the kind you wanted to run your fingers through, a little longer than last time she'd seen him but it softened the sharp line of his jaw and his cheekbones. His eyes were the same black, like polished onyx and framed with lashes so thick they made grown women weep with envy.

But there was nothing the least bit feminine about Liam Benedict. Oh, hell no. Quite the opposite. For a man she would label a geek considering what he did, he oozed masculinity from every pore.

Careful, girl, or you'll be drooling all over yourself.

The moment she'd met him, every hormone in her body had come to attention and saluted, and they hadn't returned to parade rest yet. Every time she and Liam bumped into each other it spiked again. It frustrated her that they both had such insane schedules that carving out any personal time together was impossible.

Anyway, it had been so long since she'd had anything that passed for a personal life she might just be painting him with a broad brush. Graduating from law school at the top of her class and passing the bar exam with a perfect score were what had gotten her into one of the top criminal defense firms in the southeast. So many of her friends had gone into financial litigation, real estate law or other fields that seemed so dry to her. She had toyed briefly with the idea of applying for a spot on a prosecutor's staff, but then in her senior year something happened to a friend and she'd been committed to criminal defense.

She had stuffed everything else in a virtual closet while she focused one hundred percent on her career. Then she'd used her connections to snag a couple of high-dollar, high-profile clients, insisted on being first chair in their trials and won acquittals for them. After that she'd pretty much been able to write her own ticket and had recently made junior partner.

She knew there were male counterparts in the firm who would gladly have done whatever to get rid of her. Her own profile, however, was so visible now that all they could do was gnash their teeth and send dirty looks her way. She had her own law clerk, two associates who reported to her and a personal assistant she swore had been created in heaven.

But none of that kept her very warm at night.

Of course, she hadn't met any men who'd inspired her to make changes in her schedule. Not, that is, until Liam Benedict. Even with as little time as they'd spent together, she had a sense there was something special there if they could just find time to get to it. Somehow, she'd carve out that time after this trial, even if it was just for a lunch, to see where this could go. *All work and no play,* she reminded herself. And she definitely wanted to play with Liam Benedict.

With a sigh, she hurried through her nighttime routine, pulled on a sleep shirt and crawled into bed. With so much racing through her mind, she was sure she'd have trouble falling asleep, but ten seconds after her head hit the pillow, she found herself falling through a cloud of black velvet into a dream.

"I wanted you the minute I laid eyes on you." Liam's voice was rough with need. "I damn near crippled myself trying to keep my hard-on from showing."

"I can feel it now," she half whispered, pressing her hips forward so she cradled his erection.

The scent of his aftershave tickled her nose, something fresh and citrusy. Whenever they'd been together, usually with other people, she'd maneuvered to sit beside him and managed to content herself with inhaling a deep breath and, drawing it into her system.

"We have too many clothes on." The words were almost a growl. "I've wanted to do this since the first time I set eyes on you."

He unbuttoned the tiny pearl buttons on her blouse, cursing them as he popped each one through its buttonhole. His cock flexed at the sight of her beasts filling the satin and lace cups of her bra, the dark nipples like shadows through the material. The hunger she saw in his eyes poured fuel on the fire already burning inside her.

"I want to taste every single inch of you," he growled, running the tip of his tongue across the swells of her breasts. "Lick your nipples and bite them. Lap that pussy I've been dying to dive into."

He used his hands to tug the drape of her shirt down her arms and toss it to the side. Next to go was the bra. He flicked the catch open and eased the straps down her arms. Liam sucked in his breath at the sight of her bare breasts with their swollen nipples, swiping the tip of his tongue across each one. Then he pressed his mouth to the valley between those breasts and strung kisses down over her abdomen until he was stopped by the constriction of her skirt. He took her mouth in a rapid kiss as he eased down the zipper of her skirt and pushed it past her hips. When he touched the material of her pantyhose, he stopped and groaned.

"Pantyhose. Jesus, Sydney. You'll make me come before we even get to the main event here."

He lifted her and placed her on the bed, where he'd already tossed back the covers. Disposed of her shoes then hooked his thumbs in the waistband of her pantyhose and ever so slowly eased them over her hips and down her thighs. Sydney closed her eyes, giving herself over to the feel of his hands on her skin. When he stopped with the garment only down as far as her knees, locking her legs together as if a rubber band had been tied around them, she opened her eyes to look at him.

"Liam?"

He was staring down at her, such intense hunger in his eyes her breath caught in her throat.

"Do you know how sexy pantyhose are?" His voice was hoarse and ragged. "My cock is so hard right now I'm amazed I can even stand here like this."

Then he bent forward, placed a kiss on her navel and traced a line down to where the waist of the pantyhose rested. Sydney wriggled her hips as much as she could, signaling him not to stop there. His low, raspy laugh was like a match to her body, igniting the nerves in her pussy and making her walls flex with need.

As much as she wanted Liam to hurry, he seemed just as determined to take his time. At last he pushed the pantyhose farther down her legs, one inch at a time, until he could finally pull them free. Still fully clothed, he kneeled between her thighs, parted the lips of her sex and took a long, slow lick with his tongue.

Sydney was already so aroused from the little bit of foreplay that his touch brought her right to the edge of release.

"Not yet," Liam insisted and placed his mouth on her delicious cunt again.

He nibbled the swollen nub of her clit, tugging it with his teeth before soothing it with his tongue. He lapped greedily at every inch of her core, fucking her with his tongue and drawing her toward release until she was strung tighter than a bow. He held her thighs wide apart, nibbling and licking and sucking so every nerve was tormented and spasms began deep inside her.

"Please," she begged, teetering on the edge of release. She was sure her pussy was already dripping, her body responding to the teasing and tormenting and arousing.

Liam leaned forward and touched his lips to hers, carrying her taste with him.

"Please what?" he murmured.

"Please let me come."

His laugh was low and raspy. "Is that what you want? But I'm having such a good time."

"Yes." She tossed her head from side to side,

"Then we'll have to do something about that."

He lifted her legs to his shoulders, a position that made her feel so completely open to him. Then he proceeded to use his very clever tongue and fingers on every part of her pussy, teasing and tormenting, bringing her to the edge before easing back, until she was ready to cry with the frustration of it. At the moment she was sure she would lose her mind, he thrust two long fingers inside her, pumping them, and bit down on her clit.

She screamed as the orgasm shook her in its grasp, her inner muscles convulsing and every nerve firing. Her body shuddered as her inner walls spasmed over and over. Liam held her in place, his mouth busy, his tongue lapping every bit of her cream.

The shudders subsided and she lay there, limp, her breathing erratic.

"Your body is so beautiful when you orgasm." He licked each nipple, twisting his tongue around the tips. "Your nipples darken and get so hard. I can see the beat of your pulse at the hollow of your throat that tells me how aroused you are."

He lowered his head and pressed his tongue to that spot, licking it gently.

"But what about you? Your clothes are still on."

His laugh rumbled from his chest. "Not for long."

With an economy of movement, he stripped off his shirt, his slacks and his boxer briefs. From beneath the heavy lids of her eyes she admired the lean, muscular line of his body, the curve of his ass, the long, toned legs. And, when he turned around, the impressive size of his cock.

She caught her breath. "I don't think it will fit."

He chuckled and wrapped his fingers around his shaft.

"You'd be surprised. Tonight, I'm going to feel the walls of your sweet cunt grasping it and milking it. Feel your cum bathing it."

And he proceeded to describe in filthy, erotic details exactly how he was going to fuck her. With each word, each phrase, her need increased. As exhausted as she was from her orgasm, her body was already responding to his words and the rough tone of voice.

He adjusted her on the bed so she lay flat with her legs splayed. Then he took the condom he'd moved from his wallet and placed on the nightstand earlier and rolled it on with practiced ease. Sydney watched fascinated, as he managed to cover the entire length of him.

Positioning himself between her thighs, he reached with his fingers to press open the lips of her core, his gaze focused on her wet flesh. He teased at her opening with the tip of his shaft, heat blazing in his eyes, the muscles in his body tightening as he slowly eased himself inside.

The fit was tight, but she was so well lubricated from before that he was able to slide into her hot passage with minimal effort. He moved slowly, inches at a time, his gaze locked with hers, watching her for signals that it was too much or too little. The moment every inch of him filled her, she clenched her inner muscles around him.

"Yes. Do that more," he urged in a taut voice. "God. Your cunt is like a tight fist around my cock. I could stay like this forever. Tell me how it feels for you."

"Full," she breathed. "Like you fill every one of my empty spaces. And hot."

"We can do better," he told her. "Wrap your legs around my waist."

When she did, she crossed her ankles and dug her heels into the small of his back, pulling them together even more tightly. Liam leaned forward, bracing himself on either side of her, and began the slow glide and climb up that ladder to the pinnacle.

Then he began to move, slowly at first, letting her body adjust to him. Then faster. With every increment in speed, her body responded even more, until she was pulling him as deeply inside herself as she could.

Liam was thrusting harder now, an accelerated in-and-out glide, the muscles of her sex gripping down on him like a vise. Desire spiked as his eyes darkened.

For a long moment, their gazes locked and she was sure he could see right into her soul. Then, hips pistoning, cock filling her, he drove them both to completion.

By the time her body had stopped shuddering and Liam's breathing had steadied, they were both covered with sweat. They lay there, glued together, while their racing pulses and their heart rates slowed.

Liam eased himself from her body, taking care with the condom. Sydney lay where she was, exhausted, while he disposed of it. Then he lifted her and placed her on the bed so her head was on the pillows. Sliding in beside her, he spooned around her and tugged the covers over them both.

Sydney sighed in satisfaction as she nestled against him. She had never felt so replete, so fulfilled or satisfied. She thought she could lie in Liam's arms forever. If only that pesky little noise that had suddenly drifted in from *somewhere would go away. She pressed her head into the pillow, willing the whatever it was to silence but instead it kept getting louder.*

"Liam?" she murmured. "What's that sound?" When he didn't answer, she nudged him, with no effect, so she finally pushed herself, unwillingly, to a sitting position and –

"Fuck!"

Sydney shoved her hair out of her eyes. The first thing she realized was that Liam Benedict was not in bed with her and she had not just had the most incredible sex of her life. The second thing was the insistent sound of her alarm, letting her know that it was business before pleasure and she'd better get her ass into gear.

With a heavy sigh, she climbed out of bed and headed for the shower. Trial prep waited for no man. Or woman.

Damn!

She wondered how Liam's day was going and if he'd think it odd if she called later to find out?

* * * *

Shan sat in the coffee shop, forehead pinched in a frown, speaking softly to the man opposite.

"We do not have to kill him, you fool." The words were spat out in a clipped, angry tone. "Just incapacitate him. Besides, since when have you been so squeamish about disposing of anyone?"

Aaron Huang looked across the booth, his body rigid with controlled anger. "What's the point in just injuring him? He could still get to the meetings. Still proceed with the merger. Still sign the papers. It defeats our purpose."

"Our purpose," Shan said, in a slow, measured voice, "was to incapacitate him long enough to delay the signing of the papers until our project is finished. Or at least that was the point when we last discussed this."

"Yes." Huang glared at her, his face set in an implacable expression. "Because when the idiot you hired failed to kill him on the first try, we had to alter our plans."

"I don't see why." Shan took a slow, deliberate sip of hot coffee. "What's the difference if we had to make another try to kill him or just knock him out of the action for a while?"

"First of all, in case it didn't occur to you, too many attempts to kill him would have negative results. It would raise questions. He could call the police. Or hire a security firm to guard him. You said Eight told you he is big on security, right?"

"Yes, that's true. But why would it not have the same effect to just injure him? I don't understand."

"The method of driving the car changes. It is less direct. You can't brush off someone who heads a car directly toward you. But an accidental sideswipe? He could chalk it up to a careless driver."

"Well," Shan sneered, "it doesn't matter, because your drivers didn't succeed, either."

Huang curled his hands into tight fists. "If your friend Eight wasn't so stupid and had realized how important this merger is and told you about it when Benedict first announced it to his staff, we would have been better prepared. Now it is my neck on the line as well as yours, you idiot."

Shan kept his voice low and even, although the undertone of rage was detectable. "I don't think you want to start pointing fingers. You are the one who pointed me toward Eight to begin with."

"Because Eight is the most talented of the coders. For what we want, we need someone who can do this without leaving any trace whatsoever, either in the program itself or the files stored on Software By Design's server. And who, by the way, could hack into that server if necessary."

Shan took a moment to answer. "If you think that, you are a fool. Eight has already told me that Benedict is such a talented and sophisticated code writer there is no way to get into the server once the files are locked. And any attempt to do so trips a number of warnings that would lead right back to Eight and complicate our situation. I thought you knew everything there was to know about this."

Huang rested his forearms on the table and leaned forward.

"Do not think to criticize me, not for this or anything else. My position is such that I can replace you at any time." He paused for effect. "And bury you so deep in the organization no one would ever hear of you again."

At that moment Shan knew why people committed murder and was very glad for the absence of a weapon. There was already enough trouble brewing in this operation that needed to be kept way below the radar.

"Fine. Since we cannot do anything to sabotage the meeting, we need to discuss ways to accomplish what we need before Benedict begins making changes."

"I have some thoughts on that matter." Huang leaned back, lifted his cold drink and took a sip. "Listen carefully."

Chapter Four

Liam looked down the length of the long table around which his staff were gathered, trying to read the expressions on their faces. They all looked so youthful to him, all of them in their twenties, which to him at his age seemed decades younger. Was that how he'd been ten years ago? Five?

He wondered if that had been the way the partners at Winters and Pryce had looked at him. Lord knew they'd been shocked senseless when he'd told them he was leaving. The first couple of years had been lean, with just enough contracts to take care of Rosalie and the two software engineers who had left to join him. Rosalie was pure gold, working for a smaller salary until the contracts began rolling in, and keeping every end of the business running smoothly so he could find clients and design programs.

Then one of his clients had recommended him to someone and his name had gotten passed along again and his client base had begun to build. Now, with this new security program he'd designed, with its ability to be reconfigured for each individual business, his client base was exploding. The Arroyo deal was not just the frosting on the cake; it offered him unlimited opportunity for growth and opened the doors to international expansion.

He wanted his staff to be as excited as he was. Last week he had explained to them what was happening, wanting to give them a heads-up, with the proviso that anything could sidetrack it at the last minute. Now he was able to tell them it was a done deal and he waited for their reaction.

"Okay, people. This is it. A new chapter for Software By Design. The deal with Arroyo is done. Agreements signed. It's all official."

For a long moment, no one said anything.

Finally, Teri LaGrange broke the silence. "So, we're officially part of Arroyo now?"

Liam smiled and nodded. "Everything's been signed and we're good to go."

Teri, Phil Hamilton and Sy Fantip were the three software engineers who had left Winters and Pryce to join Liam's startup company. In the beginning before the first check came in, he had paid them even when he was not drawing a paycheck himself. They had worked long hours to satisfy each client. To Liam, they were his extended family and were paid more than the three people Liam had hired subsequent to that. They had a vested interest in whatever happened.

Teri leaned forward, her eyes filled with a questioning look. "We know that means a hugely big deal to you and, trust me, we are all celebrating for you. But exactly what does it mean for the rest of us?"

"Yeah." Pete Herriot shifted in his chair. "What's gonna be happening here? I'm guessing a lot of changes, but how will they affect us?"

Liam had done his best to keep them in the loop from the beginning. And Pete's question was one that no doubt everyone else wanted to ask.

"Yes." Liam nodded. "There will be some changes, but good ones."

"Like how?" Teri again. "What kind of changes?"

Tall, with masses of dark hair that she wore in a long braid, she was usually dressed in jeans and what he called her T-shirt du jour. Today's said, *Keep calm and don't fuck up your program.* She always took the lead in a meeting and kept the questions coming.

"To start with, we'll be moving to larger quarters, which should make all of you happy. When I rented this space, there were just four of us. Now we are seven and sharing space not meant to be shared. Plus, with the increase in our client base, I'll need to hire more software engineers."

Liam could almost feel everyone's brain vibrate with that.

"Are you saying we can't handle the load?" Teri demanded.

"Not even a little." He chose his words carefully. "But I think we can all agree everyone is struggling right now under the tremendous increase in workload. The reason our client base has exploded is because of the quality of our work. I don't want anyone so overloaded they can't give the proper attention to every project. This is no reflection on any of you. I hope you know that."

Pete nodded. "We do. So where are we moving to? And when?"

"As to where, once I knew this deal was going through, I spent time checking out possible locations and I narrowed it down. There's a new building in the West Shore district that will be a perfect fit for us. We'll have an entire floor, so more room for everyone, like individual workspaces. We'll also have a bigger room for the servers. The rest will be office space plus that bigger break room you've all been asking for."

"Yes. Thanks." Pete looked around at the others. "I think all of us will be happy with more space."

"You'll also have a lot more places for lunch. You can get almost any kind of food within minutes of where we'll be."

The news was received with laughter, as he expected.

"Do they deliver?" Teri asked.

Liam took a moment to frame his answer. "They do, but not to us. That's one of the changes we'll be making in the move."

"Why?" Sy frowned. "What's the big deal about getting food delivered?"

"The entire building will now be secure, not just our offices." Liam looked around the table to make sure everyone was listening. "Each one of you will use a digital fingerprint to open the building's external doors, front and back, along with a coded key card. Same card gets you into the elevator and same thumbprint gets you into our offices. We'll have cameras set up front and back to cover the parking areas. There will also be two guards on duty, including one in the lobby, and cameras at the front and back entrances."

"Why do we need guards if the building is that secure?" Jason Hamill was the first person he'd hired when his client list had begun to grow. His work was incredible and Liam considered it a feather in his cap he'd enticed him away from the larger firm he was with. "Isn't that overkill?"

"Yeah." Carl Lopez, one of SBD's newer and best coders, sat forward in his chair at the far end of the table. "Who are we so afraid of all of a sudden?"

Liam had expected all of this and was prepared for it. Software engineers whose sole function was to create the codes for specific programs had a tendency to look at the world through a narrow lens. It was up to him to make them comfortable with changes and create the best work environment for them. While he was still happiest, as were most of them, locked to a computer in jeans and a T-shirt fueled by coffee and sugar, he had moved well beyond that. He might handle the more delicate programs and created the base codes from which many other programs sprang, but he could still get into their heads. He wanted an environment in which they felt comfortable to do their best work.

"It has to do with the nature of the other businesses in the building as well as ours," he explained. "Besides SBD, there are only three other tenants. Two are defense contractors—one of whom happens to be a client— and the other is a firm that specializes in data recovery and backup systems. There may be some rare times we work a project together. But in each case, the firm is required to have a security clearance for the business and each of its employees. You know that. You all went through that when we got our first government contract. Right?"

Heads bobbed in acknowledgment.

"Becoming part of Arroyo," he added, "also means that more of those lucrative government contracts will be coming our way. You know the security those demand." He grinned. "But it also means bigger salaries for everyone."

"You won't hear anyone complaining about that," Jason assured him. "So is the new location confirmed? Do you know when we'll move?"

"Arroyo is taking the lead on this," Liam said, "mostly because they have the clout and the power to make things move fast."

"You mean the money," Teri pointed out. "Are we selling ourselves to them?"

Liam had been waiting for this to crop up. From the time he'd made the announcement about the change, he'd known there was apprehension running through the staff. Everyone was territorial about what they had built here and not too happy with anything that might change that.

"Not at all. But we are definitely taking advantage of their resources. I had started negotiating a lease on a new building when Arroyo first approached me, but I wasn't getting anywhere fast. So, they did the expedient thing—they bought the building and will be setting our floor up to our specs."

"What about existing tenants?" Jason wanted to know.

"They stay. Arroyo will work with them to make sure they're happy, but I think that's a given. Their work is as sensitive as ours. Maybe more so."

"What do we do about our work during the move?" Jason again.

"Good question. We will have a twenty-four-hour shutdown and reboot. I'll go over the specifics with you when we get to it. You'll have plenty of notice and we'll secure all the files digitally. I'll meet with each of you individually to see where we are with your particular project and take it from there."

"Won't that put us behind?" Jason persisted. "We'll lose time and momentum while we're down."

Liam wanted to tell him all that had been taken into consideration, but he had to remind himself that Jason, like the others, looked at it from a different perspective. They were focused on their particular project and didn't do well with interruptions. He was well aware of that and had made arrangements to minimize the disruption.

"No. Arroyo is sending us a trained crew to help with the physical move and an experienced tech to help me with the digital move. I will personally oversee the situation to make sure nothing happens to corrupt the servers." He looked around the table. "Anyone else on this particular subject? Okay, kids. Let's talk through the rest of this and then I'll let you get back to your work."

When the meeting ended, Rosalie Mercado, his assistant, walked back to the office with him. A force at the age of fifty, she had left Winters and Pryce with him, telling him she was ready for a challenge. She was sharp, savvy, could control the programmers who came to work for him and kept things running smoothly.

"Big changes around here, Liam. Exciting times."

"I hope that's a plus," he told her. "You've been very positive about Arroyo from the beginning. I hope that hasn't changed."

She shook her head. "Not a bit. I think this is a great thing for the firm, especially with those new contracts sitting on my desk that need to be addressed."

"Yeah." He sighed. The thing he hated the most about the business was…the business. He loved meeting the clients, probing their minds to find out exactly what they wanted the creating their specifically tailored software. It was the paperwork that did him in. For the most part, Rosalie handled it with Hank Freeman, but he was the one who costed it out and set the pricing.

"I'd say you've got another day's grace with some of them," she told him, "before they start getting antsy."

"I promise I'll get to them today." They had reached their suite of offices. "How about if I take the top three right now and get to it?"

"After you phone Taylor Cantrell back. She called just before the meeting and wanted a report on how everyone reacted to the move and any possible changes." She cocked an eyebrow. "If she's this hands-on with every unit of Arroyo, the woman must never sleep."

"I think she has a lot of backup with her husband," Liam told her. "He doesn't say it, but when you're with them, you can tell she's his primary focus. She did tell me the other night, however, that her father was killed because he trusted the wrong people and maybe took his eye off the prize there. She's determined that will never happen again."

"From everything I've read, she's doing a damn fine job." She picked up three folders off the stack on one corner of her desk and handed them to Liam. "You said you'd start with three projects, so here they are."

"And I'll get right to them." He grinned at Rosalie. "Whoever thought when it was just you and me and three software programmers that this would happen?"

"I did." She winked at him. "Now go get to work."

"Yes, ma'am." He gave her a sharp salute.

Rosalie burst into laughter. "Work, Liam."

He had been at his desk digging into the hated paperwork when he heard a knock on the doorjamb. He looked up to see Teri standing there.

"Rosalie said it was okay, if I didn't take more than five minutes." She laughed. "I have the feeling she'd toss me out if I took more. You're very lucky to have her. *We're* very lucky."

"She's a force of nature, for sure. Okay. Then five minutes it is. What's up?"

"About the new people you'll be bringing in." She stuffed her hands into her jeans pockets.

He studied her face for a clue. "You have someone you want to recommend?"

"No." She shook her head. "I just wondered if you'd be assigning them to any of the projects we're already working on."

"I don't expect to." Liam motioned her forward. "Is there a problem I'm not aware of?"

"Not that I'm aware of, and I'm sure I would be." She tipped her head to one side. "But you know how obsessive we all get working on a project. We have a sense of ownership."

"I hope you know I'd never do that. I spend too much time with each of you making sure you know what's required to stick someone new into it with you. Besides, I thought I was clear that I'm hiring new people because we have a sudden wealth of new clients. Where is this coming from, anyway?"

She shrugged. "Some of us were just gabbing about it after you left the meeting, that's all."

He quirked an eyebrow. "*Some* of you? Do I want to know which ones?"

She shook her head and stood up straight. "Forget it."

"Just tell me this. Was it Carl?" He was the newest addition to the staff and Liam was still figuring him out.

"No. It doesn't matter. I knew this was a bad idea. I told them they were nuts, but I figured I'd ask you anyway. We're good to go."

"I hope so, because there's a lot riding here." He pointed to the files on his desk. "Now that we're part of Arroyo, we're only going to get busier. There are some great opportunities for all of you here, to make a name for yourselves and also get some healthy salary increases."

"I know, I know. I hear you. Listen, I'm going back to work, so just forget I ever said anything, okay?"

"Forgotten already."

But, after she left, he sat staring at his desk, wondering just where this had come from. He had built SBD on the Winters and Pryce model, where each software engineer had his own projects supervised, in this case, by Liam. Often, if a project was too massive, there would be collaboration, but by and large everyone worked on their own. Liam was the only common denominator. It was his responsibility to know each project well enough to step in if need be.

He wondered what they would think if they knew about his failsafe. Once each piece of software was complete and passed beta testing, he locked it digitally on the servers, so no one could access it. He was the only one who had the password to open it, although Hank Freeman had a thumb drive with copies of all the passwords on it, in case anything ever happened to him. It was always best to be prepared. But before he did that, he opened the program and inserted a special code that would trigger an alarm if anyone tried to access it without permission. A message would be sent directly to his computer, his cell phone and his special watch.

Not that he didn't trust his staff, but, well, as he'd learned early on, shit happens. And now that they were part of Arroyo, he could not afford a misstep.

Chapter Five

"We have to find a way to delay this, but my people will not be happy." Shan took a sip of tea. "Still, if what you tell me is true, Benedict will personally be checking each and every ongoing project to make sure the move does not disrupt anything. That means he will be hands-on with everything. I see no opportunity for you to insert the back door."

Eight took a healthy swallow of the bourbon the waitress had brought. Tonight, alcohol was called for more than something as mild as tea or even beer.

"I can take care of it." Pause. "I told you I could and that still stands."

Shan snorted. "Yes? And how exactly do you plan to do this with him all over everything?"

"That's my business."

Shan's fingers curled around the cup of tea. "No, it is ours. This has been a key operation for my people since we first learned about the drone Campbell Avionics had been contracted to develop."

Eight frowned. "Why is this particular drone so important? This isn't the only one being developed."

"But it's the only one with special equipment and the ability to evade radar tracking. We need that for two reasons." Shan looked hard at Eight. "And none of this is to be repeated. You know what happens to people who blab."

Eight shrugged. "Who's blabbing? I'm just curious. We never get the specs of what we're writing a program to protect, only the type of antivirus and security software needed to build the cyberwall."

"I find it amazing that you are able to write software for each individual project."

Eight waved a hand in the air. "It's just words and numbers that you put in a specific order to get what you want."

"Even so. It takes clever brains like yours to know the order to arrange them in. And don't get a big head because I used the word clever."

"But we are." Eight's mouth curved in a nasty smile. "Without us, no one's programs would be secure. Look. You came to me because out of all the coders at SBD, you managed to find my weak spot. Fine. I get it. But it's still my brains you're buying."

"Only if we get what we want," Shan pointed out. "Meanwhile, you have to get me the schedule of the move and how things will be handled. Most of all we want to know when your project is to be delivered to the client."

Eight nodded. "That will be when beta testing is complete. I have a short window after beta testing to access the files and insert a back door."

"And you are certain it is undetectable? They won't know this happened until we have our own drone in production as well as a method to take control of theirs?"

"Do I look like an idiot?"

"I'm just constructing the timeline in my head. What if something happens to Benedict? Does everything grind to a halt?"

Eight stared at the person across the table. *What the hell?*

"What's going on here?"

"Just answer the question."

"The software still has to be delivered to the client. We would take turns beta testing. But—"

Shan held up a hand. "That was a rhetorical question. We like to be prepared for all eventualities."

But Eight knew there was nothing rhetorical here.

"You will let us know once the back door is inserted," Shan continued, "and the software delivered."

"As long as I get my money."

Shan's eyes narrowed. "We are paying you a great deal of money to do this. If it fails, you won't need the money because you won't be around to spend it."

Eight fought back a shiver at the words' cold delivery. There was no doubt this had come with a great risk, but the money was definitely worth it.

"I said I'll take care of it. And Benedict won't know who did it, if it's ever discovered."

"Oh, rest assured." Shan snorted. "That's the first place they will look once their drone is compromised. But you will have your money by then and be long gone, if you wish. But tell me this. What happens if somehow the defense contractor discovers they've been compromised? Anything can happen, you know."

"But I told you—"

Shan held up a hand. "Just humor me. What happens?"

"You know damn well. The first thing Liam Benedict will do is come after all of us. I hope by then I've been able to completely erase the ghost files."

"Ghost files?" Shan scowled. "Explain."

"I will have erased all traces of the back door from the server by then, but those files can still linger out there in outer space. A good forensic data specialist can search for them." Eight took a sip of bourbon and let the flavor roll around on her tongue. At least it settled her nerves.

"Timing is going to be everything on this. When is the big move scheduled for?"

"Benedict wants it completed before Gasparilla, which is less than three weeks away. The software is scheduled to be delivered to the client no later than the week before."

Eight had lived in Tampa for ten years and loved the annual festival celebrating the supposed invasion of Tampa by the pirate Jose Gaspar. For one week the city went crazy, with parties both private and public. She and her friends loved it and always took in as much of it as they could. They never missed the big parade as it wove its way down Bayshore Boulevard and into downtown Tampa. Parade day was always barely controlled insanity, with people drinking, float personalities tossing beads and candy and people trying to run along with them.

"You must let me know when you have a date certain," Shan insisted. "Do you think he'll make the deadline?"

"Count on it. He's determined to get the software delivered and the move accomplished before Gasparilla week. He doesn't want this hanging over his head. He rides on one of the parade floats, dressed as a pirate, if you can believe that. And is involved in some of the events."

"You don't think the chaos of preparing for the move will interfere with finishing the project?" Shan asked. "We have our own deadlines. It is imperative that we have the back door to the software and that we stay on schedule."

Eight pushed aside the empty glass, signaled the waiter and ordered another drink, ignoring the displeasure on Shan's face. A long swallow of the icy liquid did a lot to soothe jangled nerves.

"I told you. Everything is on schedule. Arroyo is sending a crew to facilitate the move. I will let you know when the program has been installed on the client's server and tested there. Then it's up to your people. Is there something new I should know about?"

"That's no concern of yours," Shan snapped. "You just give us the back door. If it works, you'll get your money and we'll be done." Shan tapped a cigarette against the ashtray. "Just keep me up to date on everything—and I mean *everything*—especially changes in the schedule. My people will prepare for all eventualities.

"What are you thinking?" Eight demanded. "Something that will fall back on me? You said there'd be no heat for me on this if I did what I was supposed to."

Eight was beginning to have a bad feeling about this. Once Shan had the back door and could access the design programs on the client's computer, there was no guarantee Eight would even see one penny of the promised payoff.

"And there won't be. You will be paid once we know it works."

"Half on delivery, the other half after you test it." Eight was not going to budge on that, not with Shan bringing uneasiness to the situation.

"We don't go back on our word, but you need to be sure to keep yours."

"Fine." Eight wanted to know what the big rush was, but figured the less known, the better.

"You still have sufficient phones so you can continue to dispose of them after each use?"

"I do."

"Then that is all for today. One week from tonight for an update. Go ahead. You leave first."

Fuck, Eight thought, heading out of the restaurant. *This is getting to be a real pain in the ass. If the money wasn't so great...*

But it is, and you need it to get your ass out of the crack you stuck it in. So shut the fuck up and get on with it.

Fine. As long as I get paid.

Chapter Six

The day felt as if it had been a week long and Liam was ready for it to be done. Since the dinner with the Cantrells and the meeting where all the documents had been signed, it seemed he'd been running nonstop. Noah Cantrell had asked him which of the buildings he'd been looking at for the move was his preferred choice. They hit it early in the morning following the dinner, and by the end of the day, Arroyo had had a sale pending.

Since then, Liam had been on a fast track. He'd signed six new clients and met with his staff to set up a schedule as to who would start which project when. Two of them, he kept for himself. When he'd set up Software By Design, he'd made a promise that, unlike his former employers, he'd never remove himself from the actual business of writing software.

His days were filled either meeting with new clients or checking on ongoing projects or trying to focus on his own projects. Many nights he didn't get home until midnight, after starting out at six in the morning. But at least things were moving along at a rapid clip.

All of this he ran by Taylor Cantrell, although she'd been insistent that the business was his to run as he saw fit. Her only input would be to steer major clients his way, to recommend divisions of Arroyo that she thought would benefit from SBD, or step in if she saw things were for whatever reason going downhill. That, he vowed, was never going to happen. So he went about the business of running his firm, only tapping into Arroyo when necessary

But despite the fact that he scarcely had a minute to himself, now and then he got that same eerie feeling he was being watched. It didn't happen in any one place. Sometimes he'd sense it while backing out of his garage. That was stupid, because how would he spot anyone? He lived in a place that saw a lot of traffic day and night. Other times he'd get that little shiver down his spine when he was getting coffee to go, or gassing up his car. Once he'd even felt it at the deli where he'd stopped for takeout.

But he never spotted anyone who looked out of place, or seemed to be showing unusual interest in him. Not only that, he'd never spotted the same person twice. So, if, in fact, someone was stalking him, they were doing a damn good job of it. At least no cars had tried to sideswipe him again.

The date of the move was set from the time he'd signed the Arroyo agreements. It would happen just prior to Gasparilla week. He hadn't expected the floor they'd occupy would be ready to their specs by then, especially moving the computers and servers. A good example of the phrase 'money talks, bullshit walks'.

Arroyo made things happen that Liam knew would not have if he was doing this solo.

He'd sent an updated schedule of projects to everyone's computer. It included due dates of each one in process as well as the dates of the move and how each coder would be individually affected. He'd been so consumed with everything that he was stunned to realize four weeks had passed and the date of the Cantrell barbecue was almost on top of him.

"I don't suppose I can beg off this, right?" He was standing by Rosalie's desk, running down a list of things with her.

"You can't say no to this, Liam," Rosalie said. "It's almost a command performance. Anyway, why would you want to? It sounds like a spectacular event."

"Yeah, yeah, yeah." He grinned at her. "Maybe you could go in my place."

Rosalie snorted. "Yeah, right. Besides, you're the one they want. I'd be a poor substitute. And anyway, you need to rub elbows with the people you're now occupying Corporate Central with."

"Corporate Central?" He winked. "Do I get a badge and everything?"

"You don't need one," she joked. "It's written all over you. This is the big deal, Liam. The one that will put you at the top of the heap."

"Let's hope it doesn't turn out to be the top of the trash pile. Okay, it's this Sunday. That's three days from now. Gives me time to tie up some loose ends."

Rosalie tapped her keyboard and brought up an email. "They're sending the plane for you. Their executive assistant said it will be at Tampa Executive Airport and ready to go wheels up by nine o'clock. I believe the pilots will be here overnight Saturday."

"Okay. I'll be sure to get there in plenty of time. There's parking there, which works out great."

"Also, there will be two others on the flight with you. John Martino and an attorney, whose name I don't have."

"Attorney?" He wrinkled his forehead. "Did she say who? I know Hank had to cancel because one of his high-ticket clients had a legal emergency."

Rosalie shook her head. "I'll bet he's pissed about that.

"No kidding. He's already sore from kicking himself." Liam smiled. "But it's great that John is going. I'll have a chance to spend some time with him."

"I have a note here that you'll be leaving to come back about six o'clock San Antonio time. They're an hour behind us. Taylor Cantrell's secretary said John and whoever the other person is requested to leave then, but if you wanted to spend the night, they'd accommodate you in one of their guest suites."

Liam lifted an eyebrow. "No kidding? That's very nice of them, but I think I'll leave when the others do. There's still a lot to do here. Okay, what's the latest on the move?"

Rosalie had been coordinating everything for him with her usual quiet efficiency.

"It's all set," she assured him. "You've checked that building out six ways to Sunday to make sure everything's been done right. Besides, Arroyo's got their people all over it. Really, you only had to tell them what you needed when you had that meeting and they were on top it."

"Two more weeks," he reminded her.

"And your meetings with the existing tenants went fine," she added. "I'm sure it helped that one of them is a client."

He nodded. "No kidding. Okay, I have about another hour's worth of work to do and then, surprise! I'm going to go home, order a pizza and watch the ball game on television."

"Surprise is right. Well, you certainly deserve it." She winked at him. "Maybe a hot woman would make it even better. I could suggest one or two."

"Why, Rosalie, are you trying to fix me up?"

She snorted. "If I thought it would do any good. One of these days, Liam Benedict, some woman will come along and you won't know what hit you."

He wanted to tell her he'd already met that woman but that he was so obsessed with the business right now he couldn't even manage a date with her. Anyway, she had her own obligations at the moment. He'd been following her trial online and on television and she was right, her client was a real pisser. He didn't envy her the job.

More than once, he'd thought about picking up the phone to call her. Then he'd realized what a dummy he was. He hadn't even gotten her number. All he had was the one for the firm and he did not want to call her there. He'd checked for a home phone, but it was unlisted. Not a bad idea when a lawyer defended the kind of people she did. He also didn't want to ask anyone for it and have to answer a million questions.

So, he was going to do something that he'd deny no matter who asked. He knew how to do everything with computer programs and searches and everything in between.

"Just let me know when you leave," Liam told Rosalie.

"I checked on the staff before. I think a few of them are working late tonight." She shook her head. "Don't you people know it's Friday night? Why aren't you all out on a date?"

He chuckled. "I'm not sure any woman would have me in the middle of all this. And I'm guessing the others will make up for it over the weekend. Who's staying?"

She clicked her keyboard and pulled up a note. "Teri, Carl and Jason." She looked up at him. "The newbies. Trying to earn extra points with the boss, I'd guess."

Liam chuckled. "Rosalie. They've been with us for three years. They're hardly newbies anymore."

"I know, I know. I just keep thinking of them that way. Anyway, I told the guard downstairs and made sure they had their key cards with them."

Because of the nature of their work, all SBD employees had a specially coded card that had to be used to both enter and leave the offices. Because they shared the building with so many other tenants, Liam changed the codes for SBD every month, just as a precaution.

"I'll check on them before I leave, too. I don't want them to burn themselves out."

"Good thing we're hiring more people. Okay, I'll let them know you're still here."

Seated at his desk, Liam called up one of the search engines he used designed for this purpose. A few clicks of the keys gave him both Sydney Alfiore's cell and home phone numbers and he programmed them into his own cell. Then he leaned back in his chair. Right after this barbecue at the Cantrell ranch, he was going to give her a call to at least see how she was. And maybe, if he was lucky, she might have time for a cup of coffee or a drink. His own social life had been abysmal for months, but if he was going to break the fast, he wanted it to be with Sydney.

A rap on the doorway had him looking up to see Rosalie holding her purse and her key card.

"I'm out of here, boss. You should go soon, too."

"I will. I have one thing to finish up. Then I want to check on the workers still here. And then, I promise cross-my-heart-hope-to-die that I will go home."

"Good." She winked at him. "And don't miss that plane Sunday morning."

"Word of honor."

"All right, then. Good night. See you Monday."

Liam spent the best part of an hour cleaning up some details on a presentation he was doing next week. One of their new clients was an identity protection firm, and the very last thing they could afford was for someone to hack their database. Eventually his brain began to tire, so he closed out the file, saved it to his very-well-protected hard drive then backed it up to his external hard drive. Satisfied he'd done what he could, he locked away the external drive and called it a night.

After locking the door to his office suite, he headed down the hallway to where his three coders were working. At the moment, they were all sharing a large room, created by combining two existing offices. The lighting was dimmed and they all wore headsets as they focused on their computers. Not wanting to startle them, he flicked the lights on and off to capture their attention. As one person, they blanked their screens and turned to see who was in the room.

"I'm leaving," he told them. "You all should do the same. Burnout doesn't do anyone any good."

They all nodded.

Finally, Teri said, "I just want to finish this one particular section. I've had trouble getting the codes I want to work. Then I'm gone."

"Same here," Jason echoed.

"I'm leaving when they do," Carl added.

"Okay. Good night, then. See you all Monday."

As he let himself out of the offices and waited for the elevator, he wondered why he had a sudden itch between his shoulder blades. There was absolutely nothing happening here to give him that feeling. Still, it stayed with him all the way home and into his townhouse.

Maybe he'd go in tomorrow and do a check on their work, all three of them. He did that occasionally, just to make sure they were on the right track, and he didn't expect his search to turn up anything. But Saturday he got sidetracked when an old friend showed up in town unexpectedly, then it was Sunday morning.

Liam was up early to shower and shave and head for the airport, fueled only by a stop for his favorite coffee in a go-cup. He couldn't help watching the traffic, looking for…what? Someone trailing him?

Come on, Liam. Would you even know if someone was? What kind of car they were driving? Get real.

Still, that nagging little itch along his spine just would not go away. He was spending so much time looking over his shoulder that he was getting a crick in his neck. He deliberately forced it out of his mind, however, when he reached the airport.

At Tampa Executive Airport, he followed the directions Rosalie had texted him to reach the hangar. On the tarmac in front of it stood a gleaming Gulfstream corporate jet, cream colored with the

Arroyo logo painted on the side. A man in pilot's uniform was walking around the plane with a clipboard and, as Liam pulled up close to it, two more men came out of the hangar. He lowered his window as one of them walked up to his car.

"Mr. Benedict?" When Liam nodded, he held out his hand through the open window. "Gary McGuire, Tampa Executive Airport. Mr. Cantrell told us to expect you. If you just leave your keys in your car, we'll park it for you. When you return, one of us will fetch it for you."

"Thanks." Liam climbed out of the car. "Are the others here yet?"

"The gentleman has and the woman we're expecting should be here with in the next fifteen minutes. She called to say she was running late. But, please, go on up into the plane and make yourself comfortable."

As Liam climbed the stairs, he wondered what kind of female would be late for this. He couldn't see either of the Cantrells putting up with some of the privileged women he'd met at different events. They didn't seem the type to suffer bullshit easily, but then, one never knew. It probably didn't concern her that she was holding up the parade. Oh, well. He just hoped she didn't make a pain in the ass of herself on the flight.

John Martino was seated when he entered the cabin, and rose to come forward with his hand outstretched.

"Good to see you again, Liam."

"Same here. I owe you a huge debt of gratitude, you know."

Martino lifted an eyebrow. "Because of Arroyo? Taylor's been a friend of mine for a long time. I knew you'd be a good fit there. I seldom have clients rave about someone the way Reed Molloy did about you."

"Well, thanks for putting them on my trail. It's a great opportunity." Liam looked around. "Nice plane."

Martino laughed. "That's an understatement. It belonged to Taylor's father. They did some upgrades but basically it hasn't changed. He was a man who liked his comfort."

"I understand we're waiting for some woman to join us?"

"Some woman?" Martino cocked an eyebrow. "You don't know who she is?"

Liam shrugged. "Taylor's secretary didn't leave a name. Between you and me, I hope it isn't some privileged society female, although I don't know who else would be rude enough to keep people waiting."

Martino leaned over to look out one of the windows. "Well, you're about to find out. Here she is."

Liam heard the voice before she emerged into the cabin and the sound of it shocked him. He couldn't help staring at Sydney Alfiore, whose eyes widened at the sight of him, apparently as stunned as he was that they were going together to the same place. That bolt of electricity he'd felt before shot through his body again and he sent a mental warning to his cock to behave.

"So, you didn't know we were both going to the Arroyo party," he guessed.

She shook her head. "Not a clue, although it should have occurred to me. I mean, now that you're part of the Arroyo family. Of course, it's not as if we've seen much of each other lately, right?"

"Right. A situation I damn well hope to rectify as fast as possible."

"I can get on board with that."

She winked and just like that, he wanted her. Badly. He had to move so one of the seats blocked his body and kept him from embarrassing himself. He certainly hoped he got some private time with her before he self-destructed.

"Hey, Sydney." John moved forward to shake her hand. "Glad you could take a day off from your latest circus."

"Circus is right." She snorted.

"Excuse me." They all turned to look at the man standing in the cockpit doorway. "I'm Dwayne Robertson, your pilot. Welcome aboard. If you could all take your seats, we'll get ready for takeoff."

The cabin had a variety of seating arrangements. Liam sat on one of the couches and motioned to Sydney to join him. John sat across from them. The copilot came out to make sure they were buckled up and tell them they'd be in San Antonio in about two and a half hours.

Liam stole a glance at Sydney. Today she was dressed in fancy jeans, Western boots and a blouse of some silky material that outlined her breasts too clearly for his comfort zone. He had to tamp down the urge to run his hands over her body, mapping each of her curves. Tell her how glad he was to see her, even though they weren't even close to that stage in their hardly-a-relationship. But suddenly he felt like a tongue-tied teenager. And, shit, even his palms were sweating.

What the hell?

He was a grown man about to become a person of some magnitude in both the business and tech worlds and he felt like a teenager lusting after the head cheerleader.

Smooth, Benedict.

And, of course, there was John, sitting across from them, watching and doing his best to hide a smile. He should tell the man there was nothing going on with

Sydney—damn it!—but whatever he said probably wouldn't come out right. Then the noise of the revved-up jet engine as they hurtled down the runway precluded any conversation. At last, they reached cruising altitude and the noise throttled back.

He looked at Sydney, then glanced at her boots. "I'm guessing you've been to one of these shindigs before."

"Taylor Cantrell and I are old friends. I don't know if you're aware that she grew up in Tampa, a member of a very old Tampa family, and was a successful financial analyst until she inherited Arroyo."

He shook his head. "I knew about her financial background, but other than that, I really don't know much about her personal history except what I found on the corporate page and in Wikipedia. And what my attorney learned and related to me. That she inherited Arroyo and stepped into the role of as if she'd been born to it. That she makes sure to know what's going on in every division at all times and is ruthless if she thinks someone is trying to screw her over."

John Martino burst out laughing. "I think I'll pass that along to Taylor. She'll want a T-shirt with that on it." Then he sobered. "But there's a lot more to the story than that." He looked at Sydney. "I'm not sure…"

"I think it's safe to share with Liam," she told him. "We can both vouch that he's trustworthy."

Liam frowned. "Is there something about her background that I should be leery of?"

Sydney shook her head. "Not at all. Taylor just doesn't broadcast it."

At that moment the copilot came back into the cabin.

"Just checking on y'all. We have a little more than two hours before we land. We aren't carrying a steward on this flight, too short, so I'm doing double duty today.

Anyone up for coffee? Breakfast rolls? Mrs. Cantrell keeps a fully stocked pantry on the plane."

"I think we could all use some coffee," John Martino told him. "And if you'll just plate some rolls and leave them out here, we'll be good."

The copilot smiled. "Coming right up."

In scant minutes, everyone had a mug filled with the steaming, aromatic liquid and a basket holding a variety of rolls had been placed in easy reach of all of them. When they were settled in their seats, Liam looked over at John.

"You were about to give me Taylor Cantrell's background," he reminded the man. "Don't let me stop you."

Martino and Sydney exchanged looks.

"Okay, now my curiosity is really hot. If I'm going to be joined at the hip with Arroyo, I don't want to be blindsided, so give."

Sydney took a healthy swallow of her coffee.

"Okay. As long as you remember she doesn't like to discuss it. Ever."

"He's good, Syd," Martino told her. "I'd trust him with anything."

"All right." She exhaled slowly.

And Liam listened carefully to the story about a runaway daughter of a high-society couple whose parents found her and dragged her home. Had the marriage annulled, but could not persuade her to have an abortion. How miserable Taylor's mother had been all her life, so much so that the day after Taylor's college graduation, she overdosed on sleeping pills. Then Taylor's grandfather passed away and a couple of years ago her grandmother followed. Only she'd left a letter for Taylor explaining the whole thing.

"Jesus." Liam let out a soft whistle. "But then how —
"

"She went to San Antonio to meet her father, who thought she was a scam artist. Then, three months after that, he was murdered and it turned out he'd changed his will and left everything to Taylor."

"That must have been a shock." He took a quick swallow of his coffee while his brain tried to sort out what he'd heard.

John chuckled. "No shit. But she jumped in like she'd been born to it. That woman has quite the smarts." He looked at Sydney. "Like you, Syd."

"Oh, please." Sydney flapped a hand at him. "I can't see myself running a worldwide empire the way she does."

"No, you just take impossible cases with extremely high-profile clients who no one else will touch and, against all odds, you win."

She laughed. "I don't know if that's a compliment or not."

"It is," Liam told her. "Take it from me. I'm a long-time admirer of yours."

"Uh, thanks."

He was surprised to see her blush, then concentrate on her coffee.

The story about Taylor Cantrell was interesting and helped him to understand the woman better. But the woman he really wanted to get the details on was sitting next to him and he knew nothing about her except public information. But as they all chatted for the rest of the flight, more and more little pieces of her began to emerge. He made a mental note to take John Martino to lunch and make him cough it all up.

It was late morning when they arrived in San Antonio, landing at Skyplace FBO at San Antonio International Airport. The moment the cabin door was open and the stair released, a man in khakis and a collared shirt with the Arroyo logo on it jogged up to the cabin.

"Mornin' folks." He grinned. "I'm Greg Nagle, helicopter pilot for Arroyo. If y'all will come with me, the chopper's all set just waiting for us."

Liam stared at the man. He wasn't unsophisticated by any means, and many of his clients had a lot of dollar signs attached to their names. But a helicopter? Not a vehicle?

John rose and shook hands with the man. "Good to see you again, Greg."

"Always a pleasure, Mr. Martino. You, too, Miss Alfiore." He looked at Liam. "Welcome to Texas, Mr. Benedict."

"Liam, please." He did the handshake thing.

"Let's get going, folks. The barbecue's already heating up."

In what seemed like seconds, they were all in the chopper that, like the plane, bore the Arroyo logo, and lifting off over the busy city of San Antonio. Soon they were over the sprawling hill country with its quaint towns and busy ranches. Then they swooped over what looked to him like the most massive ranch he'd seen yet. Pastureland that went on forever, several acres dotted with cattle and directly below them the massive stone house that Liam now remembered seeing pictures of.

The party was set up at the side of the house, with a tent as well as tables and chairs on the lawn, and two open barbecue pits smoked away. They were all barely out of the chopper before Taylor hurried toward them, her lips curved in a wide smile.

"Hello, John. Sydney. And Liam, I am so very glad you came. I have a lot of people I want you to meet."

"Uh-oh." Sydney winked at Liam. "Taylor's in matchmaking mode."

"Matchmaking?" *What the hell?* "I don't—"

Sydney laughed. "Not people, Liam. Businesses. Taylor has a well-earned reputation for matching up businesses since she took over the reins at Arroyo. She hasn't been wrong yet."

"I'll look forward to seeing who she matches me up with," he told her.

Taylor Cantrell seemed to be everywhere at once. She never lost her smile, never looked ruffled, all the while talking to her guests, making sure the bar and buffet were kept replenished, checking that everyone was having a good time, and introducing Liam to people she thought he should meet. But it was all done so smoothly Liam wasn't even aware of it happening until hours later when he had a stash of business cards in his pocket and several numbers added to his cell. He'd been caught up in the swirl of people drinking at the bar inside the big tent or feasting from one of the very long buffet tables set out there. He could say without reservation that this was the most impressive and productive party he'd been to in a long time, if ever. It gave him a good sense of the way Arroyo was run and Taylor Cantrell's knowledge and control. He owed John Martino at least a case of aged whiskey for hooking him up.

Every so often he caught a glimpse of Sydney in one small group or another, chatting away, looking comfortable. It was obvious to him that she had visited before and knew several of the people. Once or twice he tried to catch up with her, but then Taylor would tug him away to meet someone.

Noah, less gregarious, was the solid presence making sure it all worked. Liam thought he'd be an interesting guy to sit down with if the opportunity ever came his way.

The April sun was showing no signs of descending any time soon and the barbecue didn't look like it was winding down when Noah came to fetch Liam.

"The helo is getting ready to leave, but Taylor wanted me to let you know if you'd like to stay the night we've got plenty of room."

As tempted as he was to accept the invitation, and get a first-hand look at how the Cantrells operated, Liam knew he should leave.

"Thank you, and thank Taylor for me, but I have an early morning meeting. Then I blocked off the rest of the day to get at the software program I'm writing for a client. So, much as I'd love to accept your great invitation, I'm afraid I'll have to pass."

"Another time, then," Noah told him. "Meanwhile, let me round up the others and we'll head over to the chopper."

Noah unclipped a two-way radio from his belt and spoke softly into it. Taylor broke away from her guests long enough to come say goodbye to them and thank them for coming.

"We'll be in touch," she told Liam. "I have big plans for your firm."

"I look forward to it."

It seemed like only minutes before they were lifting off in the chopper and soon setting down at the FBO at San Antonio International Airport. He followed

Sydney and John up into the plane. They fastened their seat belts and they were off, heading east toward Tampa.

"Quite the experience, Liam," John said. "Right?"

"I can't even count how many people were there," he said. "How does she keep them all straight? They weren't all from Arroyo, were they?"

John shook his head. "A good many were, but you also had local bigwigs and representatives of major corporations Arroyo does business with. A lot of people want to eat at that table."

"I imagine so," Liam agreed.

"Taylor's actually the person who sent me my first high-profile client," Sydney told him. The head of one of Arroyo's divisions who was charged with laundering money. Turns out it was his treasurer, who was very clever about it." She grinned. "But not too clever for John."

"So you've all known each other for a while."

"We were all active in the Tampa financial and legal communities. Believe it or not, it's a very close-knit group."

"Oh, I do." Liam rubbed his jaw. "When I was with Winters and Pryce, we designed software for a lot of them. Craig Winters hosted a lot of events, but none of this magnitude. The amazing thing is I really enjoyed myself."

Sydney laughed. "That seems to be the signature of all the Cantrell parties."

Conversation faded off after that. Liam would have liked to pick John Martino's brain, but he'd save that for another time. He contented himself with watching Sydney, who had curled into a ball on the couch and dozed off. She was one of the few women he'd met who didn't need a lot of makeup. Her thick lashes, now brushing her cheeks like long curtains, needed no enhancement. Her cheeks were a natural soft pink and he thought bright lipstick would only detract from her full lips. Lips he was dying to kiss, and lick and nibble on.

Holy shit!

He'd better slam that door shut in his brain or he'd be sitting there with an embarrassing hard-on. He leaned back and closed his eyes, doing his best to clear his mind of an image of Sydney Alfiore naked in his bed. He was damn glad when the plane finally landed.

Chapter Seven

As they deplaned, an attendant jogged out to let them know their cars would be out in a moment. By the time they reached the FBO building, two of the vehicles were just pulling up.

"Talk to you both soon." John Martino waved at them as he climbed into his vehicle.

Liam paused with a hand on the door of his and realized there were no more cars being driven up.

"Sydney? Did they forget yours?" Liam glanced at her and noticed her searching for something on her cell phone. "They don't leave you alone for a minute, do they?" he teased.

"What?" She looked up. "Oh, no, this isn't business related. I'm ordering an Uber."

"You didn't drive to the airport?"

She shook her head. "My car had a problem, so it's being serviced."

Liam's brows lifted. "On a Sunday?"

She grinned at him. "I've learned, sadly, that money will buy anything. But it's not a problem. Not when there's Uber."

"Don't bother ordering up a car," Liam told her. "I'll drive you home."

"I'd hate to make you go out of your way this late at night," she protested.

"Where do you live?" John asked. "Maybe it would be more convenient for me to drive you, Sydney."

She laughed. "I feel like I'm in high school and the popular boys are fighting over me."

John chuckled. "If only we were back in those days. So, what's your address, Syd?"

In the end it turned out Liam was closer. Despite Sydney's protests that she was inconveniencing him, and with John Martino doing his best to hide a grin, he just steered her over to his vehicle. As they pulled out onto State Road 60, the faint essence of her perfume tantalized his nose. Something flowery, but not overpowering. As long as the day had been, the scent still made his body sit up and take notice. Not that he needed much enhancement where Sydney was concerned.

He wondered if it was too late to ask her if he could come up for a drink? Coffee? Conversation? Incredible sex?

Fuck, Benedict.

He glanced over at Sydney leaning back in her seat and couldn't help noticing how the lights from the highway outlined her body, making her breasts stand out in relief. His palms itched with the need to cup them, feel their weight, but he was hardly a teenager horny enough to make out in a car. Horny, yes. Teenager, no. But he couldn't help wanting just the same, imagining her without her clothes, there for the feasting. He could run his hands over her, slowly mapping her curves. Taste every bit of her, from her nipples to the cream in her sex. Suck her nipples and bite them—

"So, you'd say today was a worthwhile event for you?"

Sydney's warm voice startled him out of his erotic reverie, and he unconsciously jerked the wheel.

"Liam? Are you okay?"

He cleared his throat. "Yes. Of course. There was just some kind of trash in the lane and I didn't want to hit it."

"Oh. Okay. Back to my question."

Question? Liam had to push the thoughts of Sydney's naked body from his brain so he could give her an intelligent answer.

"Yes. Worthwhile on a lot of fronts. I got a pretty good feel for the spread of Arroyo and the mixture of businesses that make up the conglomerate. And I met some very nice people who seem interested in contracting Software By Design."

"That's part of the reason for this annual shindig. Taylor likes people to make personal connections and take it from there. She feels most times it works better than just bringing them together via Skype or even a business meeting."

"It amazes me how she carries so much information in her head and still makes everything she does look so easy."

"She was like that when she was a financial advisor," Sydney told him. "That's why the firm she was with hated to see her leave."

"I'll bet."

"Oh, here we are. It's that building right there." She pointed to a tall brick and glass edifice. "You can just let me off in front."

"Not on your life. I always walk a lady to her door." *And maybe at least steal a kiss.* "And look. There's a parking space right near the entrance that I think has my name on it."

She laughed, that musical sound again that hit every pocket of testosterone in his body.

"Well, I'd hate for it to go to waste."

Sydney's condo was on Bayshore Boulevard, what many called the Tampa Gold Coast. He could have just stopped at the entrance and let her out. Through the glass surrounding the entrance, he could see a security guard on duty so she'd be safe. But he wasn't quite ready for this short time he had with her to be over so he pulled smoothly into the space, shut off the ignition and climbed out, sending a message to his cock to stand down. If he was smart, he'd walk her inside and over to the elevator then say good night.

But, apparently, he'd left his smarts at the office, because when they reached the elevator, he placed his hands her shoulders and turned her to face him.

"You can tell me to go to hell afterwards," he told her in a low voice, "but I have to have one kiss, Syd. I've wanted to do this since the first night we met."

He lowered his head and touched his mouth to hers, gently at first, aroused by the softness of her lips and their delicious taste. Then he pressed a little harder, and, when she didn't draw away, he let himself trace the seam of her mouth with the tip of his tongue. When she drew away, he mentally kicked himself.

What class, Benedict. I should at least take her to dinner before making a move.

"I'm sorry," he began. "That was —"

"Far too public," she finished for him, her voice low and husky. The elevator door stood open. "We should probably take this upstairs."

The invitation stunned him. "Really? I mean, don't you have to get up early in the morning for your feisty client?"

Her tempting lips curved in a smile that made him want to lick them. Along with every other part of her body. "I've stayed up later than this for him. I might as well stay up doing something I think I'm going to really enjoy." The elevator doors slid open and she leaned against one to hold them there. "We had something click the first night we met. I felt it and saw that you did, too. Our insane schedules have kept up from doing anything about it, but I'm tired of waiting. This is an unexpected opportunity and I want to take advantage of it."

She took his hand and drew him into the elevator. When the door closed, he turned her to face him and cupped her cheeks, studying her face. He wanted to be sure she wasn't making a mistake. That *he* wasn't making one, either.

"Are you sure about this, Syd? Really sure?"

"The only thing I'm sure of is I'll kick myself if I don't see where this goes." She inhaled and let the breath out slowly. "This is just who I am. I want you, Liam. I have since that first night we met. You think I'm being too forward?"

"No, I don't. I like it. I'm too old and too busy to play games and I'm glad you are."

"If this — us — is a mistake, I want to find out now."

"It's not a mistake." He brushed his mouth over hers. "I believe that."

She breathed a sigh. "Good. Really good."

At that moment the elevator doors slid open. Sydney took his hand and led him down the hallway to a door at the end. He found it interesting that instead of a standard lock, there was a keypad right above the door handle. He watched as Sydney punched in her code then followed her into the condo. She had barely closed and locked the door before he pulled her into his arms.

"Be sure, Syd." *God.* He didn't want her to have any second thoughts.

"I am sure. I think Fate created this opportunity and I don't want to waste it."

He wasn't waiting any longer. He couldn't. He cupped her face and brought his mouth down to hers, not tentative at all this time. He licked the smooth surface, tasting the faint vestiges of her lipstick, before urging her to open for him. God! She tasted like heaven—all the flavors of the day plus her own distinct essence. Liam licked every inch of the inner surface, brushing his tongue over hers and coaxing it to do an erotic dance with him. When she closed her lips around it and sucked him deeper inside, he thought he would lose it right then.

He threaded his fingers through the silk of her hair, using them to hold her head in place while he savored the taste of her mouth. He slid his tongue over hers and heat jolted through him when she closed her lips around it and did the sucking thing again. He hoped to god he didn't come in his jeans just standing here in her little hallway.

Calling on every bit of restraint he could find, he lifted his mouth from hers. Her eyes were glazed with passion and the pulse at the hollow of her throat was beating frantically.

"I don't think I want to do this standing up." He wasn't sure he'd last if he tried it.

"We don't have to, you know."

She took his hand and led him through what appeared to be a vast living room, down a hallway to her bedroom. A flick of a switch and the bedside lamps came on, giving the room a warm amber glow.

Liam was so turned on he couldn't figure out where to start first.

The boots, idiot. You can't make love to a woman with her boots on.

"Sit down." He could hear the gravel in his voice as he picked her up and sat her on the side of the bed. "Yes. Like that."

Then he figured out how to maneuver the boots, tugging them off one at a time. Sydney chuckled at his efforts, a slow, heated sound that made his cock twitch and his balls ache. Finally, he managed to get both of them free and tossed them in a corner. Then he pulled out his wallet, drew out two condoms and dropped them on one of the nightstands.

Sydney glanced over at them. "That all you've got in you?" she teased.

"All I was prepared for." He brushed her hair back from her face. "I wasn't expecting to have my fantasies come true tonight."

"Fantasies, huh?" She looked up at him. "Maybe I have a few of my own."

Jesus!

Liam gritted his teeth and reached for his control. The first thing he wanted to do was unwrap her and see every inch of the body that had starred in his nighttime fantasies. With the boots disposed of, he lifted her back to her feet and with slow deliberation unbuttoned her blouse, brushing the silky material aside so he could drink in the sight of her firm breasts lovingly cupped by lace and satin. He ran the tip of one finger across the creamy swells, the feel of her skin like satin beneath his touch. Her dark nipples, shadows beneath the flimsy material, teased him and made him salivate. He closed his lips around one of them, fabric and all, and slowly sucked it into his mouth.

"Oh, god." Sydney clutched his arms to steady herself as she leaned into his touch.

That was his thought exactly. The nipple was firm and tight, and he couldn't help closing his teeth around it and taking one tiny bite. Her little moan vibrated through him and went straight to his cock, which was sending him desperate messages. Not yet, he told himself. He wanted to savor this, to relish it, enjoy every single second.

He gave the other taut bud equal attention before sliding his hands down to the waist of her jeans. *Pop!* And the snap was open. A soft metallic slide and the zipper was undone. He pushed the denim fabric past her hips and down her legs, crouching down until it was all the way to her feet. Wrapping his fingers around her slim ankles, he lifted her feet, one at a time, to help her step out of it.

He took a moment to indulge himself. Grasping her hips and pressing his face to her mound, so he could inhale her scent. And damn! He'd be lucky if he didn't lose it all right there. Her scent was like seven kinds of sin, exotic and spicy and mouthwatering. He couldn't wait to get his mouth on her and lick every inch of her slick surface.

Pulling himself together he rose to his feet and took her mouth again, a short kiss but deep, so he could hold the taste inside him. Then he unclasped her bra and tossed it to the side with her other garments, cupping her bare breasts in his palms and brushing the nipples with his thumbs. Sydney's breath hissed between her teeth and she leaned into his touch.

But then she stunned him by moving away.

"What?" He stared at her. "Please don't tell me you changed your mind."

"Not even a little." Her lips curved in an impish smile. "But one of us has too many clothes on."

He chuffed an unsteady laugh.

"That's because one of us is probably going to lose control if he takes his clothes off."

"I don't care. I'm close to losing it myself. Time to get naked."

In all his fantasies about Sydney Alfiore, Liam had never expected her to be this forceful, this much of a participant. An equal partner. He wouldn't have thought it possible for something to turn him on even more, but damn! It heated his blood and made it pump through his body.

He started to unbutton his shirt, but Sydney brushed his hands away.

"My turn."

He forced himself to stand as still as possible, while she slowly stripped his shirt from him then ran her hands over his chest. The soft feel of them as they brushed the hair on his chest and coasted over his nipples cranked up his desire even more, if that was at all possible. He prayed that he could maintain control as long as possible to make this better for Sydney than it had ever been.

When she leaned forward and ran her tongue over each nipple with a light caress, he had to clench his hands to maintain his control. He was already so aroused that it wouldn't take much for him to explode before they even got to the main event. The rasp of his zipper being lowered sounded so loud to him, magnified because he was so acutely aware of everything Sydney was doing. Her fingers brushed his skin as they grasped his jeans and pushed them past his hips down to his ankles. In seconds he had kicked off his shoes and gotten rid of the jeans pooling around his ankles.

Sydney took a tiny step backward and let her gaze roam over his body. He could not have been more aroused if she'd grabbed his cock and begun massaging it. Just the idea of her devouring him with her eyes and sweeping her hands over his body sent him to another plane of excitement. He wanted to ask her if she liked what she saw, but was sure that would come off too egotistical. Anyway, he wanted the focus to be on her, not him. He wanted to give her so much pleasure that every other man she'd ever been with would be wiped from her brain.

And so he stood there, rigid, while she explored his body with those graceful hands. Fingertips skimmed the waistband of his boxer briefs, their feathery touch sending needles of heat straight to his cock and his balls. Every muscle in his body tightened, and he bit down on his lip. It took every ounce of control not to toss her onto the bed on her back and thrust himself deep inside her. He'd waited so long for this and wasn't going to screw it up. But when she lowered her head and pressed a kiss to his navel, then traced his curled flesh with her tongue, it was damn fucking hard.

With agonizing slowness, she dragged his boxer briefs down his thighs and to his ankles. As he'd done with his other clothing, he stepped out of them and kicked them to the side. She stroked the curve of his hips and his thighs, then reached around to scrape her fingernails along the cheeks of his ass. He was okay until she wrapped her slim fingers around his throbbing shaft and slid them up and down.

"Okay." He bit the word off. "That's it."

He dragged the covers back on the bed then lifted her and placed her with her head on the pillows, then knelt between her legs. He took a long moment to study her breasts, the gentle swell of her stomach and the trimmed lines of dark hair bracketing the lips of her pussy. Kneeling between those lush thighs, he traced the line of her slit with the tip of a finger, up and back, pleased to see her tremble with pleasure at his touch.

Liam licked her cream from his skin, the taste better than any aged bourbon he'd ever had. And he wanted more. Nudging her legs apart and bending them at the knee to give himself full access, he lowered his head, spread the lips of her pussy wide and treated himself to a long, slow lick of the tongue over her slick, soft flesh. He used his tongue to tease her clit again and again, her little sounds of pleasure making him hotter and hungrier.

When he thrust his tongue fully inside her, she arched her hips and moaned with pleasure. *God!* She tasted like seven kinds of sin, better than any woman he'd ever been with, and he wondered if he'd ever be able to get enough of her. He thrust in and out with his tongue, curling it to scrape against that sweet spot, that special place that would give her extra pleasure. He shifted one hand to pinch her clit between thumb and forefinger, rubbing and squeezing it as he fucked her with his mouth.

"Oh, god!" The words were as much a shout as a plea, her body rocking in a steady rhythm, her hands fisted on either side of her head.

The more he fucked her with his tongue, the louder the sexy sounds she made and the more she rocked up to his mouth. Her muscles tightened, she lifted her hips toward him and came on his tongue.

He never let up, keeping his tongue and fingers busy as she shuddered through the orgasm. When the last spasm had subsided, he kissed his way up her body, taking tiny bites out of her hip, her belly, her breasts. Then he captured her mouth, sharing her taste with her, plunging his tongue into her mouth, clasping her head in his hands to hold her still while he fucked her mouth with his tongue.

She lay back on the pillows, her gaze languid, her body relaxed. But Liam, not so much. He was hard as a spike, his balls ached and he was hanging on to his control by a thread. He was going to make sure, however, that she was damn well satisfied before he took his own pleasure. He couldn't remember the last time, if ever, he'd been so focused on a woman or so attracted to her. More than a physical attraction. Maybe that was why it was so important to him to take proper care of her.

Bracing himself on his forearms, he trailed his lips across the line of her jaw and down the slender column of her neck, taking little nips here and there. He captured her earlobe between his teeth and tugged on it before releasing it and tracing the shell of her ear with the tip of his tongue. She sighed and ran her hands up and down the muscles of his back, her touch igniting all the little nerves just beneath the surface of his skin.

Liam began to kiss his way down her body again, paying particular attention to what he'd discovered were the sensitive areas just behind her ears and where her neck and shoulder met. He took his time again when he got to her breasts, licking circles around them before taking each nipple, in turn, into his mouth. When his teeth closed down on the pebbled flesh, Sydney arched up to him, making soft little sounds of pleasure.

God, he loved those sounds. He was sure he could worship her with his mouth forever just to hear them. But right then, he had more important business. He slid down her body until his mouth was aligned with her sex and he could take the swollen nub of her clit into his mouth. He closed his teeth around it gently and tugged, moving one hand to stroke the wet flesh of her pussy.

Sydney eased her thighs apart, and when she did Liam slid two fingers into her hot, tight channel. The slick flesh closed around his fingers as she tightened down on him. When he set up a rhythm thrusting those fingers in and out, Sydney moved her body with him, pushing down on his hand even as he continued to tease her clit with his teeth.

Liam added a third finger, stroking her inner flesh, feeling the orgasm rising within her body. Delicious little sounds were drifting from her mouth and she kept thrusting her hips at him. At the moment she pushed down on his hand, hard, he closed his teeth around her hot nub again and sent her into orbit. The walls of her pussy convulsed around his fingers, gripping them as spasm after spasm rocked her body.

At last the tiny aftershocks subsided, and Sydney sprawled limp against the pillows, face flushed. He eased his fingers from her and, lifting them to his mouth, deliberately licked each one clean. She watched him from beneath heavy lids, running her tongue over her bottom lip. He moved up her body so he could put his mouth over the delicate hollow of her throat where her pulse still beat in an erratic rhythm. She moaned softly at his touch.

Okay, that was it. He'd held off as long as he could but he needed to be inside her right then more than he needed to breathe. He shifted his weight so he could rise to his knees and leaned over to fetch one of the condoms from the nightstand. His movement put his cock directly within her reach. When she closed her slim fingers around it and gave it a gentle squeeze, he had to grit his teeth to hang on to his control.

"Honey, if you don't move your hand now, it'll be over before we get to the really good part."

Her little laugh was light and breathy. "I don't know. The first part wasn't too bad at all."

"I'm so close to the edge…" he groaned.

"Next time," she promised, running the tip of her tongue over her bottom lip. "Next time I get to play first."

He rolled the latex on with one smooth move and knelt between her thighs. The sight of her face, flushed with a combination of satisfaction and need, of her eyes darkened with desire, her lips so full and tempting and he had to have a taste. Right then. He lowered his head and brushed his mouth over hers, running his tongue along the soft skin. She tasted so damn good everywhere he didn't think he'd ever get enough of it. Of sampling all her flavors. When he urged her to open her mouth, she did and slid her tongue over his.

Jesus!

He'd worried that he'd worn her out with the two body-shaking orgasms, but he could tell by the way she moved against his body that she was ready for him again.

He kept his eyes locked with hers as he moved and adjusted her body. Wrapping his fingers around his very swollen shaft, he nudged the head at her opening. She spread her thighs wider as he eased slowly into her slick pussy, sucking his breath in at the tightness of it even after two orgasms. He eased forward in increments, the heat of her making his blood race and his breath quicken.

He sucked in his breath at the tight grip of her sex around him, taking a moment to just let the pleasure roll through him. He threaded his fingers through Sydney's and pressed her hands back against the pillows. Then he drove into her, slowly at first but then moving faster. She wrapped her legs around his hips and held him to her, locking her ankles at the small of his back. Then, as the rhythm increased, they moved together in synchronicity, flesh slapping against flesh. She matched him stroke for stroke, his balls striking against the curve of her ass.

He gritted his teeth, determined to wait for her not to be a jackass and leave her half-finished, but holy shit. He was so close to the edge. Then he felt it, the beginning of the tremors in her inner muscles. He picked up the pace, thrusting harder and deeper and faster.

The orgasm hit them both with unbelievable force, her pussy squeezing him while his cock pulsed and pulsed and pulsed. Nothing existed except their two bodies caught up in an enormous erotic whirlpool.

The downward slide began, spasms turning to tremors, breathing not so labored, heartbeats returning to normal. Liam collapsed forward, catching himself on his forearms and touching his mouth to Sydney's in a barely there kiss. He brushed the damp strand of hair from her forehead and looked directly into her eyes. He saw satisfaction and pleasure but no regrets.

Thank god.

"This wasn't a mistake." She said it before he could.

He smiled. "No, it wasn't. I just wish time wasn't our enemy."

"Me, too." She placed her palm against his cheek.

The gentle caress went right to the middle of his heart. "We lead crazy lives, Syd. Especially right now. But I don't want to wait months to get together again." He stroked her cheek with his thumb. "And I'd at least like to take you to dinner."

She chuckled. "But this is so much more fun."

He studied her face for a long moment, desperate to make sure he wasn't misreading things.

"It is, but I want it to be a lot more than this. Agreed?"

He held his breath until she nodded.

"Agreed."

"Okay, then. I know we probably won't be able to talk every day, but even if it's just before we fall into bed at night, we can exchange one text. Okay?'

"Okay." She swallowed and he saw a trace of uncertainty in her eyes. "Liam, we aren't moving too fast here, are we?"

So he wasn't the only one who hoped this was more than a tumble or two in the sheets.

"Not at all." He brushed a soft kiss on her mouth. "The way our lives are, we need to telescope things and take shortcuts when we can. All we need to know is that this is the start of something very good."

"It is." She giggled. "I guess I should thank you for being as overworked as I am."

He smiled at her. "It just makes every moment together that much more important and special." He shifted away from her body. "And now I think I need to get out of here. When I have a sleepover with you, I want time the next morning for breakfast in bed and some playtime in the shower."

She reached up and ran her fingers through his hair. "Yes. It will be special."

Special, indeed. He discovered when Sydney Alfiore took off her professional suit of armor, beneath it was a warm, loving, giving and slightly vulnerable and very desirable woman. He needed to be sure he didn't do anything to screw this up.

The moment he rolled away from her and pushed himself to his feet, he felt the loss of her presence. He almost crawled back in bed with her but reminded himself of what they'd just agreed on. She watched him as he pulled on his clothes, and when he was fully dressed, he kissed her, a hot, open-mouthed kiss that included lots of tongue. Then he lifted his head,

"Just so you won't forget." He winked.

"Trust me. That won't be the case."

She insisted on getting out of bed, pulling on a robe and walking him to the door.

"It locks automatically, but I wanted a chance for one more kiss."

"And here it is."

This one was more emotional than erotic and he hated to break the contact.

"One text tomorrow," he reminded her before he turned down the hallway to the elevator.

The feelings of satisfaction and fulfillment stayed with him as he drove home. But they would have stayed a lot longer if that sensation of being watched hadn't interfered. But all the way back to his townhouse, he wondered if every car was one of the ones that had tried to run him down, or carried someone spying on him.

I've been watching too many reruns of old James Bond movies. I need to get over this.

But damn it, the feeling just would not go away.

Chapter Eight

"A couple of weeks at most then?" Robert Hoffman, CEO of Hoffman Contractors, smiled at Liam.

"You have my word."

"Great!" Hoffman grinned. "Excellent, in fact. We've been keeping the components of the design sequestered on free-standing computers just waiting for this to put all the pieces together and move forward."

"Will that give you enough time to prep for it and have your key people there when we install it on your server?"

"It will. We're more than ready."

Liam looked across the desk at the man. Average height, average weight, average looks but off-the-charts brain. His company was anything but average, designing highly sophisticated defense equipment for the government. Software By Design was just completing an equally sophisticated security software program that, once loaded into the Hoffman system, would prevent hackers from accessing the classified design for their newest project. He had asked Teri, Sy and Jason to each try hacking the program at various stages, and they'd been stymied. Not that he didn't trust all his people, but those were the ones he had the longest history with and felt the closest to.

"I promised we'd get it done before Gasparilla and I like to keep my word."

"Liam, I hope you realize we would not use anyone else to design this program."

"I appreciate that."

"You did an excellent job for us last time." Hoffman picked up the pen he liked to twiddle with when he was talking. He'd once said it settled his nerves better than anything except a stiff shot of bourbon. "And I appreciated you explaining to me why we should not use the same security software for another project." A tiny grin quirked his mouth. "Uncle Sam appreciated it, also."

"Most people don't think about it." Liam shifted the tablet on his lap. "You're on a supposedly secure classified network. Only you and the Department of Defense."

"You use that word 'supposedly'. That's what caught my attention the first time we talked."

"Because it's the correct adjective. As long as you are connected via a network that goes beyond your physical premises, there is plenty of opportunity for someone to find a way to hack into it."

Hoffman shook his head. "It continues to baffle my mind. If these hackers have such sophisticated skills, why don't they use them to make a lot of money?"

Liam shrugged. "For some it's just the thrill of getting over on what they consider the establishment. For others, they make way too much money hacking for profit. We work hard just to keep ahead of them. But that's why we advise our clients to use different protocols for each project. There is always the chance some hacker has figured out the previous one by the time you get to the new project."

"I have to admit," Hoffman said, "when you first brought it up I thought maybe you were just trying to squeeze another fee out of us. But I talked to my contacts at DoD and they said they wished all their contractors would do this."

"We always insert what we call duress words to alert us of any intrusion into the system," he assured Hoffman. Liam used those duress words to trigger a special alarm. "But that's just an extra precaution because our software is very strong. That just means someone is making the effort. And a hacker would have to penetrate that to actually get to your design software."

Hoffman's lips twisted in a lopsided grin. "I suppose you think I'm nuts to keep going over this with you, especially since this isn't our first rodeo together."

Liam shook his head. "Not at all. The stuff you did, as with many of our clients, is so sensitive it requires utmost secrecy. We're happy to provide it. Of course, safety would be one hundred percent if you used an isolated computer, or one that was only part of an in-house network."

"I hear you, but that's impossible. Often when we work on a design for them, we need input along the way. And they want their eyes on the progress."

Hoffman studied him for a long moment. "You know, you never asked the details of our project."

Liam shrugged. "I know it's top secret. I figured it was none of my business. I didn't need the details to write the software."

"Even though you have high-level clearance from the DoD?"

"Yeah. Even though."

"Well, I think you should know what we're so paranoid about." Hoffman leaned forward, resting his arms on his desk. "We're creating a brand-new drone that can be armed as well as disappear from tracking software like radar."

Liam's brows rose at that. "Damn! I know a lot of foreign nations would salivate to get their hands on the design for this."

"You know it. So now you understand how important it is that the security software you install has to be airtight."

"Agreed. And it will be." He rose from his chair. "We'll start beta testing next week. That will give us time to run it through its paces. You said you wanted it before Gasparilla, right?"

Hoffman nodded his agreement.

"Okay, then. My goal right now is to get it to you before then so your own people can also test it."

"Looking forward to it." Hoffman stood and the two men shook hands.

"I'll touch base the beginning of the week to keep you in the loop."

Excitement was still sizzling through Liam as he rode down in the elevator and walked out to the secure lot where his car was parked. His mind was whirling with the idea of the drone Hoffman Inc. was creating. He'd damn well better be sure the software keeping their computers secure was airtight. In theory, there shouldn't be a problem. The computers the designs were created on were only linked to a secure connection with the Department of Defense. But Liam knew that once those codes were out in the Internet stratosphere, there was always a danger of hacking.

Sometimes he thought the old ways of doing things had been better. Save it all to discs, then have the client send someone to deliver it to DoD or whoever. But he knew of at least two instances where the messenger had been killed in order to get the discs and others where the messenger had been compromised and sold them to the highest bidder.

It was his job to create an electronic safety net around the project's design software so it was safe from beginning to end. It was exactly the kind of challenge Liam liked and what he had built his reputation on.

He had three of his people working on the program with him — Teri, Jason and Brad. He would put all the parts together before the beta testing. When that was done, he'd put the software behind a digital lock and wipe the files from the main server. Finally, he'd save it to a hard disk and lock that in the office safe. He'd learned early on in this business that there could never be too many safeguards.

As he climbed into his car, memories of his night with Sydney flooded his senses. That had been happening to him a lot lately. He had to figure out a way to see her again before he lost his mind. Not just for sex, either. A meal. Coffee. Anything.

Shit, Benedict. Acting like a teenager much?

But he knew, especially after their night together, that they had something special between them. They just had to find time to nurture it, which wasn't too easy these days. And texting wasn't quite doing it for him, especially when they couldn't always answer each other right away. He knew her trial had begun two days earlier but when he looked at his watch, he realized they were on break until two o'clock. It was now one. Maybe he could catch her for a quick message.

Hi. At lunch?

It was a full two minutes before she answered him.

Is a courthouse hot dog lunch?

He sent her a smile emoji. *We'll have to fix that.*

Please. I might have to kill my client & I need sustenance.

He thought for a minute.

Can u do a late dinner 2nite?

Another long pause.

Maybe. Text u as soon as we are done for 2day.

K

And he'd have to be satisfied with that, at least for the moment. He had plenty to keep himself busy with in the meantime. As he drove out of the lot, he waved at the guard in the little gatehouse, who nodded at him. The street was a busy one, lined with a mix of businesses and office buildings so he had to ease into the traffic. Some of the buildings were already flying Gasparilla flags, the famous pirate symbol. This time every year, Tampa went crazy with Gasparilla events leading up to the big parade.

He was glad the Hoffman project as well as two others would be finished and delivered before then. Some of his project designers were huge fans and attended everything. He smiled, glad that he'd pushed everyone to stay on target so this would be possible.

Then, out of nowhere, like a physical blow, that sense of being watched grabbed him. *What the hell?* At least a week had passed without that sensation, long enough that he'd chalked it up to his imagination. Thoughts of Sydney and immersion in the program he was writing and planning the move had left little room for anything else. Still, he was sure he would have noticed a feeling like that.

As casually as possible, he lifted his eyes to the rearview mirror, but really, what could he tell? He had pulled out into traffic and there were a number of cars both behind and beside him. The street was two lanes in both directions. He hadn't been looking for anything, so if someone was following him, they were already in place. And of course, they wouldn't make it obvious.

The next traffic light was red. He jerked the steering wheel to the right and cut in front of another car — the driver blaring his horn at him — and made a sharp turn into the cross street. More horns squawking at him, but no one tried to pull out of line to follow him. About ten blocks down the street, he pulled into a drive through line for a Joltin' Java. Probably the last thing he needed was coffee. His nerves were already twanging, but he had to get off the road so he could get his shit together.

As he sat in the usual very long line, he couldn't help constantly looking left, right and behind him. It didn't do him any good to tell himself if someone was indeed following him, they couldn't just cut into this line. Or even bracket him, as full as the parking lot was. Distracted, he almost forgot to give his order and settled for an iced tea, some flavor that would settle his nerves.

Go-cup in hand, he pulled back onto the roadway and blended in with the traffic He didn't see anyone suddenly pull in behind or around him, but he was on edge all the way back to the office. He decided, at the last minute, to check on how the new building was coming.

Having a lot of disposable income must be nice, he thought, as he walked up to the building. Then he realized the Arroyo income was hardly disposable. They just had a lot to invest, and this was one of the areas. He was damned sure Taylor Cantrell expected to make all of this back and more as his firm expanded.

A man in khaki pants and a sweatshirt stood at the building entrance. Liam knew to passersby he looked like a man passing the time. Or supervising construction, what with the materials visible in the parking lot. But Taylor had let him know the man had done three tours with Delta Force, knew at least ten ways to kill without using a gun and was a crack marksman. And was also heavily, if not visibly, armed.

The parking lot was surrounded by a chain-link fence, accessible only with a coded key card. The other tenants in the building were also involved in businesses that required secure protection. Taylor had met with them and gotten them on board with all the additional security measures, which they wholeheartedly bought into.

As he pulled up to the gate, Liam waved at the man standing at the entrance, a protection Taylor was paying for.

"How's it going, Andy?"

The guard winked at him. "Oh, having the time of my life, Liam. You know that."

What Liam did know was that Andy was recording the faces of everyone who passed by or walked up to the gate or asked permission to enter the building.

The building doors could only be opened and the elevator accessed with specially coded key cards. Then each business had its own cards for its floor. At night there were two guards inside who took turns manning the desk in the lobby and patrolling the floors. All of them were former Special Forces and every business had been more than happy for Arroyo to vet them and hire them.

As Liam pulled into the parking lot, he breathed a sigh of relief. If someone was tracking him, they'd have a fucking hard time doing it here. He just wished he knew who it could be. The clients Software By Design served were certainly high profile and their projects would be worth a lot of money on the black market. That was something he was always aware of, which was why he took so many electronic safeguards. The Hoffman drone was probably the most valuable project of any they had going right now, but neither he nor anyone on his staff ever discussed it outside their offices.

That was something he'd made clear when each person was hired. They were also told that if they breached security, because of the nature of their clients, they could end up in prison. He figured that was enough to deter anyone.

He'd vetted them all at hiring, out of necessity. Maybe he should run another check on everyone, just to be on the safe side. He'd discuss it with Taylor in their next Skype session, which was just a few days from now. He couldn't figure out, however, what anyone would want with him.

To write a special program for them? Good coders could be bought more easily.

To get him out of the way? But the work wouldn't stop just because he was taken out of the game.

So, what the hell would anyone be following him for?

With a deliberate effort, he shook it off, used his key card to open the back door and took the elevator to the third level. When he stepped out into the small reception area, he was pleased to note that there was a lot less chaos than usual. He walked the hallway slowly, stopping into each work area and doing a visual check. Most of them were complete, as was the room that would house the server.

Good!

He knew how complicated moves like this were, and his staff was more than double what it had been when they moved into their present quarters. More people, more computers, more everything.

He wanted to be finished before the Monday of Gasparilla week. Festival insanity reigned in the city and he knew the week would be crazy. And Taylor Cantrell had insisted on sending Arroyo's head of computer services as well as a technical team to make the move that much easier. That meant they would only be offline for less than twenty-four hours. His staff would be there, also. By the time the tech people were finished, they would be ready to rock and roll.

"I can't thank you enough," he'd told Taylor when she called to check up on the process.

"It's the way we do business with our people," she'd said. "I promise you, it will all come together. By next Monday you'll be sitting in your office, drinking coffee and elbows deep in your next project. Or entertaining the next swarm of clients."

It certainly looked as if all the prep work was on time.

He poked his head in the room housing the electrical connects, where he found Esteban 'Stan' Contreras, supervising organized chaos. Stan had handled all the wiring before the move into SBD's present offices and Liam had contacted him as soon as this move was confirmed. Stan knew what the hell he was doing and how to prep the new quarters for everything they'd need.

"Looking good," he told the man.

Stan flashed him a smile and nodded. "Coming together nicely. We'll be all set when the movers and the tech team arrive."

"And twenty-four hours will do it?"

"*Absolutamente!* We'll be ready next Friday morning. You've got all my numbers and I plan to make myself available if your tech people need anything from me."

"It's a weekend," Liam reminded him.

"No weekends in my business," Stan joked. "You break down on Saturday and by Sunday you'll be in business again."

"I take your word for it," he told Stan as he backed out of the room and headed toward the elevator.

He glanced at his watch and realized it wasn't five o'clock yet, but he was done with business for the day. There was a cigar store in the Town and Country area where he bought gifts for special clients. Robert

Hoffman certainly fell into that category, so he decided to head out that way and do some shopping. He left the building and headed out State Road 60, and damn! That itch between the shoulder blades was back.

This is stupid. No one is watching me. Why would they? I'm out here on a busy highway in the middle of the city. There are lots of cars here, right?

He was telling himself how ridiculous the whole thing was when bam! A car hit his right rear bumper. Hard!

Shit!

He spared one second for a glance to the right and saw a gray sedan veer right and speed away. But then he was eyes front because the hit had sent him spinning around and he was jolted toward oncoming traffic. He stomped on the brakes as hard as he could and jerked the wheel, but it wasn't enough. In the blink of an eye he'd collided with the front of an oncoming car, the hard contact enough to jar his entire body. His vehicle shuddered as it made contact, and came to a full stop. Then came the chain reaction, cars behind the one he'd hit who couldn't stop in time, and cars behind him in the same predicament.

And the asshole who'd caused it was long gone.

He moved to open the driver's side door and discovered two things. His knee was jammed into the steering column and his shoulder hurt like a motherfucker.

Fuck! Just fuck!

Horns were blaring and people were shouting. He heard heavy pounding, and he realized someone was yelling at him and pounding on his window. He pushed down in the door handle again, shoved harder when the door resisted but finally, with creaking and crunching he got it open. Of course, pushing on it didn't help his shoulder any that now felt as if someone had stuck a medieval lance through it. He managed to climb out of the car, bracing himself against the door when his knee threatened to crumple. His leg nearly buckled and sharp pain stabbed his knee when he put weight on it and he gritted his teeth as he forced himself to stand. It took him a minute to pull himself together enough to assess the situation.

The highway was a mess everywhere he looked. Cars in both directions, either trying to avoid him or trying to avoid each other, had caused chain reactions. People whose cars had not been involved were trying to inch by without much success.

The man who had pounded on his door was standing so close Liam had trouble getting the door open, and barely moved back enough for Liam to get out of the car. He looked to be in his fifties, his stocky body clad in Bermuda shorts and a Tampa Bay Buccaneers T-shirt. He was shaking his fist at Liam and still shouting.

"You asshole! You fucking asshole! What the hell did you think you were doing?"

Liam gritted his teeth against the pain and dug for his best conciliatory tone.

"I'm sorry, but another car slammed into my right rear and knocked me into traffic. If you take a look you can see where he hit me."

"I don't care about your fucking car," the man raged. "What about mine? Look at it. Just take a look."

Liam looked at where the other man's car was locked to his front bumper. Shit. And behind him were six or seven more cars that hadn't been able to stop.

"I'm sorry," he repeated. "Let me give you my card and my insurance information."

"You're gonna need to give that to more than just me, jerkwad. I'll sue your ass." He held up his cell phone. "I'm calling the cops right now. You hear me?"

"I called the cops." A man standing by a vehicle three cars back yelled at him. "They'll haul your ass to jail."

"I did, too," someone else shouted.

More horns joined the honking until the cacophony made Liam's head hurt. He wanted to tell them all to just shut the hell up. A woman whose car had plowed into the side of Liam's because she hadn't been able to stop had finally climbed out and was adding her two cents to the conversation. Liam thought the whole thing resembled a bad movie that he couldn't turn off.

Shit! Shit! Shit!

The shrill sound of sirens cut through the noise. Liam watched as three police cars — one from the direction in which he'd come and two from the direction he was facing — made their way along the shoulders of the road. They parked, lights flashing, and headed into the chaos.

The man whose bumper Liam's car was currently lip-locked with started in right away, cursing Liam and telling the cops to "fix this damn mess." Others began adding their voice.

The cop held up his hand, then introduced himself. "One at a time, please. We need to find out what happened."

"I told you what happened," the man snapped. "This asshole over here slammed right into me going the wrong way and look at the mess."

Although to Liam it seemed like an entire day passed before the whole thing got untangled, it was really more like an hour. An hour in which he attempted to mask his pain, hold on to his temper and try to be aware of everything around him. Because that same sense of being watched still clung to him like a coat. He had no idea who the fuck might be watching him or why? He kept scanning the other cars looking for…what? What did he expect to see?

The cops radioed for an ambulance to at least administer first aid. Blocked off the highway in both directions and directed people to the closest off ramps. Figured out whose cars were drivable and who needed tow trucks and what kind. Took down everyone's information and told them they could ask for a copy of the report.

In the midst of it all, Rosalie called him and he had to tell her what happened and assure her that no, he did not need to go to the hospital. And yes, the cops were there handling it. He also gave her his friend's number and asked her to tell him today was off. Oh, and by the way. Could she send an Uber for him since his car was at that moment being loaded onto a wrecker. And also arrange for a loaner starting tomorrow. He'd cab or Uber over to pick it up in the morning.

And yes, he was going straight home as soon as Uber got there. Provided, of course, the cops were finished raking him over the coals.

And that was a nightmare itself. His knee and shoulder throbbed, his entire body ached, and if they asked him one more time to explain exactly how and why he crashed into incoming traffic, he might be arrested for murder.

When things finally wrapped up, Liam had a traffic ticket along with insurance information from the other drivers, a pounding headache and his shoulder and knee felt as if they were on fire.

He had told the tow truck driver to take his car to the body shop he used and now he Ubered back to his townhouse. Still wrapped in paranoia, he had the driver take him to the garage entrance rather than the front. In the kitchen he dropped his briefcase on the counter, grabbed a glass from the cupboard and carried it to the bar in the living room. He didn't even bother with ice, just poured two fingers of Jack Daniel's into it and took a healthy slug. The liquor burned on the way down but he hoped it would numb some of the pain, and maybe settle his nerves.

Ice, he told himself. And not just for the drink.

He was about to top off his drink and carry it upstairs so he could run a hot bath or maybe just take a shower when his cell rang.

Fuck.

He wasn't in the mood to talk to anyone right now. He answered without looking to see who the call was from, a rarity for him.

"Yeah?"

Silence, then a soft voice. "I caught you at a bad time."

Oh shit. Sydney.

He blew out a breath. "Hi, Syd. Can we start this call again?"

Her easy laugh drifted through the connection and rolled over him like a tranquilizer.

"Sounds like someone's had a rough day."

"You don't know the half of it," he snorted. "But just hearing your voice makes things better."

"We finished early today," she told him. "And I needed my client to have a night off, from me as well as the trial. I wondered if you could squeeze in dinner at the last minute."

Hell and damnation. The one night she was free, he was a physical wreck.

"Uh, listen," he began.

"If you're tied up, I understand," she said quickly.

"No, you don't understand." He made himself take another deep breath. "Let me tell you what happened today."

By the time he finished giving her the details, the Jack Daniel's had begun to work and at least mellow him out a little. Holding the phone in one hand, he added a touch more Jack to the glass.

"Liam, you need to see a doctor. You could have some serious injuries."

"No," he assured her. "I'm more sore than anything. And it would have to be the one night you can get free. Damn."

"No problem." He could hear the smile in her voice. "Go get in a hot shower and stay in it as long as you can. I'll bring over Chinese takeout and my skills as a masseuse."

At the thought of her massaging his naked body, his cock hardened and tried to push its way out of his fly.

He started to tell her this wasn't the best night, but then he thought, *fuck it.* They had to work so hard to find time together. She had a rare free night and he wasn't going to waste it, no matter what.

"You've got yourself a deal," he told her. "There's a great new Chinese place about two blocks from me. Let me call in the order, if you'll pick it up. And I warn you, Syd. I'm pretty damn useless tonight."

"We'll see. Okay, give me the name of this place."

"And Sydney?"

"Yes?"

"Don't ask me a bunch of questions, but just please do me a favor. Park your car in the garage at your condo and Uber over. I'll make sure you get home okay."

Silence hummed across the connection for a long moment.

"What's going on, Liam? Are you in trouble?"

Damn!

"Are you asking as my friend or an attorney?"

There wasn't a lot of humor in her chuckle. "For right now, let's say a friend. A special friend, though," she emphasized.

"Okay, let's go with that." He paused. "For now."

He also gave her the code to his back door lock. He'd stopped using keys a long time ago, knowing how easy they were to steal and or duplicate. He called the Canton Palace, gave them his order and his credit card number. After he hung up, he realized he hadn't asked Sydney what she liked, so he'd gone with some pretty standard dishes. Figured he couldn't go wrong that way.

Chapter Nine

This is a weird way to dive into a relationship. He'll think I'm nuts.

And maybe I am.

Wait. I've done crazier things before, right?

But not on such a personal level.

She wasn't an impulsive person. Earning her stripes as a highly successful attorney had taught her that impulsive usually led to trouble. But this was different, and she knew it. Felt it. Their one-night together had made her more positive than ever that whatever was between them definitely needed to be nurtured. The physical connection with Liam had zinged her from the start. But it wasn't just sex, even though somehow that was what lack of time kept turning it into.

No, it was a lot more than that. They connected on all levels. She didn't need him taking her out to dinner to know that.

Leaving her car in the condo building garage, she ran up to her apartment and took a minute to strip off her work clothes for jeans and a T-shirt. Tonight, she wasn't being glamorous Sydney Alfiore. Tonight, she would be just Syd. She grabbed a few things she thought she'd need and stuffed them into a tote bag, then headed downstairs to wait for the Uber driver.

What in the hell was going on in Liam's life that that he didn't want her to bring her car? Or that he couldn't discuss over the phone? The questions rattled around in her brain on the ride to his townhouse, preoccupying her so much she almost forgot to pick up the takeout. And why couldn't she come in through the front door?

She paid the Uber drive and got out, juggling the takeout bags and her tote as she punched in the code for the garage entrance. When she opened the inside door and stepped into the kitchen, she nearly bumped into Liam.

"Oh!"

"Sorry." He flashed a quick grin as he lifted the takeout bags from her. "I heard the door and came downstairs to meet you."

He had changed into sweatpants and a T-shirt and as she dished up the food, she was mentally drooling over him. For a guy who basically spent most of his life behind a computer, he had a body that would make most men weep. The sight of his broad shoulders, flat abs and sculpted muscles made her nipples tighten and the muscles in her core throb with insistent need. She couldn't recall the last man who'd made her senses react so quickly and so intensely. She wanted to plaster herself to his body and feel every inch of him.

She could put the hot sex on hold for the next time and do what she could for his anxiety.

And maybe just a little sex, enough to make him feel good.

As they carried dishes and the takeout cartons to the table, she noticed that he moved stiffly and had acquired a slight limp, favoring his left knee.

After dinner, she'd make him let her look at it. She pulled out a chair, but before she could sit, Liam grabbed her, turned her to face him and planted a hot, open-mouthed kiss on her. She was so startled she just opened her mouth automatically, allowing his tongue to sweep in. The flavor of him permeated every part of her, heating her body and for a moment making her forget everything else.

When he lifted his mouth from hers and stepped away, she had to blink to bring the room back into focus.

"I just had to have one taste." He blew out a breath. "I needed something to blunt the day."

"I gather it was a bitch." He held her chair as she seated herself at the table.

"In spades. But let's eat. If I talk about it now it'll ruin my digestion." The grin he tried fell way short of its mark.

"Fair enough. We've got time later, after I make sure you're relaxed."

"And exactly how do you plan to do that?"

She was pleased that he could at least joke a little. "After dinner. Food first."

She thought it was a miracle they could make easy small talk as they ate, but at last they were finished. They cleaned up together in silence. Then she made him sit and pushed up the leg of his sweat pants, frowning when she saw the swelling around his knee and the ugly bruise.

"Did you ice this at all?"

"Not yet. I figured I'd do it in a little while. I planned to take a hot shower first."

"Hmmm. Let me see your shoulder."

It didn't look much better than his knee. *Damn! That must have been some hit his car had taken.*

"Okay." She winked. "Tonight, I am your therapist. Here to give you therapy after a bad day."

"That sounds great, Syd, and I want to take advantage of that more than anything." He shook his head. "But I don't think—"

"Right. Don't think." She lifted her small duffel that she'd dropped by the door when she came in. "How about showing me the way upstairs."

"Oh, okay, but—"

"Shower, Liam. We're going to shower and then I'm going to take care of your bumps and bruises. After that, maybe we can talk about what's got your head in a twist and see if we can make sense of it."

Sydney managed a cursory glance of the place as they moved toward the stairs. The townhouse was spacious, with most of the bottom floor a big open family-room-type layout. She had a brief glance at the comfortable furniture before he led her up the stairway.

His bedroom was huge, no less than she expected. But it was the bathroom that made her eyes widen. The shower itself was as big as some bathrooms she'd seen, taking up one wall, with a long sliding glass door. And the tub, if the time ever came to use it, could hold them and any activities they chose very nicely.

"All right, buddy." She grinned. "Strip and get the shower going."

He gave her one long, slow look before dragging his clothes off and padding into the bathroom. He tested the water until he was happy with the temperature then stepped inside and leaned against one wall, his head on his forearm.

And god! Didn't he just look a wreck? Her heart ached for him. His entire posture screamed anguish and the marks of the accident stood out in bold relief. She could better see the purpling of a bruise on his left knee and his left shoulder. She could imagine how sore he was. Well, she was there to try and make it better, at least as much as she could.

She slid open the door slowly, not wanting to startle him. As it was he jerked, knocked his sore knee into the tile wall and swore loud enough she could hear him over the running water.

"Sorry, sorry, sorry." She stepped under the water with him.

He raked his gaze over her naked body. "You're a welcome sight, but be warned. I don't think I'm in proper shape to appreciate you tonight."

"Right now just being with you is enough." She cupped his cheeks and studied his face, noting the deep lines cut by tension and the anguish in his eyes. "Okay. Let's get you soaped and showered. Then I'm going to tend to your obviously aching body. Those are some bruises you've got, so come on. Turn around. Try to relax while I do all the work."

The fact that he didn't laugh at her weak joke or protest, didn't do the macho thing where he insisted he was fine, told her more than words that something was going on with him that was more than just daily stress.

She poured some of the body wash from the bottle on a shelf into her hands. Lathered it up and began to smooth it over the rigid muscles on his back. He was so tense she wondered why the muscles didn't just snap like overstretched rubber bands. She took her time massaging from neck to waist and down the length of each arm. She took extra care when she came to the injured shoulder, feeling the heat of the injury beneath his palms.

Damn! Whatever happened, he wrecked himself pretty good.

When she reached his ass, she had to put her hormones in park and pretend she was soaping a mannequin. She crouched down to take care of his legs then nudged him to turn around. It took every bit of her self-control to soap and rinse the front of his body without letting desire poke its head into the process.

When she got to his cock and his balls, the corners of her mouth inched up in a tiny grin.

"Apparently the rest of your body hasn't gotten the message that your mind is dealing with some bad stuff," she teased.

"No shit." He chuffed a laugh. "I need to send it a message because I'll tell you, tonight it's—"

"Not a problem," she interrupted. "That's not why I'm here." She looked up at him. "We'll have plenty of other opportunities for that. Right?"

"Right," he agreed. "And thank you."

"No thanks necessary." She placed a soft kiss on his swollen, bruised knee and stood up. "Okay, I think we're done with this."

She made sure they were both rinsed off before turning off the shower. Then she wrapped both of them in two large bath towels, tucking the corner of hers so it would stay in place.

Sydney stood on tiptoe to plant a light kiss on his lips. "Let's move into the bedroom.

Liam chuckled. "Any other time, I'd say bring it on."

"Any other time I'd let you. Come on."

In seconds she had the covers folded way back on the bed and Liam stretched out on his stomach, the towel draped across his hips. When she pressed gently on his shoulder, he groaned.

"Fuck, that's sore."

"It looks it. How did it happen?"

"Auto accident." He stifled a groan. "Wrenched my shoulder and jammed my damn knee into the steering column."

"This will help. Just close your eyes and try to think of anything but this."

"Normally I'd think about sex," he joked. "But…"

"Think about a trip to Hawaii and lying in the sun. Where was the last vacation you took?"

"Would you believe me if I told you it was so long ago I'm not sure I remember? Pathetic, right?"

"Might be, if I wasn't in the same boat." She uncapped one of the small bottles she'd brought with her, poured some into the palm of one hand and began to gently massage it into his left shoulder.

Liam let out a tiny moan of pleasure.

"Damn, Syd. What is that stuff? Is smells almost as good as it feels."

"A magic lotion I got when I wrecked my knee waterskiing." She chuckled. "Serves me right for doing something so idiotic. A turtle is more coordinated then I am." She dripped a little more onto her palm and began the circular motion again. "So, while I have you at my mercy, why don't you tell me what's got you so upset? And why I had to Uber here and come in the back door? Is this part of the same feeling you had the other night at the hotel?"

"Uh-huh. But it may be all in my imagination," he told her, "and I don't want you to think I'm a stupid idiot."

Sydney began to gently knead the flesh of his shoulder. "Then maybe talking about it will put it in proper perspective. Come on. A man doesn't get where you are in the world of technology by being easily spooked. Let's have it."

"It started about a month ago," he began. "Remember I mentioned it when we were in the hotel bar? It hasn't gone away. Just a feeling. A sense of being watched."

By the time he'd given her most of the details, she was finished with the massage. *Damn it!*

He'd had his eyes closed while she was working her magic, but now he opened them. "So, what do you think?"

"Turn over and I'll give you my opinion."

When he did, she covered him from waist to lower thighs with the towel. She didn't need to be distracted by the sight of his incredible shaft. She grabbed a second bottle, another one a doctor had prescribed for her knee. With careful, gentle strokes she began to rub it into his knee and the area around it.

"Okay." Liam closed his eyes as if he couldn't watch her while she told him what she thought. "Let's have it."

Sydney weighed her words carefully. She was pretty sure Liam wasn't someone who was easily spooked, or jumped at shadows. Something must have triggered it, so she needed to figure out what.

"Has anything significant happened lately besides the Arroyo deal? Not that it isn't significant enough by itself, but I can't see anyone following you or causing an accident because of it. So what else? Anything with any of your clients?"

"Not any more than usual, except for the recent flood of new accounts. Oh! Ouch!" He flinched when she squeezed his knee a little harder.

"Sorry. I just want to make sure this gets to the bone."

"Well, whatever you're doing feels good. I don't want to take advantage, so you can stop any time after the next three or four days."

She laughed. "You wish."

"Yeah, a guy can hope."

"I'm going to get something to ice that knee in a minute." She sat back on her heels. "You may be imagining things, as you said, but I've learned to trust people's intuition. So, let's get back to your clients. Anything special that night trigger this?"

"Possibly." He shrugged. "Maybe. I write software for defense contractors as well as high-profile financial firms."

"Which one's at the top of the list right now?"

"I'd have to say Hoffman. They're doing a hush-hush project for the Department of Defense. We're just finishing up their security program now so they can load everything onto their servers. I'll be delivering it the week before Gasparilla."

"I don't suppose you caught that guy's license plate today, did you?" She shook her head. "Stupid question. I think we'll go with deliberate because that's what the logistics say. I don't think whoever this is wants to kill you, or they would have done it."

"What good would killing me do, anyway?"

"What happens if you're out of commission? How does it affect your ongoing projects?"

He frowned. "Not a lot. We're structured so any one of the staff can jump into any project if necessary. If I couldn't finish the Hoffman project, there are three others on my staff who have worked on it with me who could complete it, beta test it and deliver it."

"So, harming you wouldn't accomplish a thing, right?"

"Right. That's why this is so hard to understand."

Sydney nibbled on her lower lip. "Does the outside world know that?"

"I have no idea what they know." He started to push himself to a sitting position, then groaned and fell back.

"Easy, big boy." Sydney shifted on the bed to kneel beside him. "You've got some mighty big bruises here."

"I feel like I got hit by a giant fist."

"Looks like it, too. Maybe we need to come at this from another angle, but not tonight. You need to get some sleep and I need to ice those bruises." She eased off the bed. "Do you have gel packs in your freezer?"

"Yeah. I always keep a couple handy."

"Good. Better than ice." She took a sleep shirt out of the little tote she'd brought with her and pulled it on over her head. "I'll be right back."

She fetched two gel packs from the freezer. She'd score a hand towel from Liam's bathroom to protect him from freezer burn. He was still in the same position when she hurried back into the room. To Sydney, it didn't look as if he'd moved an inch. She did notice, however, the glass on the nightstand that she figured had held the Jack Daniel's was now empty. *Good.* He'd be relaxed. She had a special treat to finish him off and he'd be able to sleep.

"This is cold," she warned him, as she settled one gel pack on his knee.

He jumped. "No shit."

Even though she wrapped it in a towel, when she eased the other ice pack beneath his shoulder, he jerked again and cursed softly.

"We need to leave these on for twenty minutes. If you're a good boy, you'll get a reward."

It was a testament to the electricity between them that even in his present condition, his cock flexed beneath the towel and when he spoke, his voice was husky.

"I can hardly wait." He sighed. "Damn. It's a good thing I do most of my work sitting down." He studied her as if suddenly aware of what she was wearing, and his mouth curved in a little grin. "You came prepared to spend the night?"

She shrugged. "Of course. You sounded as if you needed me and I wanted to be here for you." Watching his face, she could almost see him processing everything in his mind.

"So, let me see if I understand, because I don't want to make a mistake here. We've been together twice. Three times, if you count the party where we met. Neither of them were what I'd call dates, but the last time was better than any other date I've ever had. And instead of me taking you out on a real date tonight, here you are tending to my wounded body and prepared to spend the night. Even though I know damn well you have an early meeting before court tomorrow. Did I get that all right?"

Sydney had been adjusting the ice on his knee, but she stopped and stared at him. "Is this okay? I know I have a tendency to telescope time lines, so did I get our signals wrong?"

"No, you didn't." He smiled and linked his fingers with those of her free hand. "Not even a little. There's something here, Sydney. We have the kind of careers that don't leave a lot of openings for personal time. Time to build relationships, so if something's there we need to jump into it with both feet. Otherwise we risk losing it. But make no mistake here. This isn't anything close to casual. We had something going from the minute we met. And I want to make sure we do everything we can, however different this might be, to be sure we don't lose out on it."

"Good." She blew out a breath and felt the tension ease from her body. "Me, too. Now, how about you just close your eyes and let me work some of my magic on you?"

He arched one eyebrow. "Magic?"

"Uh-huh. Go on. Close your eyes."

As soon as he did, she shifted to kneel beside him. Tossing aside the towel draped over his hips, she slid one hand between his thighs to cup his balls and wrapped the fingers of the other hand around his now rigid cock.

He started to sit up, but pain slashed across his face and he fell back onto the pillows.

"Jesus, Syd. Way to startle a man."

"But a good way, right? Just close your eyes. I'll do all the work here."

As soon as he was relaxed again, she began a slow up-and-down glide of her fingers on the hard cock, gently squeezing his balls in rhythm with her strokes. The more she stroked, the harder the pulse at the hollow of his throat beat.

She bent lower and took one stiff nipple in her mouth, sucking it before giving it a gentle bite. A low groan rumbled from his throat, so she closed her teeth on it again before moving to the other bud. Then she trailed the tip of her tongue along a line down his abs, paused to ease the indentation of his navel then continued on through the curls at his groin. When she reached his cock, she swiped her tongue across the velvety head, catching a tiny bead of fluid sitting right at the slit.

"Jesus, Syd." Liam tried to lift his groin closer to her.

"Uh-uh. No moving. Can't lose the ice packs. Can you hold absolutely still?"

He chuffed a slightly hysterical laugh. "I can't believe I'm letting you do this while icing my body."

She winked at him. "It'll keep you from getting too hot too fast."

"Not possible. *Oh, god!*" He spat the words out as she shifted her fingers and took the length of his shaft into her mouth.

He tasted of shower and body wash and just plain Liam, the skin soft, but beneath it, he was hard as steel. She timed the movement of her mouth with the rhythmic squeezing of his balls, not too fast but just enough to push him slowly up that erotic climb. She alternated scraping the length of him with her lips and her teeth and stroking him with her fingers. It wasn't hard to tell the need was building rapidly in his body. His breathing became choppy and his hands clenched into fists at his sides. He made exciting little noises as she pulled him closer and closer to a climax, keeping everything deliberately slow and steady.

"Jesus, Syd. God! Please. I need to— Holy fuck!"

The words flew from his mouth as she used both her hand and her mouth on his cock. Now she moved faster, sucked harder, felt the heat of him against her palm.

And he was there, his body rigid, back arching, shouting as he erupted into her mouth. She massaged his balls as she sucked every bit of fluid from him, swallowing it as he came and came and came. At last he went limp, his shaft softening against her tongue.

She eased him from her mouth, smiled and kissed her way up his body to his lips. He threaded the fingers of one hand through her hair, anchoring her head in place so she was looking directly into his eyes.

"That was…incredible."

"For me, too." The kiss she gave him was more emotional than passionate. "Did it get your mind off what's going on with you?"

His laugh rumbled up from deep inside his body.

"Damn straight. Although I might need the same kind of treatment every night until we find out what the hell is going on."

She chuckled. "Don't push your luck, buddy. Tonight was an unexpected gift."

"I know." He pulled her head closer to kiss her again, a soft touching of lips, no tongue, just that affirmation of connection. "But I can hope, right?"

"Well, keep hoping. I can't wait to get to closing statements in this damn trial. My client is a horse's ass and the prosecutor is obsessively detailed. He's insisted on bringing in an army of forensic accountants to testify to each minute transaction. Which of course I then have to rebut with my own expert witnesses."

"Not much fun," he commented.

"No kidding. But Gasparilla's in a couple of weeks and I'd like to be finished by then so I can party a little. If I've done my job right, the jury won't take long to return a verdict of not guilty."

"I'm close to delivering the Hoffman project." He stroked her shoulder, his touch warming her from the inside out. "The move to the new building is all set for right after that. What do you say we celebrate Gasparilla together?"

"I'm all for that."

He chuckled. "Come to the parade and I'll wave to you from my float and toss you some beads."

She stared at him. "You ride in the parade?"

"Uh-huh." He told her the name of the group he was with. "Been doing it for about five years. There's a private party after. We can have a couple of drinks, do the glad-hand thing and then have our now private celebration. How does that sound to you?"

"It sounds terrific." She sighed. "Especially the private part."

He chuckled. "And I won't be so banged up by then, either."

His smile hit something deep inside her. None of the men she'd ever been with had smiled at her quite the same way.

"Then after that maybe we can actually go out on a real date," she teased.

"Or five or ten," he joked.

"Meanwhile you need a good night's sleep."

She eased the gel packs away from his body and helped him slide beneath the covers. Then she slipped in next to him, cuddling close on his uninjured side. He curled his arm around her to hold her as close to his body as he could. She tried to relax but her brain wouldn't stop poking at her.

Should I have left him alone tonight? Would it have been better if I had stayed away?

But she couldn't deny the connection between them, and the chance for something she'd never had before. She had never wanted to make time for a personal relationship before, mostly because no one had ever come along that made her want it. For the first time in her life, she felt this intense connection and she wanted to build on it.

"Syd?"

"Mm-hmm?"

"Thanks."

She opened her eyes and looked at him. "For?"

"Just being you." He kissed the top of her head. "Good night."

"Yes." She smiled. "It really is."

Chapter Ten

Shan had chosen a different restaurant this time, one in a northern suburb of Tampa, where they would be much less likely to run into someone they knew. They had been lucky so far, but Shan had deliberately chosen meeting places not frequented by people they knew.

Eight had ordered beer again, ignoring Shan's displeasure. To each his own. Besides, who was the one risking life here, anyway?

Shan took a sip of coffee, set the cup down carefully and looked across the table. "Your boss must have a body made of steel. I cannot believe the accident didn't keep him out of the office."

Eight snorted. "Only death would keep him out of the office. That was a very stupid thing for you to do. He's been paranoid all last week about the security for this project. He insisted on checking all the work at the end of each day. Some nights he was there almost until midnight beta testing each phase."

Shan had been playing with a cigarette. The restaurant did not allow smoking, so this apparently was the next best thing. But at Eight's words, Shan's fingers snapped it in two and scattered tobacco on the table.

"I expect you made sure that did not interfere with your ability to do what you have to."

Eight almost choked on a swallow of beer. "I did what I had to. I'm very good at my job. You and your people are the ones who fucked it up because you insisted on doing things that called attention to the situation."

Eight did not want to tell Shan that one personal project she'd been working on was a new way to hide the back door in the software. She was testing it on the Hoffman project. Someone would have to be very sophisticated in the field to be able to detect it. There hadn't been a way to test it yet, because Liam had hardly left the office until the Hoffman software was delivered. She couldn't have copied it to a laptop because it would have left an electronic footprint. It had just meant picking the right morning to go in extra early and take care of it.

And taking advantage of the fact that Liam trusted Eight without reservation.

Oh, what fools people can be.

And that was almost a problem. Eight heard from Rosalie that when the head of Arroyo heard about Liam's 'accident', she wanted to hire security to drive him everywhere. Thank god Liam had managed to squash that. So, there had still been a narrow window — narrow being the operative word — to install the new, more sophisticated back door. If it worked, perhaps that would generate an even larger payoff when everything was complete.

Don't get ahead of yourself.

But the devil that sat on Eight's shoulder was calling with its seductive voice and the secret vice was demanding to be let out.

Soon. Very soon.

"So, the program is in place at Hoffman's. Good. Let's give it a few days before we test your back door."

"The best time would be when we're in the middle of the move," Eight pointed out. "There will be a point in time when the entire system is down."

"You will text me when you have that information. When did you say the move was scheduled for?"

Eight swallowed an irritated sigh. "This weekend. Tomorrow."

"But most likely he will begin dismantling things today. Correct? My people are most impatient to move forward on this. Time is critical."

"Just don't do anything until at least late tomorrow." Eight's gut burned. This thing would produce ulcers before it was finished. If only self-control wasn't such a problem when the devil beckoned.

At last Shan finished the last of his coffee and signaled their meeting was over.

Eight slid out of the booth and hurried to the door, wanting to get out of there as fast as possible.

What a clusterfuck this was turning out to be.

* * * *

Liam popped a couple of ibuprofen in his mouth and washed them down with the water left in his bottle. He had become accustomed to the constant dull ache in his body and the twinge in his knee that stabbed him whenever he got up or sat down. The residual ache was

147

taking a long time to go away, most likely because he pushed himself at work for hours longer than she should. If not for Sydney's wonderful massage last week, he'd be in much worse shape.

Sydney.

Just thinking her name called up all kinds of erotic images. It had thrilled him to discover that beneath the take-charge image she projected to the world was a softer, more feminine woman who made him want so many things. And now he was right on the verge of being able to enjoy those things and – he hoped – a lot more.

He'd finally taken care of all the paperwork on his accident. Gotten the police report that contained his statement about another car pushing him into oncoming traffic. The damage to his vehicle spoke loudly to that. He'd picked up the rental, his own car now out of commission for at least a week because the body shop was so backed up.

Teri and Phil had offered to stay late to do a last work-through on the Hoffman project. Sy was at a client's tweaking their program, but the two were more than enough. They put the software through its paces, finally satisfied that it was locked up tighter than a drum.

After the others left, Liam added his own special tweak in there. No matter how much he trusted Teri or Phil or Sy, he wanted to be the only one to know about this little gimmick. By the time he locked down for the night, he was exhausted but satisfied he and his team had done their job more than well.

He delivered the new software to Hoffman Contractors on time and installed the system on their server while Hoffman and his staff watched. Then, with everything in place, he tried to again crack it to access their files, without luck. It had worked without a hitch. He stayed long enough to watch them load all the work files, especially those involving the new drone project, and to make sure all was in working order.

Today, just to satisfy both himself and his client, he'd tested it again, trying to hack it from his office, then from a cyber café near Hoffman's building. Nothing got through. He kept getting the same programmed screen: *Incorrect password. Try again.* When he left, everyone was happy, including himself. This was a weight off his shoulders.

Tomorrow morning they'd begin the move, a process he wasn't looking forward to, but he could do it with that pressure gone. Plus, Taylor's assistant was working with Rosalie and had told her Mrs. Cantrell insisted he get a large enough crew that everything would go smoothly. Everyone would be in early, including the tech specialist Arroyo was sending him. Max Something. He hoped the guy knew his stuff.

He called Rosalie after he left the Hoffman offices. "I'm done for the day."

She was silent for a moment. "Before midnight? You don't think the world will stop spinning?"

He laughed, and the laughter felt good. "It might, but today I don't care. Tell everyone else they can quit at five."

"Wait! I have to alert the media." Then she chuckled. "Do something nice for yourself tonight. You've earned it. But don't forget you told everyone this morning to be here at seven sharp tomorrow. The big move. Someone from Taylor Cantrell's office called while you were out and said the crew was ready and they'd be here at seven sharp."

Liam nodded. "I'll even be early."

"And I'll arrange for the coffee and pastries." She chuckled. "Go have fun."

As he rode down in the elevator, he was already texting Sydney. They had communicated every day since that night at his place. She was concerned about his shoulder and also his situation. She always asked if there had been any other out-of-the-ordinary incidents. Had anything happened to trigger that sense of uneasiness again? And how was he feeling?

He always wanted to say not as good as if she was with him, but he knew her situation. She expected the jury in her trial to return a verdict today. Hopefully, they'd both have something to celebrate.

Dinner and a sleepover tonight? Today went well.

Jury still out and I'm hand holding. Will let u know.

K

Damn! He'd sure hate to have to spend tonight alone, but he understood her situation, just as she understood his. Maybe she could at least meet him for a sandwich or a drink.

Do you think u can steal a half hour later?

He was at his car behind the wheel before she answered.

Ten-thirty. Too late?

His thumbs flew over the keys.

No. I'll take whatever I can get. Where?

Hotel DaCosta. I have everyone staying there. Meet you in bar.

I'll b there.

He had hoped for a sleepover, but he understood her circumstances. Probably just as well, since he had such an early call in the morning.

He showered and changed into khakis and a soft collar shirt. Made sure to strap his special watch back on. He'd designed it with an engineer when he began designing software for defense contractors. Unknown to his staff, the last thing he did before delivering new software was embed a warning alert. He trusted the security of the code, but he never left anything to chance. Just in case some outrageously smart and clever hacker tried to hack into the program, the alert would go off and send the warning to his computer at work, his laptop and his watch.

Then he sat in front of his television icing his knee until it was time for him to leave for the hotel.

"Are you in disguise?" he asked when she walked into the bar. She'd exchanged her power suit and heels for slacks and an embroidered T-shirt. Her thick ebony hair was pulled back in a ponytail and she wore very little makeup.

The corners of her mouth turned up in a tired smile and fatigue was in every line of her body.

"As a matter of fact, yes. I left Sydney the lawyer up in my room. For a few hours, I can be just plain Syd." She studied his face. "That okay?"

"More than." He reached across the table and took one of her hands in both of his. "I hate to see you killing yourself like this. No verdict today?"

She gave a tired shake of her head. "I wish. I don't know what they're waiting for. We refuted every bit of evidence the prosecution presented and even gave them some alternatives."

"So, he's not guilty?"

"Not as far as my case is concerned, and, at the moment, that's all I care about. I just want this done and over with."

A waiter came to take their order, interrupting them for a moment.

Maybe a drink will give her a lift.

"So why are you staying at the hotel tonight?" he asked.

"Because it's the better alternative to locking my client up in my house with me. He's going absolutely nuts. His friends and business associates are keeping their distance until a verdict is in and his wife and teenage kids took a powder until this is over. I'm holding his hand over the weekend."

"Nice support system," he snorted.

"Yeah, no kidding." She rubbed her forehead. "I am going to be owed so many favors when this is over."

The waiter delivered their drinks and Liam touched the neck of his beer bottle to Sydney's glass.

"Here's to a verdict of innocent delivered early tomorrow."

"Amen to that."

They each took a swallow of their beverage.

"So, let's forget about my trial for a minute." She leaned forward and rested her elbows on the table. "I know you delivered the Hoffman software. That has to be a huge relief for you."

"It is. We beta tested that sucker six ways from Sunday. If there's someone who can break through it, I want to hire him." He winked. "Right after he gets out of jail."

"And the move?"

"We're launching at seven tomorrow morning. Arroyo hired the crew for us and sent their head technical engineer to help with the electronics."

"What about your shadow?" She took another sip of her drink. "Any more off-the-wall incidents? Or funny feelings?"

He shrugged. "No incidents, but that damn feeling just won't go away. I guess I'm just becoming permanently paranoid."

"I never shrug off or discount feelings. Maybe once you're moved and settled in, new quarters, it will go away."

"One can only hope."

He had just taken another sip of beer when his watch beeped at him and a red devil on the face flashed at him. Every muscle in his body tensed and he felt as if all the blood had drained from his body. For a moment he actually thought his heart had stopped.

No. This is just not possible.

"I have to go, Syd. I'm sorry, but I have to leave right now."

Her eyes widened at his reaction. "What's wrong, Liam? What's happening?"

"I have to go right now." He threw money on the table and strode toward the lobby.

"Okay, okay. I get it. But what happened? I thought you were going to keel over dead."

"I might yet." He stopped and turned to face her, resting his hands on her shoulders. "An attempt has been made to breach the Hoffman security software. I built in an alarm that alerts me if anyone tries. This has never happened before." He planted a quick kiss on her lips. "Good luck tomorrow. I'll call when I can."

He raced into the garage, thankful the elevator came right away and he was in his car in less than two minutes. As he headed down to the street, his cell rang.

"Benedict, what the fuck is going on?" Robert Hoffman's voice was gravelly with anger.

Liam had also installed software on their head tech engineer's computer that would signal him if a breach had been attempted. He was sure the man had been in touch with his boss the minute the warning sounded.

"That's what I'm on my way to find out right now. Call your security and tell them to let me in."

"You're supposed to be the best at this," Hoffman growled. "If you or your people fucked this up, there won't be a place on this planet you can hide."

True that, Liam thought to himself.

"I'll be there in less than ten minutes, Robert. This could just be a one in a million glitch that I can fix on the spot."

"You damn well better. I'm on my way, too. I'll see you there."

"Good."

Not good.

Shit. Shit. Shit.

The night watchman at the lot at Hoffman's building had obviously gotten the word, because he passed Liam right through. Ditto the guard on duty in the building.

"They're up on three, Mr. Benedict," he said. "I held the elevator down here for you."

Liam just nodded as he stepped into the elevator car and pushed the button for the second floor. The ride up took mere seconds, but to him it felt like hours. When the doors opened, he strode down the corridor to the big central IT room. The building was divided according to specialties. The top floor was all office. Below it was the huge technical section, with cubicles for the individual computer specialists, large spaces for the actual project engineers, and a huge room where all the servers were housed. The door was open, light spilling out into the corridor and he could hear angry voices.

"...as soon as he gets here." Robert's voice, loud and angry. "Ah. Here he is now."

"I'm here," Liam acknowledged.

"You'd damn well better be. What the fuck is going on?"

Liam let out a breath and looked around. Besides Hoffman, there were three other men in the room. He'd met George Eisner, the project engineer, and Barry Felton, their technology guru whose job it was to see that shit like this did not happen. Nobody introduced the other man and at the moment Liam didn't care.

"Just give me a minute here," he told everyone.

He sat down at the computer Barry routinely used to troubleshoot and check everything running on the servers. His fingers flew over the keys as he typed in commands. At once code began scrolling on the screen. He watched it as he typed in more and more commands. He never looked at anyone else, keeping his focus just on what he was doing. Finally, he sat back in his chair, his shirt soaked in sweat, his head throbbing. He took a minute to massage his aching temples before turning to his client.

"Okay. There's good news and bad news."

"The first thing I want to know," Hoffman ground out, "is if someone actually got into this system and into the files. Shit, Liam. That would be a fucking disaster, in a whole lot of ways."

"I know. And no, they didn't get into anything. The alarms and failsafes I built in just before I delivered it to you worked and set off the alarms. They also locked out whoever is doing this."

"Explain, please," Hoffman demanded. "In language I can understand."

"I know what he's talking about," Barry Felton said.

Hoffman held up his hand. "I want Liam to tell us."

"Think of the security system as a big fence around your design software and your actual plans, those completed and those in progress. There's a gate in the fence. A visible one and one that can't be seen. Someone tries to breach the fence. They might get through the visible gate, but then the invisible one drops down and slams them shut."

"Would they know that?" Hoffman asked.

Liam shook his head. "We don't want them to. They might regroup and try a different hacking software, one that's so new we don't even know about it yet."

"But they get a message, right?" Stan obviously couldn't help himself.

"Yes. One that says the system is down, please try again later."

"So, then they'd wait," Stan jumped in again. "Give it a while to reset and try again, right?"

Liam nodded. "And that's where they are now. So, we have some decisions to make."

"I want to know how the fuck this happened," Stan demanded. "You're supposed to be the best in the business. Everyone sings your praises. No one ever said they had a glitch like this."

"That's right," Liam agreed. Only extreme self-control was keeping him from tearing his hair out or banging his head on the desk. Hoffman was right. This had never happened before. One of his hallmarks was his ability to create unhackable software. Usually by the time hackers got to the first gate, they gave up and went to work on something else.

"So?"

"There's a first time for everything. But the very good news is they didn't get through the invisible barrier. Didn't get into the system and nothing was disturbed."

"But we have to start all over, right?"

Liam shook his head. His breathing had finally returned to somewhere east of normal and ideas were spinning in his head. "Not at all. We know the software holds, right? So, let's see if we can set a trap."

George jumped in. "We can't afford anything that'll screw up this project. We're on a tight timeline and the Department of Defense isn't going to be happy if we have to give them a bunch of excuses or ask for more time. Don't forget once we're satisfied with the design, we still have to build the prototype, test it and work out any kinks."

Liam nodded. "I understand. This will not interfere with the project at all."

"So, what do you propose?"

"I'd like to install a ghost program. A false design. I can tweak the security protocol so if someone tries to hack in, it will send them to the phony plans. That will give me time to get a forensic data specialist in to take apart the program on my end and see if there's a problem."

Hoffman quirked an eyebrow. "I didn't realize there were people who did that."

"You bet. Like forensic accountants, only they dig through coding instead of accounting."

"So you think there's something wrong with the software that I just paid you a fortune for?"

Liam's headache was building in force again. "No. I beta tested it multiple times. Then tried to crack it again when I installed it here. But that's the logical place to start."

"Can we keep working or do we have to stop?"

"Can you hold off until noon tomorrow? I know time is tight, but that will give me a chance to create the ghost."

"Better to take the time and make sure we're foolproof," Barry told his boss. "We'll make the time up. No sweat."

Hoffman looked at each of them in turn before he nodded.

"Fine. But only until noon tomorrow."

"I'm going to fix this, Robert," Liam assured him. "I'll find the problem and take care of it."

"You do that."

Anger, shock and fear coalesced inside Liam as he left the building. He was so uptight he almost forgot to keep an eye out for any strange cars following him, easy to spot at this time of night. And oh, yeah, that feeling of being impaled on a virtual sword managed to stick itself into the mix with everything else.

But nothing caught his attention or made the hairs on the back of his neck stand up. Still, he did his best to check both the rear and side view mirrors on the drive to the office. He hoped like hell whoever this was, if in fact there was someone, would leave him alone while he tried to solve a problem that could kill the Arroyo deal and destroy his young company.

Chapter Eleven

"I'm sorry to bother you so late," Liam apologized as soon as Taylor Cantrell answered the phone.

"Don't be ridiculous. One of the first things I told you was emergencies don't run on a clock. And I'm assuming this is an emergency."

"Unfortunately, yes."

He took a hit of the strong coffee he'd picked up on his way to the office. He was too wired to go home. He wouldn't sleep anyway and he itched to get started tackling this disaster, so he'd called from the car as he headed for the office. And shit! He remembered tomorrow was the big move. How the hell was he going to get everything taken care of?

"Okay, let's have it." Her voice was blessedly unruffled. "And tell me want I can do to help."

Her steady voice and quiet words did more to calm his jittery nerves than anything else could have. One of the reasons, he realized, that she ran a giant conglomerate as well as she did. He kept his recitation brief but made sure he gave her the complete picture.

She was silent for a moment and Liam's gut knotted. But when she spoke, there was no censure in her voice.

"Do you think someone on your staff could have manipulated the security program you wrote after the beta testing? I thought it was foolproof."

He swallowed a sigh. That was the first thing that had occurred to him, also.

"Like I said earlier, this program is like a concrete barrier. Any hack would bump into it and be stopped. No further progress. I only put the alarm in as a failsafe — I never thought would be tripped. It means someone got through that first barrier. So yes, to get that far someone would have had to build in a backdoor. And that would have had to happen after the beta testing."

Damn! His staff was like family to him, especially those who had been with him since the beginning — Teri, Sy and Pete. If it was anyone it had to be a newer hire, someone who did not have personal loyalty to him. But even considering that made him sick.

And what the hell would have happened if he hadn't put that failsafe in with the alarm?

"It has to be one of them, Liam. No one else would have had the chance. Or even the skills."

"God, Taylor. I just hate to think so. A couple of these people have worked with me for a long time. And everyone's been vetted carefully."

Or maybe not as carefully as I thought.

"All right. We can go over personnel records after we get this problem fixed."

Just like that. No yelling or finger pointing. Just right to the heart of the matter. Not that the other might not come later.

"Right. I'd like to get a top-notch forensic data specialist in to go over every line of code in the program. That's top priority. He or she can find the aberration, if there is one. And hopefully where it came from."

"Where it came from?"

"Yes." He swallowed another hit of coffee. "I have everyone's computer tagged so I know who writes which code." He paused. "Uh, Taylor, they don't know that."

She laughed. Really laughed. "Liam, you are a man after my own heart. I don't trust anyone a hundred percent, either. Except for Noah, that is. Okay. I have just the person for you. I know him personally."

"I'd hoped that was the case, because my calling someone might not be able to get them here right now. And I need someone like yesterday."

"Okay. Let me make a call and I'll get right back to you."

Liam was almost at his office building.

"I'll be at my office in about five minutes," he told her. "But don't call me on the landline. Use my cell. I know it's protected."

"Got it."

Once inside and at his desk, he booted up his computer. He had an isolated, locked file on his laptop, which at the moment was at his townhouse. He'd check that as soon as he was finished here. The first thing he wanted to do was unlock the files on the server and see if there was anything hinky that for whatever goddamn reason did not show up in the beta testing.

There was about a ten-minute gap between the time he finished with beta testing and was actually able to install the digital lock. He was working to reduce that time, if not to zero at least to one minute. Theoretically anyone could go in and change it then, but they'd have to have left some kind of digital footprint.

The sky outside his window had turned from black to gray by the time he finished with that chore, frustrated because he could not find a thing. He copied the software onto a thumb drive and sat back in his chair. Just as he wondered when he'd hear from Taylor, his cell rang and her name popped onto the screen.

"Got something for me?" he asked. He figured she wouldn't care if he did away with the niceties of answering phones.

"Many somethings. But first, Noah says to tell you to take a deep breath. We've got your back."

"Taylor, I want you to know—" He stopped, rephrased what he was going to say. "I am shocked by this, because at least until now I have utmost faith in my staff."

"You know what they say. Shit happens. You won't be the first one to be fooled nor the last. It happened to me when I took over the corporation, if that makes you feel better."

"That's hard to believe, but I guess you are right."

"Okay." She cleared her throat. "Some information for you. Max Bowman just happened to be in Miami, on another job for us. A marketing agency we just brought into the fold. They moved to new quarters and she supervised all the technical equipment. We sent a helicopter for her and as we speak, she should be landing in Tampa. I gave her your cell number so you should be hearing from her ASAP. She'll take that off your shoulders."

In Miami? Helicopter? He really had become part of a corporate family that made things happen.

"Do I need to arrange a car for her? A hotel room? I can—"

"Already taken care of," Taylor assured him. "Now for your forensic data specialist. We are damn lucky, Liam."

"Lucky?" His eyebrows reached for the sky, even though no one was there to see them.

"Eric Braun, who I'm told is the best in the industry, happens to be a friend of a friend. They reached out to him, put him in touch with me and we just sent the plane to Denver to fetch him." She gave a short little laugh. "We're lucky. His job just before this was in Madrid. That's a long plane ride back."

Liam breathed a little easier. "I have no idea how to thank you for this."

"No thanks necessary," she told him. "This is happening to an Arroyo company. I want whatever bastard is doing this as much as you do. So. My secretary is also arranging for his hotel and transpo while he's in Tampa. He also has your cell and will call you as soon as he lands. I'd say by midmorning he should be at your office."

Liam rubbed his forehead. "How are we going to do this and move all the equipment at the same time?"

"Eric and Max will figure it out. Just be ready with whatever they need."

"You can bet on that. Oh, and one more thing." He told her about the ghost program he wanted to install on Hoffman's system.

"I'll make sure Eric knows that. I'll check in with you later."

He disconnected the call, leaned back in his chair and pressed his fingers against his eyes. How was it possible that just when his life was taking a huge uptick, a shitstorm loomed on the horizon? Who in the hell on his staff would do something like this? He considered them family, certainly those who had come with him from Winters and Pryce. He'd need to get to Robert Hoffman again today and assure him that experts were on site and everything was being handled. Something like this could destroy Software By Design just as it was sailing up the ladder of success.

Fuck!

His cell phone buzzed, signaling a call. He looked at the screen. Sydney. And at six-thirty in the morning.

"You're up early, counselor." He tried to make his voice as even as possible.

"I need coffee and aspirin before I start my day. Besides, this trial is giving me fits."

"Your client driving you nuts with no verdict yet?"

She made a very unladylike sound. "You have no idea. Anyway, I'm probably going to be tied up all weekend holding his hand and preventing him from doing something stupid."

"He can't stay by himself?"

"I don't *trust* him to stay by himself. God, I can't wait until this is over." Her sigh carried over the connection. "Anyway, I wanted to see how you were and if you figured out the problem."

Just the sound of her voice was soothing to him, like a sip of fine aged brandy. God, how he wished she was next to him right now.

"Someone did, in fact, try to hack the system at Hoffman Contractors, but the security cyberfence held." He raked his fingers through his hair. "Thank god, is all I can say. Robert Hoffman was sputtering like a Roman candle."

"That's because the cyberfence you built was perfect."

"Or damn close to it, thank god."

There was silence for a moment. "Liam, are you okay?"

Not yet, but I will be.

But he didn't want to say anything to Sydney that would put her off-balance.

"Yes. I am. That's no bull."

Okay, so a little white lie.

"I'm crossing my fingers for you. Listen, I have to go now. Is it okay if I text you later and see how everything is going?"

"I'd be mad if you didn't." He paused for a moment. "Anyway, don't worry. Taylor is sending me someone to straighten this out. A data forensic specialist. It's probably just someone in Siberia who's bored and perfecting his hacking skills. Or hers. I'll talk to you later. You go chew 'em up today, Syd."

After their conversation ended, he sat there for a moment, just thinking about her, the vision an oasis in the storm brewing around him. It was the only thing that prevented him from tearing his hair out and having a meltdown. How the fuck could this have happened?

At eight o'clock, he called Robert Hoffman on his cell phone to give him an update.

"The expert will be here about midmorning," he told him. "I'd like to bring him right over to your place to install the ghost program so we can begin monitoring any outside activity."

"Fine." Hoffman's voice was a cross between a bark and a growl. "This damn well better fix the problem, Benedict, or your name is in the toilet in my industry."

Yeah, Liam figured that.

"The good news, Robert, is that they were unable to pierce the cyberwall. This will put another layer between you and whoever this is and allow us to trace back activity."

I hope.

"Fine. Call me when he gets here."

He had barely disconnected when the phone on his desk rang, startling him. He picked it up, frowning. Who the hell would be calling him on his private line? Better yet, who knew his private umber?

"Yes?"

"Mr. Benedict?" The voice was somewhat familiar. "This is James in the lobby."

Oh, yeah. The overnight security guard.

"Yes, James. What can I do for you?"

And why are you calling me on this number at – he looked at his watch – *six-forty-five in the morning?*

"There's a lady down here that says you're expecting her."

Liam frowned. He wasn't expecting any women except those on his staff, and they had their coded key cards.

"Not here. What's her name?"

"Bowman. She says she's from Arroyo."

Click!

Taylor had sent him a woman to ride herd on this?

Chauvinist much, Liam? Asshole.

He had very talented women working for him. It was just... *What?*

His brain flaked out.

"Send her up. I'll get her a key card today."

He was waiting by the elevator when the doors opened, trying not to show his shock when the woman walked out. She was tall, maybe even six feet. Her black hair was pulled back in a tight ponytail, emphasizing the dark eyebrows and high cheekbones. She was dressed in a black T-shirt and jeans that emphasized her long legs and toned body. She carried a large messenger case with a cross-body strap, and a boxy briefcase.

She held out a hand to him. "Max Bowman. No one but my grandmother is allowed to call me Maxine, but I wasn't sure what name Taylor had given you."

"Pleasure to meet you, Max. And I mean that in every sense of the word."

"Here. Just so you know it's really me." She pulled a wallet out of her back pocket, flipped it open and showed him her Arroyo identification.

"Feel free to call Taylor for verification."

He supposed someone could have faked this whole thing or waylaid the real Max and sent in a ringer, but his senses were telling him this wasn't the case.

"We're good. I know you're basically here to oversee the technical aspects of this move, but did Taylor tell you what else is going on?"

She nodded. "Said someone's fucking with new software you wrote for a client. Hate people like that. But no worries. Eric will take care of it. Never saw a hidden glitch he couldn't find."

"You know Eric Braun?"

Liam was beginning to think this was all a tight-knit little group that Taylor put together to troubleshoot and handle difficult tasks.

Max nodded. "We've worked together before. Listen, I know we're tearing down this place today, but do you still have a coffee machine that works?"

"What? Oh, damn! Forgive my manners, but I didn't sleep last night."

She snorted. "With what happened? Not surprised. Just lead me to it. I don't need to be waited on."

"Ah, sure. This way." He led her down to the break room.

"Oh, single serving. Great. Hate waiting for the damn plot to brew." She stuck a pod in the machine, filled the reservoir and found a mug.

"My staff will be arriving shortly," he told her. "Along with my executive assistant, who can help you with just about anything."

"I think when your people are all here, we should meet with them and set down the outline for how this is going to work. I don't want them to think they need a babysitter for this."

Liam found himself grinning. "Even if they do?"

She laughed, a warm, natural sound. "Yeah, but we won't tell them. This was supposed to leave you free to manage all the other details, but with this new glitch popping up—"

He held up a hand. "I'm good. Rosalie will be my stand-in. I think she'll actually do it better than I would."

She laughed again. "Most executive assistants can. Okay, show me where the brains are hidden."

He led the way into the large room where all the servers were.

"I sent a schematic to Taylor when we first discussed this."

Max nodded. "Got it in my bag. Let me walk around and—"

"Liam?" Rosalie's voice echoed down the hallway. "You here already?"

He turned to Max. "Let me introduce the two of you. She'll be your contact for just about anything and she's a great problem solver." Then he touched Rosalie's arm. "A minute in my office, please?"

Concern lined her face as he ushered her in and closed the door.

"What's up, boss? You look like death warmed over. Are you sick?"

"In a manner of speaking. Have a seat." He indicated the couch against one wall, not wanting the barrier of the desk between them. This was too personal. Taking a deep breath, he laid out the situation for her from the time he'd gotten the alarm and called Hoffman. Rosalie listened, her face turning pale and her lips tightening.

"Shit, Liam." She whispered the words. "This could destroy us. Who on earth would gimmick the software and when? How? Who do you suspect?"

"Everyone? No one?" He shrugged. "That's part of the problem. All questions yet to be answered. But we're covered. I worked on it all night and Taylor Cantrell sent in a couple of experts." He explained what the next steps would be.

"And with this big move right now." She shook her head. "What can I do?"

"Just be your usual efficient self and keep your eagle eye peeled."

"You know it." She rose, brushed an imaginary speck of lint from her jeans. "All right. Let's do this."

Within the next ten minutes, the movers arrived, and Liam was happy to hand everything over to Rosalie and Max. But he needed to get his staff together and give them some story to cover Eric's sudden appearance. They began arriving even as he thought about it, and when everyone was there, he asked them to come into his office.

"We have awesome new people who will be around for a couple of days. Maxine Bowman — Max — is going to supervise the move of the computers and servers. And yes, Pete, I know we could do it ourselves, but I need you all to take care of your own equipment. She'll oversee the servers and make sure everything is up and running properly. She does this for a living and we're lucky to get her."

"And who else?" Teri asked. "You said *some* people."

He studied everyone for a long moment, watched them carefully as he gave his little speech he'd prepared. "It turns out even with all our testing, there's a glitch in a couple of the programs we recently delivered. I needed someone who specializes in this to dig them out. Eric Braun, who was referred to me by Arroyo, is a high-level forensic data analyst. It's his job to dig out these trouble spots."

"What kind of glitch?" Sy demanded.

Liam tried to decipher if that was irritation underlying the man's words or fear.

"Some things that disrupted the operating process." He was deliberately vague, again looking at each person in turn. "As soon as I know more, I'll tell you."

"Why didn't you ask us to do it?" Teri demanded. "We worked on the programs."

"Exactly."

"So, you don't trust us?" Phil barked.

No, I don't, and it's killing me.

Liam shook his head. "That's not it at all. It's the reason authors should not edit their own work. You are so used to seeing what you see that it's easy to miss something."

"But—" Teri began.

Liam held up a hand. "I'm sure it's something stupid that we all, including me, overlooked. It is what it is. So just go with it. I just ask if Eric needs any of you for anything you give both him and Max your utmost cooperation."

They all nodded, albeit some reluctantly.

"Fine. Good. Now, let's get this move done."

He watched them file out of his office and he could almost hear the buzz of undercurrent as soon as they were away from him. He'd tried to get a reading when he'd laid it out for them as to who might be involved in this. Unfortunately, whoever it was, they were very good at concealing it, which didn't help either his trust issues or his state of mind very much.

He leaned back in his desk chair and opened the top right-hand drawer in his desk. Reaching into it, he lifted out a box, flipped the top open and took out the object it was holding. The Arkansas Toothpick Bowie Knife had been a present from his father, who got it from *his* father. It usually sat displayed on his desk, but he'd put it away in preparation for the move along with some other items he didn't want to lose. He had a habit, sometimes, when he was trying to get his brain to work, of sitting there fiddling with it. Now he returned it in the box to the desk drawer and got back to work.

By ten o'clock, there was action everywhere in the SBD offices. Under Max's direction, his people were getting the server room and their individual stations broken down and packed up, using colored tape to show which parts went where. It appeared Taylor had sent a big enough crew to move the entire building, but that was good. They could not afford any down time. Furniture was stacked in the wide hallway, and movers along with his staff were hustling in and out of rooms.

If Eric Braun would just get here, Liam's nerves might settle down a bit. He wondered how close to arriving the forensic data specialist was.

At that moment, as if an inanimate object could read his mind, his cell phone chimed in his hand and an unknown number popped up on the screen.

Hesitant, he punched Answer.

"Yes?"

"Eric Braun, Liam. I just pulled out of the airport and I've got you on GPS."

"Just come to the front door. I'll take care of it now."

Instead of calling downstairs to James about their visitor, he decided to go down to the lobby himself. Less than fifteen minutes later, a man walked through the front door.

Good thing we're changing that at the new building. No one, not even clients, will be able to get off the sidewalk without verification.

The man was about his height, lean with dark hair almost to his shoulders, and a day-old scruff outlining a strong jaw. He was dressed in jeans and a T-shirt with the legend *Nerd? I prefer the term intellectual badass.* Liam swallowed a smile. Eric and Teri should get along just fine. And he had a feeling badass was a much more accurate term for this man.

He handed Liam a business card along with a fax from Taylor that said, *Trust this man.*

"This is my first job for Arroyo so you can bet I'll be on top of everything."

Liam nodded. "I agree. Did Taylor tell you about the ghost program I want to install?"

"She did. She gave me what she could, but I want to make sure what I have will work." One corner of his mouth turned up in a grin. "I wrote it on the plane."

Liam stared at the man. He'd thought he was good at what he did, but Eric Braun was obviously twenty stages ahead of him.

"Come on up to my office and I'll give you the lowdown on everything."

At SBD people were moving everywhere. Furniture was stacked in the wide hallway and movers and his staff were moving in and out of rooms. Max and Rosalie seemed to be everywhere, the calm in the midst of chaos.

"Hey, Eric." Max walked over, grinning, and stuck out her hand. "Glad to be working with you again. You take good care of our friend, Liam, here."

"Absolutely." He motioned her closer to where he and Liam stood and dropped his voice. "We're out of here for a couple of hours, but when I get back I'll need access to the server. Will you have it set up by then?"

"Of course." She looked at her watch. "Yeah, that's doable. I'll only have the one access ready. Will that be enough?"

"Yes. Great. Thanks so much."

Rosalie brought coffee to their office then closed the door. Sipping the hot liquid, Liam gave Eric every detail about the situation he had.

"I'm telling you, Eric. I tested that thing top to bottom and then some. When I installed the cyber alarm, I never thought anything would activate it."

"But in retrospect, it's a damn good thing you did." He set his coffee cup down on the desk. "All right. Let's take a look at the program. I'll make sure the ghost I wrote will work with it. Then you can call your client and tell him we're on the way. When we get back, I want to log into your server and look for the deleted files."

Liam knew that not many people realized when files were deleted from a hard drive, even when the trash or recycle bin was emptied, the original file still remained, hidden. With special software, it could be retrieved. Only overwriting it destroyed traces of it completely.

Liam frowned. "I checked them myself and nothing popped up."

Eric grinned. "Ah, but that's why you hired me. I can find the most invisible things."

An hour later, they were in Hoffman's offices with the head of his IT. Eric sat at a computer in the server room, checking Liam's software one more time before installing the ghost. Finally, he sat back in his chair.

"Okay, folks. It looks like we're ready to go here. This will work for the moment, but I want to install a more sophisticated program tomorrow."

"Wait." Hoffman dragged his unlit cigar from his mouth. "You mean, this is still not safe?"

"It's very safe," Eric told him. "Anyone trying to hack in will get the ghost which will just deliver a message that the server is not working at the moment. That's not uncommon, but we can't do it too many times. Whoever is doing the hacking will know something's up."

"So, what's the answer?" Hoffman demanded.

Eric looked at the client then back at Liam. "We need to put something in there to direct them to files for a project that failed. In other words, we want them to actually hack into the system, but it will be a false direction because once they get into the Hoffman computers, this will direct them to useless files."

It took a while to hash it all out and to convince Hoffman none of this would compromise his electronic security. Then he had to be persuaded to hand over old, useless diagrams with no connection to the current project.

"We'll take care of it," Liam assured his client.

"When?" he demanded. "This is your mess. You'd better fix it damn quick."

Liam looked at Eric. "I can get started on this while you work on taking the security software apart."

Eric nodded. "Works for me."

Liam turned back to Hoffman. "I'll be back to upload something to your server Monday morning at the latest. But your people can get back to work on your project right away. You're well covered up."

"It better be."

"Take a breath," Eric said once they were back in Liam's car. "We've got this handled. And I'm going to find your mole." He grinned. "It's what I do."

By Monday, Software By Design was settled in its new offices and back in business. Max had left, with huge thanks from Liam and even grudging thanks from the staff. Liam had already fired an email off to Taylor expressing his appreciation.

The false information was installed on the Hoffman computers so anyone hacking into the system would access files of a drone that was filled with flaws. It would also send a signal to Hoffman's system, allowing someone to backtrack where the hack came from. It was a delicate process, but Liam had seen it work twice before.

Now it was Friday. Liam had held his breath all week, waiting for something, anything, that would trigger the setup at Hoffman's, but so far nothing.

"I can't believe they haven't tried again," he told Eric. "We've got it all set so they get sent to the fake server. They'd at least want to see if he server is up and running again."

"You haven't told anyone here at the office what you've set up, right?"

Liam shook his head. "That would defeat the purpose. All they know is there was a problem and I cleaned it up. Everything is good to go."

"My guess is it won't be much longer. They want those drawings and specs before Hoffman can go into production."

"I wish to hell they'd get moving then, so you can trace it back. They've been told your job is to analyze the problem with the original software. That's all."

"Whoever is doing this I guarantee you is pissed they nearly got caught and think they are smart enough to go around you again."

Liam nodded. "I'll be they are so egotistical they think they can do a better job this time."

"Even if they hit the false server," Eric reminded him, "they may be clever enough to put up a wall that it will take me time to get through."

"Shit." Liam shoved his fingers through his hair. As much as he'd been doing that today, it stood up on end.

"Don't worry. I'm pretty sure it won't be much longer."

Eric was settled in one of the new offices with two laptops. He had one set up so if anyone tried to hack the Hoffman system again, it would send a signal and he'd be there to backtrack it. At the other, he was meticulously taking apart the code for the Hoffman program one line at a time.

Liam also spent some time making sure each of his programmers was satisfied with the new setup, had a proper workspace and wasn't feeling disrupted by the move. Then he turned them loose on their current or new projects. He continued to be amazed at the fact it had been accomplished in two days and everything was up and running again.

He was working on a program for a new client when there was a knock and he looked up to see Phil standing in the doorway.

"You got a minute, Liam?"

Well, not really, but at the moment he was acutely interested in what any of his staff had to say.

"Sure." He waved the man into his office. "What's up?"

Phil sat in the chair across form him and leaned forward.

"It's about this specialist. Eric."

"Oh?" Liam cocked an eyebrow. "Is he causing some kind of problem?"

Phil lifted a shoulder. "Not exactly. But Teri, Sy and I were talking, and we still don't understand why you went outside the firm to get someone. All three of us are more than qualified to look for whatever is wrong with the program."

"Maybe so, but Eric is a specialist in that area. Besides, he doesn't come to the table with any preconceived ideas. He's never seen these lines of code before, so it's easier for him to spot a glitch." He studied the man across from him. "You worried about something, Phil?"

"Only that you might suddenly see us as incompetent. Besides, I don't much care for a stranger digging around in my codes."

Liam's stomach knotted. Was Phil trying to hide something? Was that why he was asking the question? Was he the problem?

"He's digging around in mine, too," he reminded the man. "Let's just relax, okay? We've got new contracts that have to be fulfilled. I'd think you'd be elbows-deep in the new program I asked you for today."

"I am, I am. It's just—" He shrugged. "Forget it. I'm probably making a mountain out of a molehill. Sorry I bothered you. I'd better get back to work."

Liam rubbed his forehead. It made him sick to think Phil might be involved in this. If it had to be anyone he wanted it to be one of the newer hires, someone he wasn't emotionally invested in.

And there was this weird feeling that continued to plague him, that someone was watching him. He'd even gone so far as to check every inch of his offices and his townhouse to make sure that no one had breached his security and planted bugs. He was pretty damn sure that hadn't happened, but he couldn't get rid of the feeling.

He hadn't felt it at all since the Hoffman debacle, but he could have just been so wrapped up in this emergency it didn't register. He hadn't sensed anything this morning, either, but his brain had been so busy with everything else he might not have noticed if a building had fallen on him. Maybe whatever this was had just disappeared. A figment of his imagination.

Whatever. He was just happy to be rid of the feeling he was constantly bring watched.

He was working in his office on a new project, just the bare beginnings, and wondering if Sydney would get her jury verdict today. He had hoped to hear from her by now worried at how crazy her client had made her weekend and that jury deliberation would drag on yet another day. He was just about to get himself a fresh cup of coffee when his phone chimed with a text.

Not Guilty! Free at last! Great God, I'm free at last!

A smiley face emoticon was pasted right next to it.

Liam actually laughed, loud enough that Rosalie tapped on his door and opened it.

"You okay, boss? Not losing your mind? Because I don't think our current situation is humorous in any way."

Liam had of course filled her in on everything. There was no one in the world he trusted more than Rosalie. He motioned her into the room and showed her the screen on his phone.

"She's been going nuts with this trial. She doesn't even like her client."

Rosalie quirked an eyebrow. "Then why did she take the case?"

"As a favor to her mentor from law school. He was the one who recommended her to this firm and he's helped her with other things. I think she's more than paid him back."

"Yeah, no kidding."

Liam motioned to the door. "Close that for a minute."

She did, and leaned against it. "What's up?"

"How's Eric coming along? I don't want to keep bugging him, but I know Hoffman's about to have apoplexy."

"But you guys gave him a temporary fix so he's protected, right?"

"He was protected without it. We set it up so anyone hacking now will find that failed diagram, and also hopefully track us back to whoever is doing this."

"Have you checked it since you installed it?" she wanted to know.

Liam shook his head. "I left the alarm active and it hasn't signaled. Whoever it is may be taking a step back."

"Well, Eric's hardly left his desk. Sometimes I think he sleeps here at night. I'd say if anyone is going to find the problem, it's him."

"Let me know if he needs anything. How's everyone else coming along?"

"Oh, you know. Hard at work but tense. Everyone's looking at everyone else, trying to figure out what the hell is going on. It's a good thing you didn't confront them. We'd have a mess here."

He nodded. "I'm keeping that to myself until Eric gets the answer. Okay, I'm going to text Sydney and see if I can grab her for a few hours."

"Good idea. You need some recreation." She winked as she walked out of the office.

Liam picked up his phone.

This calls for a celebration. Are you free yet?

Pause.

Tonight. After seven.

He smiled. *"Dinner? Out? In? Your place? Mine?"*

Dinner. My place. Seven o'clock.

Sounds good.

You can get away?

He laughed. *Try and stop me. C U then.*

He was glad he had plenty to do for the rest of the day, keeping his mind busy. About four-thirty, he knocked on the closed door of Eric's office.

"Come in."

Eric looked up from his computer when the door opened, and motioned Liam inside. The man was again in jeans, this time with a T-shirt that said *Byte me*. His hair looked as if he'd run his fingers through it a few hundred times and the scruff was back at his jawline.

"Sorry I don't have an answer yet," he began.

Liam held up his hand. "Not even going there. I think we both know this one's going to be a bitch and a half to find."

"They always are. One of the things I'm doing is comparing the final product line by line with the deleted files."

Liam snorted. "Better you than me."

"In more ways than one. You're so used to seeing the lines of code that an aberration might not — probably would not — jump out at you. Listen. Your programmer, Teri, poked her head in to see if I needed help." He grinned. "We bonded over our T-shirts."

"She's one of the trio who came over with me from Winters and Pryce."

"I thanked her but told I've got this okay." He studied Liam's face. "I didn't think you wanted any of your people in the middle of this."

"Yeah." Liam scratched his jaw. "The fact that I'm sure it's one of them makes me sick to my stomach. I treat them like family."

"Sometimes family hurts you the most," Eric pointed out.

"I know. I know. Anyway, a couple of things. I won't be around tonight. You have my cell, but for emergencies only."

Eric's mouth split in a wide grin. "Got it."

"The other thing is Gasparilla. I'm sure you've seen the craziness all over the place. I have to hit a couple of evening events this week and tomorrow I have to ride in the parade. I'm a pirate." He held up his hand. "Do not even say one word."

Eric laughed. "Sounds like fun. And with this hanging over your head, you need a change. I'd hate to have to tell Taylor Cantrell if you stroked out."

"Yeah, I wouldn't be too happy, either. Anyway, I'll always have my cell with me if you need me."

"Except tonight," Eric joked.

"Damn straight. You need me to get any food for you before I take off?"

Eric shook his head. "Got it covered. I'll take a break later and walk to one of the places around here. I'll need a break and it helps me clear my head."

"Okay, then. See you in the morning. And, Eric? You get some rest, too."

"I'll rest when I get some answers." He pointed at his computer screen. "Whoever fucked with your program is very, very clever."

"The curse of hiring smart people. Since you're set, I'm leaving."

He said goodbye to Rosalie and headed out to his car. As soon as he stepped out of the building, that chilly feeling that someone was watching him crept along his spine again. He looked all around but did not see anything or anyone out of place. Damn it! What the hell was going on?

Chapter Twelve

Sydney took one look at Liam when she opened the door and wanted to ditch her plan for a romantic evening and just hold him in her arms. He looked like warmed-over shit. His thick brown hair looked as if he'd dragged a rake through it at least a hundred times. The circles beneath his golden-tinged chocolate eyes could have held a week's worth of luggage, and his face, usually so strong-looking with his square jaw and slashes of cheekbones, looked drawn, haggard even. His shirt and jeans didn't help the look. They gave the appearance he'd slept in them for a week.

"Have you been sleeping in the office?" she demanded. "My god. You look like shit. What happened?"

The smile he gave her was more pathetic than anything. "Hello to you, too."

She opened the door wider. "Come in, come in."

She closed and locked the door behind him and drew him over to the sofa by the big window.

"Sit." She pushed him onto the couch, although it didn't take more than a tiny shove with one finger. What the hell?

"At first I wasn't sure if I should inflict myself on you." His smile held little humor. "But then I realized what I needed the most was just to be with you."

She stopped in front of the couch, leaned down and pressed her mouth to his. He was a big man, a strong man, but she could feel a frailty in him that only extreme stress could cause. And so, when she pressed her mouth to his, she put everything she felt for him, all the emotion that had bubbled up in her in such a short time, into her kiss.

She licked the seam of his mouth and nudged it open before easing her tongue inside. She wanted him to know this was as much about what she felt for him as it was about wanting him. When she finally took a step back, she was pleased to see the pain in his eyes had diminished a little and was now mixed with equal heavy doses of caring and wanting.

"I have wine for our dinner but how about a real drink first?"

"I won't say no." He raked his fingers through his hair. "I think I need it. Bourbon, if you've got it."

"No problem."

She put ice cubes into a rocks tumbler and poured a generous slug of aged bourbon into the glass.

"Thank you." He took the glass from her, raised it to her in salute and downed half of it.

"Whoa!" She chuckled. "I didn't realize you were such a two-fisted drinker."

"I'm not, but today I might need to be." He took another small sip before leaning back and stretching out his arm. "Come sit with me for a minute. I need that." As if to emphasize his point, he set the glass on a coaster on the table.

Sydney curled up next to his body, leaning into the shelter of his arm, and rested her hand on his chest.

"Okay, tell me how everything stands at the moment. And how the expert Taylor Cantrell sent is doing. Did he find the problem?"

Liam shook his head. "Not yet. And if he's having trouble, it's a nasty, complicated little bugger." He stroked her arm as he spoke, his touch warming her.

"Do you have any hint or clue yet who might have done this?"

He shook his head. "I wish. The sickening part is, it has to be one of my own people, because no one else had access to the files."

"Oh, Liam." She reached up and stroked his jaw. "How devastating this has to be for you. I wish there was something I could say or do."

He moved both of them so in a moment, she was sitting on his lap, his arms around her, and he was stringing kisses along her jawline.

"I don't want to talk about it right now. I put it out of my mind as much as I could when I left the office to come here. I want to have a great dinner, some fine wine and some outstanding sex. And not necessarily in that order."

Beneath the cheeks of her ass, she felt the length of his cock harden as it pressed against her. She wriggled a little, just to tease him, and was rewarded with a slight groan. Just being this close to him, feeling the hardness of his shaft against her body, his mouth stringing kisses down her neck, was enough to set her body humming. He wound his fingers in her hair, tightening the stands and holding her head in place as — at last — he pressed his mouth to hers.

His lips were firm and warm, and the touch of them made her body tingle. Her nipples hardened, pushing against the flimsy silk of the top she wore, and the walls of her pussy contracted with need. When he teased her mouth again, she opened for him and scraped her teeth over his tongue. He moaned, a sound that made her hotter and needier.

His marauding tongue touched every inner inch of her mouth, licking and tangling with her own tongue. The kiss went on for so long she forgot to breathe and she didn't care as long as he continued kissing her like that. Every part of her cried out for his touch, and when he shifted his arm to cup one breast with the warm palm of one hand, she pressed herself into his touch.

He took her mouth again, this time more gently but just as hungrily, while he pinched a nipple between thumb and forefinger. Heat streaked right to the center of her core, between her thighs, right at the heart of her pussy. Her pulse pounded erratically and need consumed her.

She shifted so she was now straddling Liam, pressing her sex against the swelling ridge beneath his fly. She tugged his shirt from the waistband of his jeans, nudging him to raise his arms so she could pull it over his head and off.

"I wouldn't have thought someone who lives behind a desk would be so buff."

She brushed her fingers over the sprinkling of dark hair on his chest, trailing them down over his taut abs. On impulse, she leaned forward and licked the hollow at the base of his throat then scraped her nails over his hard nipples. When he sucked in his breath, she did it again.

"I'll give you an hour to stop that," he teased, his voice thick with need.

"Oh, but I have other things I want to do, also."

She flicked the tip of her tongue over each nipple, first one then the other. Liam's breathing hitched and his arms came around her, trying to pull her closer to him. He groaned when she took a tiny bite at each hard nub before trailing her hands lower, over his hard abs to the waistband of his jeans.

When she shifted her body to move from her lap, he pulled her close to him again.

"Don't move."

"If I don't, then you won't get your treat."

"My treat?"

"Yes." She nodded. "I was going to give it to you for dessert since I have such a great dinner planned. But I think maybe you need it right now."

She inched her way back until she slid from his lap and was kneeling between his legs. Then she went to work unbuttoning and unzipping his jeans. Easing his jeans and boxer briefs down past his hips, she wrapped her fingers around his now freed cock, squeezing gently.

Liam leaned back and sucked in a breath.

"Holy shit, Syd."

"Mmm-hmm," she hummed as she took him fully into her mouth.

He was solid steel beneath the covering of skin that was baby soft. The hair surrounding the base was dark and curly, and tempted her to sift the fingers of her other hand through it. A tiny bead of fluid sat atop the dark purple crown of his cock, and she collected it with one slow swipe of her tongue.

Liam groaned and thrust his fingers into her hair to grip her head, holding it as she continued to trail the tip of her tongue around the soft, purple tip and the furled flesh surrounding it. She squeezed gently with her fingers, feeling the pump of blood through the thick vein twisted around the steel shaft. When she took him into her mouth and began a rhythmic up-and-down pumping with her hand, he groaned again and thrust his hips upward.

"Shit, Syd. Fucking holy shit. That's it. Don't stop."

Pressing his fingers against her temples, he tried to urge her to increase her pace, but she was determined she would be in control here. Slowly, steadily, she slid her fingers up and down his cock, her mouth busy with the head. When she nudged her free hand between his thighs and cupped his balls, his groan vibrated through his body.

He tasted so good to her, felt so good, that she could do this forever. Wanted to draw it out so he was shaking with need by the time his orgasm crested. With her hands and tongue, she licked and sucked and rubbed and tasted until his moan was one long sound of need.

"Please, Syd," he begged. "Fuck! Now! Please now."

He was doing his best to match her rhythm with his hips, but she'd only drawn his jeans down to just below his knees, restricting his movements. That made it all the more delicious to her. Humming her satisfaction at his response, she increased the pace of her strokes, her mouth covering the head of his shaft, her tongue swirling around it.

She felt it when his body was near the point of cresting. His muscles tightened, his fingers increased their pressure on her head and his hips jerked as she stroked faster and faster.

"Goddamn!" he shouted. "Now."

In that instant he erupted, his body jerking as he spilled into her mouth. Her cheeks hollowed as she sucked harder, taking in every delicious drop. She didn't change her rhythm until she'd wrung the last drop from him. Then she gave his balls a light squeeze, slowly released him from her mouth and drew one last line from head to balls with the tip of her tongue.

Liam still cradled her head in his hands and he tugged on her, urging her to move up on his body. She crawled onto the couch with him and nestled against him, cupping his now semisoft cock with her palm.

He pulled her more tightly against him, stroked her arm lazily. When she placed the palm of one hand on his chest, she could still feel the erratic thundering of his heartbeat. Hear the stutter of his erratic breathing. At last she felt his body completely relax. He moved his head to place a soft kiss on her forehead.

"I don't know what to say," he told her, "except thank you."

"No thanks necessary." She placed a light kiss on his shoulder. "The pleasure was all mine."

They sat there like that for a very long moment. Sydney was enjoying both the cocooning intimacy and the pleasure of being able to wipe Liam's troubles from his mind even for a short period of time. He seemed perfectly content to just sit there, cock at rest, his boxer briefs and jeans down around his knees. At last she pushed herself up to a sitting position.

"I think I need to check on dinner." She kissed his shoulder. "Hope you like Cornish game hen."

He continued to rub her arm in lazy strokes. "I'd like anything you fixed. In fact, right now, I don't think there's anything I *wouldn't* like."

"Want another drink while you're waiting?"

He shook his head. "I'll wait for the wine, with dinner." He looked down at his clothing. "But I'd better get myself together before we eat."

Sydney chuckled. "I don't know. I rather like the view. Maybe you should take them off altogether."

"After dinner." He winked. "I have plans for us."

A shiver of anticipation skittered over her. "I can't wait."

* * * *

Eight twisted the rocks glass around and around, needing something to disguise trembling fingers. The summons from Shan had not been unexpected but was dreaded just the same. Not even the finest whiskey could calm a stomach in turmoil or jittery nerves.

How the fuck did I get myself into this?

Oh, yeah. Betting on everything but the weather. And maybe that would come next. An addict is an addict is an addict.

"Well?" Shan looked across the tale. "Do you have news for me?"

Eight shrugged. "Nothing that I haven't already told you."

"So, the specialist is still there."

Eight nodded. "Working away."

"I thought you told me he and Liam were at the Hoffman office over the weekend fixing whatever the problem was. And by the way, what *was* the problem? You assured me that the code you added for the back door was undetectable."

Eight nodded. "And I stand by that."

"Well, then?"

Eight took a healthy slug of whiskey, then set the glass down. "Look. He told us that there was a problem when one of the design engineers at Hoffman tried to get back into his files. That's entirely possible. He could have screwed it up himself. Or forgotten the correct password. Or there could have been a glitch in their system over there. That kind of shit happens all the time, believe me."

"I hope you are telling me the truth, because if not, you won't be around long to discuss it."

Eight's stomach knotted. Shit! Getting involved with these people had been such a mistake but damn it! The money had looked so good.

"Tell me again what happened when your people tried to access the files."

"We received a message that said the system was down and to please try again."

Eight relaxed just a fraction. "Okay. That's fine. When—"

Shan pounded a fist on the table. "Fine? How can you call it fine? It locked us out."

"If you'll just let me explain." Eight took a healthy swallow of the whiskey. "I believe that's the same thing that happened to the people at Hoffman's. That's why Liam had to run over there almost in the middle of the night. And why he has this Eric guy working on the copies of the program we keep to see if the same glitch shows up in any of the others."

Shan took a swallow of coffee and set the cup back down with careful precision. "So, let me make sure I understand what you are telling me. If we open your back door to the software again, we will not be blocked. We will not be told to try again later. We will not corrupt the software. Am I correct?"

Eight nodded. "Right on the nose. You use the codes I gave you, get into their software and you can begin downloading their files. Just one thing, though."

"What?" Shan's voice had a new edge to it.

"Do not try to download all the files at once. Space it out. The one thing it's impossible to guard against is an overload signal."

Shan lifted an eyebrow. "An overload signal?"

"Yes. This is the one failsafe I couldn't work around. If you try to download too many of the files at once, the program shuts down."

"*Now* you tell me? Why did I not know of this before?"

Eight leaned forward. "Pardon me for saying this, but I assumed that your people with all the expertise you claim they have would know something like this. I'm damn sure this isn't the first time you people have done this."

Shan's fists tightened around the coffee mug, the only sign of escalating anger.

"We must get those files before Hoffman can build and test their prototype and hand it over to the Department of Defense. And do not ask me any more questions. None of this is your business. You just have to get us into the software. We will do the rest."

Eight had a sudden feeling of quiet terror. "You aren't going to screw with their files, are you?"

Shan's smile didn't offer any reassurance. "We will do whatever we have to."

"But—"

"Not to worry. You will have your money and can be long gone before any of that happens."

Eight leaned back in the booth. *Shit!* This was going to be a fucking disaster. That money damn well better be ready.

"Are we through here? It's Friday night. I'd like to enjoy a little of the weekend."

"No." Shan pulled out a cell phone. "My people are going to try getting into that software again. You will wait here to make sure your little back door works. Then you may go."

Shan's shrug was impressive enough to make Eight's entire body cramp.

"Fine. Go ahead. I'm ordering another drink. And you're paying."

Shan's smile was enough to stop a hurricane. "Of course."

Eight sat quietly drinking while Shan made the call and gave the order. Then neither of them said a word, just waited in silence. After the longest ten minutes Eight had ever spent, Shan listened to her phone and smiled.

"Good. Continue the process."

"It worked?" Eight slugged down another gulp of the whiskey.

"Do not get drunk, my friend. You want to be sober enough to enjoy the fruits of your labor."

For the first time since arriving at the restaurant, Eight actually relaxed. Damn. The payoff was so close it was almost visible.

"So, when do I get my money? Half on delivery, remember?"

Shan lifted a small briefcase that had been almost hidden by the table.

"Half on delivery. The rest when we have completed the download of all the files."

Eight took the briefcase with a hand that actually trembled.

"I should say thank you, but I earned this."

Shan's lips curled in the coldest smile Eight had ever seen. "Just be sure you use it wisely. We would all hate for you to fall into the same pit again. Your next partners in crime might not take such good care of you."

"There won't be a next time."

"For your sake, I hope so."

Eight grabbed the briefcase and slid out of the booth. "I'll count this when I get home, but I'm pretty damn sure you wouldn't try to stiff me."

Again, that weird smile. "Enjoy the night."

"I will. Believe me."

And when I get the rest of the money I'll never have to see your ugly face again.

* * * *

The woman could cook, for sure, although Liam wasn't sure why that surprised him. Maybe because most of the women he'd dated thought cooking was heating up takeout. He had left his shirt off, at Sydney's insistence, enjoying the way she looked at him and licked her lips. He gave thanks for her excellent blow job that had eased a lot of the pressure and allowed him to make sure his cock behaved during dinner.

He had to admit that she'd eased a lot of the tension gripping him and for a short while erased the whole Hoffman software debacle from his mind. Everything on that front seemed to be proceeding as it should and he had made up his mind on the way here to just enjoy tonight. If Hoffman's computers got dinged one more time, there was no telling when he'd have this chance again. He closed his eyes for a moment and visualized putting his brain in a box and locking it away. When he opened them, Sydney was watching him with an expression of concern on her face.

"You okay?" she asked.

He grinned at her. "If I was any more okay, it would be illegal. Why?"

"You had the strangest expression on your face." She took a sip of her wine. "Like you were — I don't know — changing gears? Did you want to leave?"

"Hell, no." He hadn't meant to shout the words. He swallowed. "I was packing away every part of my brain except the part that's engaged with you."

The tension eased from her body. "Good. That's what you're supposed to do." She lifted the bottle of wine. "More?"

"Not right now."

He stared at her, enjoying the casually mussed look of her. She hadn't dressed up for tonight and he wanted to tell her how glad he was. He liked the casual look on her, the jeans and pretty pink T-shirt and the bare feet. Especially the bare feet. He planned to tell her she had sexy feet, maybe while he was carefully sucking on each toe as he worked his way up her naked body.

"You're looking at me very strangely, Liam. What's up?"

My cock.

"I'm just thinking how delicious you look and how I can't wait to taste you." He let his gaze roam every inch he could see. "Yeah, delicious and then some."

"Um, let me just get these dishes cleared away…"

Liam rose and took the dishes from her hands. "These can wait. I'll even clear the table myself." He paused to let his gaze run over her from top to bottom. "Later."

He lifted her in his arms and carried her to her bedroom, thankful that he'd been here before and knew the way.

She had left one of the bedside lamps lit, bathing the room in a warm, muted-amber glow. He swallowed a smile when he saw the covers on the bed had already been turned back.

Sydney saw where he was looking. "I just like being prepared," she teased.

"For which I am eternally grateful."

He stood her on her bare feet at the side of the bed, studied her face and nearly lost himself in her striking blue eyes. He touched his mouth to hers, brushing his lips back and forth before using the tip of his tongue to trace the seam. She moaned softly, which only ramped up his hunger and need. He'd never met a woman he felt this connection with before, or this strong a hunger. He wondered if he'd ever get enough of her.

She wrapped her slim fingers around his wrists and slid the tip of her own small tongue out to touch his. Just that tiny contact was so electric, hitting his body like the touch of a live wire. He nudged her lips apart so he could slide his tongue inside the heat of her wet mouth. Every nerve in his body fired.

He tilted her head to give him better access as he took the kiss deeper. Only when he knew they were both running out of breath did he break the contact.

Sydney gave a shaky little laugh. "We sure don't do anything in half measures, do we?"

"And that's not all bad." His own voice wasn't that steady.

He tugged her T-shirt loose from her slacks and eased it up her body. She lifted her arms so he could pull it over her head and toss it to the side. Another one of her lacy concoctions, this one in deep purple, lovingly cupped her sweet, sweet breasts. Her nipples were dark berries pushing against the silky fabric and he just could not help himself. He ducked his head, took each one in his mouth in turn, sucked them and bit down gently.

The touch of his wet mouth and the erotic pinch of his teeth stole Sydney's breath. She slid her hands around to press her palms to his naked back, her touch making him glad he'd never put his shirt back on.

He trailed his lips down the slender column of her neck, peppering her with tiny kisses then taking a soft bite at that very sensitive spot right where her neck and shoulder joined. Pulse hammering, she pressed herself closer to him, her breasts warm mounds against the hard plane of his chest.

Jesus!

Despite the fact she'd taken the edge of with her fantastic use of her mouth and fingers on him before dinner, he was instantly hard, his shaft begging for release. He dug deep for his self-control, because now it was Sydney's turn.

He unfastened her slacks, pushing them past her hips. He held her as she wriggled the garment down to the floor and kicked them aside. With his hands beneath her ass, he lifted her to the bed, placing her at the edge so he could feast on her at will. He went nuts at the sight of the teeny-tiny panties that matched the bra, gripped the lace band at the top with his teeth and dragged it down until the fabric banded her thighs together. It left the lips of her pussy and the ripe bud of her clit now open to whatever he wanted to do.

Lowering himself to his knees, he traced a line with his tongue from her navel to the top of her mound, pressing just the tip of it between her lips right where her clit beckoned. It was hot and smooth and he played it with his tongue like a toy, flicking it back and forth over and over until Sydney was moaning and twisting and trying to push her thighs wider for better access.

He laughed, a low, rumbling sound.

"Uh-uh. We do this my way. You had your turn." He lifted his gaze to her face, her cheeks flushed with pleasure, and he wanted to lap every inch of her.

He went back to work on her hot button, teasing it with the tip of his tongue then licking the closed seam of her cunt. She tried to open her thighs but Liam wasn't yet ready to slide her jeans down. Placing his hands on her hips, he held her in place while he licked and nibbled until she was moaning her pleas and trying to thrust her body upward.

"Please," she begged. "Liam, please, please, please."

"Please what?" he teased.

"Please take my clothes off and lick all of me."

He nipped her little clit again. "Do you want me to make you come with my mouth?"

"Yes." Her head thrashed from side to side. "Yes, yes, yes."

"Tell me," he insisted.

"Make me come with your mouth." She almost shouted the words.

"See." He laughed, a low, rumbling sound. "All you had to do was ask."

He hoped he could control himself because just the sight and taste of her made his dick so hard he wondered if it might snap off.

He pulled her slacks and teeny panties down, tossed them to the side and nudged her legs wide. He took a long moment to just enjoy the sight of her, that sweet pink flesh so wet and shiny, bracketed by two neatly trimmed rows of curls.

Damn!

Pulling in a deep breath, he spread the lips of her pussy with her thumbs and applied his tongue, licking the tempting inner flesh, stroking over the swollen bud of her clit. The more he lapped and stroked, the wetter she became. Her soft little moans of pleasure ramped up his own hungry need.

He lifted her legs and placed them on his shoulders, opening her even wider to him, and he thrust his tongue deep inside her.

"Oh, god! Please."

He loved to hear those little cries of pleasure. He licked deeper and faster, rubbing her clit with his forefinger in time to his strokes. Her inner walls began to flutter then contract as her orgasm rose. Then she was there, her body clasping his tongue, riding it as he drove her over the peak.

Her inner walls were still in spasms when he stripped off his jeans and boxer briefs, grabbed a condom from his wallet and sheathed himself. He wanted to climb up onto the bed with her but he was afraid his own body demands wouldn't wait that long. Instead he placed both hands beneath the cheeks of her ass, lifted her and drove into her with one swift plunge.

Jesus!

He had to stop and take a breath or he might have come right then and there. Reaching for the last vestiges of his control, he set up a rhythm, thrusting in and out, feeling her muscles grip him like a vise.

"Shit! Syd, I'm not gonna last."

"It's okay," she breathed, her voice strained. "Do it. Please."

He felt the tremors in her body as she gripped him harder, harder, and knew she was close. Faster, he told himself, gritting his teeth.

And they were both there, her cunt milking him as he pulsed into her again and again and again, until he wondered if he'd ever stop coming. When he did, he fell forward, catching himself on his forearms, his heartbeat thundering, his breath sawing in and out.

When he regained some measure of control, he kissed her, a light touch of his lips to hers. He looked into those dark blue eyes, not sure what he'd see there. A ribbon of pleasure coursed through him to see the same well of emotions he himself was feeling. He brushed damp strands of air from her cheeks.

"Syd." He breathed her name.

"Me, too." She smiled.

"I feel —"

She touched her fingertips to his lips.

"Me, too, but don't say it yet. Let's wait until your crisis is past so there's nothing affecting it."

"It's not why I want to tell you," he objected.

"I know. But wait, okay? So the only focus is us."

He understood what she was saying, but he wanted to tell her so badly how he felt. Instead he eased himself from her body, disposed of the condom then moved them both under the covers. He had enough brainpower left to remember to put his cell on the nightstand before he spooned her against him and kissed the shell of her ear.

"I'm not leaving until morning," he told her.

She sighed. "Good. Then we can do this again before you have to leave."

He fell asleep, smiling.

Chapter Thirteen

With Robert Hoffman's permission, Eric had set up a trap in the Hoffman system so that a hacker would be directed to the fake file and an electronic notification would be sent to Eric's laptop. They had discussed sending it to Liam, also, but he didn't believe that was necessary.

"I won't be available much until Sunday, anyway," he told the specialist.

"Oh, yeah. Tomorrow's the big parade." He grinned. "Too bad I can't run down there and snap some pictures to send to Taylor, Mr. Pirate."

"Uh, that would be a no." He handed Eric a folder. "In case you want a break, here's the parade route. We start down Bayshore Boulevard. If you decide to take a break, I marked the side streets where you could try to park. If we get a hit, start tracking it."

"That's what I'll be doing. Also, still working on the code for the program, looking for something that shouldn't be there."

"Take a break when you can," Liam urged.

"I will. I just want to dig out this little bugger that's driving me crazy."

Which was exactly what he had been doing most of the evening. Or waiting to do. About eleven o'clock, he got an electronic signal that someone had hacked into the Hoffman system. He logged in from his computer and began the detailed process of examining and following each line of code. As he expected, he ended up on one wild goose chase after another. Whoever was doing this was sending him all over from Venezuela to China to Russia to Alaska and on and on.

Eric sighed, pushed back from his desk and stretched his arms over his head. He needed a break or he'd be no good to anyone. He had learned early in the game to sleep wherever he could whenever he could, so he darkened the room, leaving only the light from the laptops. Then he stretched out full-length on the floor, hands behind his head, closed his eyes and in seconds he was asleep.

He was deep into a dreamless void when a beeping sound cut through to his consciousness. He woke and pushed to his feet, instantly alert. The beeping was coming from the laptop tracing the source of the hack. Sitting at his work table, he focused on the last location the machine had identified and began typing codes that had sounded wrong to him into the machine. These bastards were fucking smart. They had the trace bouncing off so many other locations it looked as if they'd designed it with a ping pong ball. He was simultaneously elated and pissed off at the complexity of it. He liked a challenge and he was at least gratified that whoever had hacked the Hoffman system wasn't the average everyday computer nerd. No, whoever was behind this had brains and money, a dangerous combination.

Late morning, his grumbling stomach sent him a message, reminding him he hadn't eaten since late the day before. Even thought he was alone in the offices and there were multiple layers of security, he still locked the door to the room he was working in before heading downstairs.

The guard who signed him out nodded to him.

"Through for the day? You must have slept here last night."

Eric barked a short laugh. "As a matter of fact, I did. Now I have to feed the beast. Any suggestions where I can a quick hit of breakfast?"

"Most every place will be jammed with parade goers." He looked at his watch. "Got a couple of hours before it starts. There's a Starbucks in the next block. If you hustle, the line shouldn't be too bad."

"Great. Thanks a lot."

He got himself out of the building and down the street. The Starbucks line was doable and he took advantage of the wait to shake the kinks out of his body. Carrying a cardboard tray holding his Grande Americano with an extra shot, and two pastries, he entered the building and went straight back to his workroom. He practically inhaled half the coffee before biting into one of the pastries then getting back to work, this time on the Hoffman software while the other laptop continued its attempt to track the hacker.

He had no idea how long he'd been working again when he entered a code and suddenly the page on the screen scrolled up and up and up before stopping. He stared at it, reading it through again and again to be sure he understood what he was looking at.

"Holy shit!" he whispered. "Holy fucking shit!"

Liam had set up a small printer for him so he could print out anything he needed to. He hit Print Now, selected the pages he wanted and sat there while they spit out.

He had also, in this case, given the passwords to both laptops to Liam. Just as a backup. He seldom did that, since too many times the client had turned out to be the bad guy who just wanted Eric to find the week spots so he could fix them and hide whatever he was hiding.

Then he took his cell out of his pocket and dialed Liam's number, hoping he could get the man before he was all tied up with parade stuff. No such luck.

Hey, buddy. Call me back as soon as you get this. I found the problem with the Hoffman software. You have someone very, very clever working for you. We need to talk and I mean now. So call me ASAP.

Fuck! Fuck! Fuck!

He checked his watch.

Maybe I can still catch him before he gets on that float.

He knew from the brochure Liam gave him where the parade started. If he could just get there in time. This could not wait, celebration or no celebration. He shut down the computer with the Hoffman project on it and stuffed it in one of his messenger bags along with the printout. He made sure the door to the workroom was locked before he headed out for the elevator.

"Which way to the parade?" he asked the guard when he reached the lobby. "I've got a thing here with the route. I'd appreciate it a whole lot if you could help me?"

"Sure. Let's see it."

He hauled out the map Liam had given him. "Just point me in the right direction."

"You'll have a damn hard time finding a parking place by now," the guard told him and stuck his finger on the map. "You can drive this far, but then you'd be better off walking."

"Okay, great. Thanks."

He snatched up the paper and raced out to the parking lot. Five minutes later, he was headed toward where the guard had told him he'd have to leave his car. He debated taking the messenger bag with him but decided to lock it in the trunk. Then he was racing down one street and another, looking for the parade start. The task was made even more difficult because the streets were jammed with people in Gasparilla gear partying and laughing and generally getting in their own and everyone else's way.

"Excuse me." He tried to push his way through a tight group of people.

"Hey, buddy, Relax." One of the men held up a beer. "How about a drink?"

"No, thank you. I just need to get through."

"Hey! You're cute." One of the woman pushed herself against him. "How about joining us?"

"Thanks but I—"

That was as far as he got. Something sharp slid into his body between his ribs and a breath-stealing pain paralyzed his body. Another sharp stick, and his legs threatened to collapse. He found himself falling to the ground.

"Hey!" A woman's voice. "Hey, you can't lie down here. I don't care how cute you are. Dino, make him get up."

"Okay buddy. Listen, you can't— Holy shit, Maribeth. He's hurt. Damn it, he's gushing blood. Someone help me here."

Eric heard their voices as if from a great distance.

Then he heard nothing at all.

* * * *

Eight was in a panic. Everything was falling apart. Coming to the office had been a spur-of-the-moment thing, prodded by a desperate need to see what, if anything, Eric Braun had dug up yet. How far he'd gotten with both his projects, especially the one breaking apart the coding for the Hoffman software.

Entering through the rear door meant being able to avoid the guard in the lobby. He was fixated on the front door only. It was supposed the people who worked in the building had already been vetted.

Eight had been disappointed the man wasn't there, but his car was still in the lot so he couldn't have gone far. Then he was back, after an obvious Starbucks run. So maybe an offer to help do the search might not be a bad idea. Score some extra points.

But not after overhearing the message he left for Liam.

Shit and damn. He could not be allowed to tell Liam whatever he'd found. And just how in the hell had he found it, anyway? This guy must be some fucking genius, is all. But now what the hell to do? Tackling him in the hallway didn't seem like too bright an idea. It would mean exposure, for damn sure. Worse than that, the end of life, as Eight knew it. Maybe even the end of Eight's life, since there would be no money to pay off the horrendous gambling debts.

Shan would be furious. Eight's death would be a foregone conclusion.

Panic surged thick and heavy. *Fuck, fuck, fuck.*

What was the saying? Kill or be killed?

Only, committing murder had never been on the agenda.

But standing here wasn't going to solve the problem. Eric had already headed downstairs and in another minute would be impossible to catch up with. But the effort had to be made. This was life or death. *Eight's* life or death. No time to be squeamish. It was amazing what fear could make a person do.

A weapon. Without a gun, something else would have to do. And that gave birth to a brilliant idea. Liam did not always lock his office, mostly because everything in it was locked in cupboards or other containers at night, with double locks. Eight rushed down the hallway to his office and blew out a breath of relief when she saw that was the case today.

And there it was, Liam's prized knife, a distinct weapon that looked like a tapered skinny dagger, sitting right there on his desk. Maybe this could kill two birds with one stone. Get rid of Eric Braun and plunge Liam Benedict into the middle of a murder investigation. By the time it was resolved, Shan's people would be in the Hoffman system and have all the files they needed and have done an electronic disappearance.

Something to hold it with so there'd be no fingerprints. Eight looked wildly around for something, anything, and finally ran to the rest room to grab some toilet paper. Scooping up the knife and pocketing it, in seconds Eight was racing out to the parking lot and trying to catch up with Eric.

Killing someone had not been on the agenda, but self-preservation was a powerful motivating factor.

Okay, there was his car, just up ahead. Following him wasn't hard, with Gasparilla traffic clogging the streets.

I can do this. It's my ass on the line.

Then the man was racing down the street toward Bayshore like his pants were on fire, and Eight had to be very careful to keep him in sight without being seen. Okay, okay, there he was. Right near the parade starting line. How the hell did he find that parking space? There was no place for Eight to go except someone's driveway. Hopefully, business would be taken care of before anyone complained about it.

Eric raced down to the broad street and started toward where the floats were lined up. The cops on duty were trying to get everyone out of the roadway so the parade could begin, without much success. He was pushed right up against a knot of people blocking his progress.

Fucking A. There were a *ton* of people in that mass.

Okay, okay, that's a good thing.

Eight was already wearing a pirate shirt and black pants, a concession to the party after the parade. A bandanna, whipped out of a pants pocket, covered the head and fastened with a knot in the back. Now no one could tell the difference between one pirate and another.

Eric was still trying to muscle his way out of the little crowd of people. Eight's hand curled around the dagger, handy in a pants pocket, and just slipped up next to him. Everyone was talking and laughing and he was trying to get them to move aside. Impulse and desperation took over, and in seconds the knife had been plunged into Eric Braun's chest not once but twice.

Slipping away was easy after that. With people pressed hard against him, Eric didn't fall at once. By the time he did and someone noticed what was happening, Eight was back down the street and heading toward the car. And didn't draw a full breath until there was distance from the parade.

Someone would find Eric. Call an ambulance. Have to identify him. Call Liam. Put everything into motion. By the time the curtain rolled up on the next act, Eight would be controlled and prepared.

Hopefully.

* * * *

Tampa Police Officer Andy Frankel didn't mind working security at Gasparilla the way some of the others did. For the most part the people, although often tipsy, were warm and friendly. In four years, he'd only had to break up two fights. And usually he got the drunk and disorderlies out of there and off with friends before they became critical. Once the parade was actually over, he and the other cops out here with him managed to get the people off Bayshore Boulevard and into downtown. The parade ended there and partygoers broke off into groups. Then it was mostly a matter of just being a blue presence. For the most part, people behaved themselves.

But the damn parade was due to start and people were still filling the damn street. Which is why he was startled when, as he tried to herd people into the first section of bleachers, he heard people shouting at him.

"Officer?" a man yelled. "Officer, come over here. Help. Hurry."

"Yes, hurry!" a woman screamed in a shrill voice.

He hurried over to where a tight knot of people was crouched around something on the ground. *Damn it.* Had someone had a fist fight? Injured somebody else? *Crap.* The parade would be coming through here in the next little bit and they needed to move out of the way. But his annoyance faded when he saw what they were all crowded around. A man in jeans and T-shirt lay on the ground and another man and a woman were using pirate bandanas in an effort to stop the blood pouring from two wounds.

What the hell?

Andy took one look and used his shoulder radio to call his precinct, giving his name, badge number and location.

"I'm at the end of the bleachers with a man stabbed and down. Send me backup and EMS now. And tell them to step on it," he added. "This guy's in bad shape."

And might not make it if the ambulance doesn't get here like yesterday.

"Anyone know who he is?" he asked.

There was a chorus of nos.

"He just got shoved into us while we were standing here," one of the women told him. "The next thing we knew he collapsed and was bleeding everywhere."

He knelt beside the wounded man, urging everyone back except the two people putting pressure on the wounds, glad to see the flow of blood had slowed but wondering if it was enough to save the guy. He did what he could but he hoped to hell the EMTs got here fast.

He was peripherally aware of the arrival of a patrol car parking askew at the end of one of the streets leading into Bayshore. The two cops who climbed out brought orange cones from the vehicle and hurried down to block off and contain the scene. That accomplished, they went to work at once containing the scene and dispersing the crowd of rubberneckers that had gathered. They also took down the names and phone numbers of the people who had tried to help the man.

Andy was never so glad to hear something as the *whoop! whoop!* of the ambulance siren as it punctuated the air. He glanced over his shoulder and saw the other cops clearing the way for the vehicle to pull up to the spot where they all waited. In seconds the EMTs were there, checking the guy, wrapping his wounds tighter, taking his vitals, contacting the hospital then lifting him on a stretcher and into the ambulance. Then they were gone, sirens blaring, off to Tampa General Hospital and its emergency room.

Now Andy and the others steered all the curiosity-seekers out of the street and back into the bleachers, or onto the sidewalk across the road if they could find room. Fortunately, the people who had surrounded the victim had seats in the bleachers, held for them by friends while they'd gone to get drinks. That taken care of, he reported back to his corporal, giving him a status update.

"See if the people who helped you will hang around just a few," he told Andy. "The detectives are on their way, but with streets blocked and parade traffic they won't get there until the parade is all the way past the bleachers. They'd like to talk to them if possible."

"I'll do what I can. And I'll hang around here until they're finished."

"Great. We've got two more detectives on the way to Tampa General. That's where they took the guy, right? Nearest facility?"

"It is."

"All right. Good job, Frankel. I'll be looking for your report."

"Thank you, sir." Andy signed off, thinking it would only be a good job if the guy survived. Which at the moment didn't look too promising.

One of the officers stayed by the blocked-off area while Andy and the others went to work getting the crowd of rubberneckers and curiosity-seekers out of the street to make way for the parade, which was already starting late, and keep them off the road until the parade passed by.

The parade had passed the starting point and all the floats and vehicles were wending their way down Bayshore by the time the two detectives arrived. Some people were leaving to head downtown, but others were still hanging around, talking, drinking, laughing.

"You still have those people here?" one of the detectives, Jay Howard, asked Andy.

"Yeah." He pointed. "Let me take you over to them."

He introduced himself and Andy noted that, for the most part, the people were happy to talk to the detective. The women were still shocked at what had happened.

"I can't believe that happened while we were just standing there," a tall redhead said. "Lordy. I'm sure I'll never forget it."

"Nice people," Howard commented when he was finished. "But the parade's already started so it's no environment to question witnesses. Listen." He read Andy's name on his shirt. "Office Frankel. Thanks for everything. You'll be filing your report when you get back to the precinct?"

"Yes, sir." Andy nodded.

"Okay. I'll request a copy. But if you could hang around until the parade is over here and help keep the scene blocked off until forensics gets here. That would be great."

"Sure. No problem."

Andy just hoped the poor stabbing victim would be okay.

* * * *

Liam was ready to tear his hair out. He hadn't bothered to check his phone once he got to the parade lineup spot, figuring he wouldn't be able to hear anything anyway. But as soon as the parade was done he leaped off the float, stepped into a Starbucks and turned his phone on. Most of the calls he could return later, but when he heard Eric's, his blood chilled. The man had not only found the glitch, he'd figured out who had installed it? The guy was a fucking genius, but that didn't change the fact that someone working for him had screwed with a client and he had no idea why.

When he got Eric's voice mail, he said, "Call me back. Now."

Five minutes later, when he hadn't gotten a return call, he tried again. He also texted. Nothing. Nada. Blank. He had left his car in a parking lot downtown, knowing he'd need it after the parade, and Ubered to the launching spot. Now he ran for the lot, fidgeting while the attendant took his damn time processing Liam's payment.

Once in his car, he turned on the Bluetooth so the phone would hook up and tried calling Eric again. Where in the hell was the guy? Liam was getting a very sick feeling about the whole thing.

He got no satisfaction at the offices. The guard said Eric had run out of there a couple of hours ago like his pants were on fire, the strap for his computer bag slung across his chest. But Eric's car was gone and the offices were empty. He opened the door to Eric's workroom with his master code key and found just one laptop sitting there. A program was running on it, but when he tried to bring it up it asked for a password. He wanted to find Eric before he did anything. If the man had found the problem with the Hoffman program, that needed attending to at once.

So where was Eric? And where was the other goddamn laptop? And the messenger bag?

Shit!

He wanted to pull his hair out. Should he call the cops and report the man missing? Most times, they wouldn't even take a report if it was less than twenty-four hours. He wanted to avoid calling Taylor and asking if she'd heard from him. He could just imagine her reaction. What kind of dumbass loses an expert doing highly specialized work for him?

But where in the fucking hell could he be?

He had just taken the elevator back upstairs, planning to go through whatever Eric had left in his work space, when he heard the phone in his office ringing. He raced down the hall but by the time he got the door unlocked it had stopped ringing. Then his cell phone rang.

"Eric?" *Jesus, please let it be him.*

"Is this Liam Benedict?"

Liam frowned, held the phone away to look at it, then put it back to his ear.

"Yeah. Who's this?"

"Detective Brian Duarte. Tampa Police Department. You're Benedict?"

Liam nodded, unable to form words for a moment. Then he realized the man couldn't see him. "Yes. I am. What's — what's this about?"

"You have a man named Eric Braun doing some specialized work for you?"

Oh. Jesus, Mary and Joseph.

Liam's stomach pitched to the bottom of his shoes and all the saliva in his mouth dried up. Whatever the detective had to say, he knew it wasn't good.

"I do. I've been looking for him and haven't been able to locate him."

"That's because he's in surgery at Tampa General." Duarte delivered the news in a flat voice.

Liam squeezed the cell phone so tightly his hand hurt. "Can you tell me what happened?"

"I think it best if you get down here so we can discuss this in person."

"But—"

"We're in the surgery waiting room. Get here soon."

The call disconnected and Liam just stared at the phone. *What the hell?*

He was so rattled he almost forgot to go through the security process to lock his office. It seemed to take forever to get to the hospital, although on a good day the trip only took fifteen minutes. Of course, this wasn't a good day, what with the Gasparilla craziness still going on. He was ready to tear his hair out by the time he got there, parked in the parking structure and managed to find his way to the surgical waiting room.

It wasn't hard to spot Duarte and his partner. They were the only two men there wearing jackets and slacks and ties. He looked from one to the other.

"Which of you is Duarte?"

"I am." The taller of the two men, dark-haired and slim, stepped forward.

"I apologize for the costume." He gestured at the pirate clothing he wore. "I rode one of the parade floats and haven't taken the time to go home and change."

"Yes." Callahan cleared his throat. "Can I see some identification, please?"

Liam stared at him even as he pulled his wallet out of his pocket and flipped it open to his driver's license.

"What the hell is going on here? And how is Eric? Is he out of surgery yet? Can I see him? What happened?"

Duarte sighed. "I'm sorry to inform you, Mr. Benedict, but your friend died fifteen minutes ago."

Chapter Fourteen

Liam wasn't sure he'd heard right. Everything around him faded until he felt as if he was wrapped inside a cocoon. He blinked, gave himself a mental shake and stared at the two men.

"Excuse me. Did you just say Eric Braun is dead?"

Duarte nodded. "I'm sorry to have to be the one to tell you. Listen, I know this is a shock to you, but – "

"A shock!" Liam interrupted. "Are you kidding me? That doesn't begin to describe it. What the hell happened? And how did you know to call me?"

Duarte exchanged a look with his partner.

"How about we go sit in the corner over there and I'll tell you what we know?"

"How about you just spit it out right now?" Liam demanded. "And while we're at it, how about the two of *you* show *me* some identification, so I know this isn't just some kind of practical joke."

They displayed their shields hooked to their belts, then hauled out their wallets and flipped them over to their ID cards.

Liam studied them.

Brian Duarte.

Dean Callahan.

"Now can we go sit down?" Callahan asked.

Without answering Liam turned and headed for the corner seating arrangement. There were only two other people in the room, both in seats by the door.

"Okay." Liam faced the two men. "Talk. I want to know exactly how this happened."

"We can only tell you what we know," Duarte said. "Your friend was in the middle of the crowd at the end of the parade bleachers on Bayshore when someone stabbed him. Twice. No one knows who it was or even how it happened."

"Parade bleachers?" Liam was stunned as the situation hit him. "He must have been looking for me."

"And why would he be looking for you there, at the start of the parade?"

"He knew I was riding on one of the floats. He'd tried to call me, but my cell was turned off, so he left me a message. He must have come there to try and find me.

"Can you tell us how you know the victim?" Duarte asked. "And why he was so hot to find you before the parade started?"

"What does that have to do with anything?" Liam studied both men.

"We don't know yet." Duarte studied him. "Why don't you answer the questions and maybe we can figure this out. We had to chase all over hell and gone just to identify him."

"Wait. What?" Liam thrust his hands in his already disheveled hair.

"You heard him." Callahan's face gave a way nothing. "The man had no identification on him, nothing to tell us who he is."

"Then how did you find out? And where is his stuff? His messenger bag was not at the office because I looked for him there first."

Duarte cocked an eyebrow. "What was on the message that was so all-fired important?"

"It had to do with business. Can we please quit playing Twenty Questions and get to the facts here?"

"That's what we're trying to do." Callahan sighed. "Eric Braun was stabbed at the very end of the bleachers on Bayshore Boulevard, right at the start of the parade. Whoever did this pushed him into the middle of a crowd waiting for the parade to start. We're lucky that a heads-up cop was right there working security."

"He knew what to do," Duarte added. "Applied emergency first aid, called it in and asked for an ambulance. Made sure your guy got taken to the hospital right away. But…"

"But?" Liam prompted.

The detective's face sobered. "The doctors did everything they could to save him, but there was just too much damage from the knife wounds. I'm sorry."

Liam scrubbed his hands over his face as if trying to wake from a bad dream. "If he had nothing on him, how did you know who he was? Or that you should contact me?"

"We took his fingerprints electronically just before they took him into surgery. Once we knew who he was, we found a phone number for him that leads to his assistant. She said he was here in Tampa on a job for you. All we told her was we needed to contact him and I left both our cell numbers. I'm sure you'll be hearing from her." Duarte studied his face. "So what kind of a job is he doing that could get him killed?"

Shit!

The last thing he could do was give them that information.

"He was analyzing some software for us, trying to find a glitch that had popped up. I doubt it was anything that cause someone to murder him."

Duarte studied him for a moment. "But you don't know that for sure."

"Let's just say it would fall somewhere between absurd and unbelievable. It's just a business situation. Very boring." *I hope.* "I've never been in this position before. I need to make arrangements about Eric's body. I have arrangements to make, and people to consult before I can do that. What happens now? When can I move forward?"

"Let me check with the coroner." Callahan pulled out his cell.

"The coroner?" Liam's eyes bugged. "But we know how he died."

"Yes, but all we know is someone used a sharp instrument. The medical examiner will be able to tell us what he was stabbed with, the size and depth of it, all things we need to find the instrument itself."

"And you think you can do that? Pardon my skepticism."

"Not unexpected. We're going to do our damnedest." Duarte put away his little notebook. "I'll be honest with you, Mr. Benedict. We're gonna be looking at everyone he came into contact with since he arrived in Tampa."

"What if it was someone unrelated to his trip here? Maybe they just saw it as a good opportunity to kill him in a place where they wouldn't be connected."

"We'll definitely get to that," Callahan assured him. "Meanwhile, the first place we'll start is your office. That's where he spent most of his time since he got here, right?"

"Yes."

And although he didn't know for certain, Liam was pretty damn sure Eric had not been in contact with anyone else in the area. He apparently lived and breathed a job when he was on it.

"Then we'll want to talk to your entire staff. Nine o'clock Monday morning. At your offices."

"You want to question all of them?" Okay, so he sounded like an idiot.

"Everyone who came into contact with Mr. Braun."

Well, he damn sure wasn't giving them Hoffman's name.

He blew out a breath and tried to pull himself together. He still had trouble believing this whole thing had happened.

"Fine. I'll get hold of them. They'll be…shocked." *To say the least.* "I have some calls to make, but I'd like to see him first."

The two detectives exchanged glances. "Are you sure?"

"Is he disfigured in some way? Will I be shocked to see him? What's the problem?"

Again they exchanged looks.

And Liam lost it. Rage replaced shock, and he had to ball his fists to keep from decking one of these guys.

"Look, goddammit. A man doing some work for me has been murdered. I am not going to call people to come in and be questioned, or notify the people who need to be, without getting my eyes on him. Now where the fuck is he?"

One of the two people sitting by the door gasped audibly.

"Okay, okay, okay." Duarte held up his hand. "Keep it down. Come on. We'll take you to where he is. We're waiting for the medical examiner's van to pick him up."

Callahan punched the button on the elevator and they rode down in silence.

They took him to an empty room at the rear of the first floor. Eric's body lay strapped to a gurney, completely covered with a sheet. Liam gently peeled it back from his face and stared at the man he'd taken an instant liking to. The man looked as if he was asleep, except for the exceptional paleness of his face. Liam stood there for a long moment, just staring at him, a chill racing through his body. Then he dropped the sheet back into place.

He took a moment to pull his shit together, settle himself down. As devastating as Eric's murder was, he had another urgent situation.

"He had a car," he told the detectives. "It isn't at the office building. I'm not sure which company he rented it from but I'm sure you have the resources to find it."

Duarte scribbled in his tiny notebook.

And fuck! The laptop with the Hoffman program on it is no doubt in the missing messenger bag, which is probably in the car.

"Please let me know when you find the car. And I'm pretty sure his messenger bag will be in it. There should be a laptop with files relating to our current projects. I need to get that ASAP."

Callahan frowned. "That becomes evidence. We'll have to make sure there's nothing that would have led to this murder."

Liam controlled himself with a major effort. "There are files on there that belong to clients. Files we're working on that cannot be viewed except by my staff or me. It's all confidential."

Duarte looked at his partner. "I hear you, but do *you* understand if it's found in the deceased's car it becomes part of a murder investigation?"

Liam ground his teeth. Eric dead. Murdered. The laptop missing. He needed more clout that he had to fix this. God. Could things possibly get worse?

"All right. I'm leaving, I have calls to make. But please. If you find that laptop, can you at least let me know?"

"I guess we can do that," Callahan told him. He pulled a business card out of his wallet. "If you think of anything we should know, give me a call."

"Or me." Duarte also handed him a card. "And don't forget about your employees. Nine o'clock Monday morning."

"We'll be there. All of us."

"We'll count on it."

He had little recollection of driving away from the hospital and heading home. He had everyone's phone numbers in his contacts list on his phone and desperately needed a drink to do this. He didn't even bother to check to see if someone was following him, although with all the traffic today how the hell would he know, anyway?

A thought slammed into him and he almost vomited in the car. Had Eric been killed by mistake? Was he,

Liam, the actual target? But who would have made such a mistake?

The moment he was inside his townhouse, he tossed a couple of ice cubes into a glass and poured a substantial amount of his favorite whiskey. He swallowed a generous amount in one gulp, hoping the burn as it worked its way down his body would erase the sick feeling that gripped him. He had one call to make before he contacted his staff and he was not looking forward to it. It was entirely possible that after this he and Arroyo would be history.

Dropping onto the couch, he took another healthy swallow of his drink and speed-dialed Taylor Cantrell. She'd insisted if he needed her and it was urgent she call her cell. He just hoped she'd be able to take his call.

"Liam? I'm gathering since you called this number there's some kind of emergency?"

"Yeah." He exhaled slowly. "I, um, am afraid I have bad news for you. Devastating news."

He could tell from the silence that stretched across the connection she was stunned by his news, and probably having a hard time absorbing it.

"Give me just a minute here. Okay, we're home today. I'm going to call you back on a landline so Noah can get in on this, too."

Liam had barely disconnected when the phone rang again.

"Give me all the details," Taylor said. "Everything you know."

"It's not much," he told her, "but here it is."

He recounted everything Duarte and Callahan had told him, in as much detail as he knew. There was a long silence when he finished.

"Taylor? You there?"

"We're both here." Noah's voice. "Go over it one more time for us."

So, he did, starting with Eric's voice mail message.

"And that's all I've got. Jesus, I don't even know what to say to you. If you want to pull out of the deal with Software By Design, I'll totally understand and there'd be no objections on my part."

"That's not our style," Noah told him.

"Unless you killed Eric yourself," Taylor added, "which I certainly do not believe is the case. There's no way we'd throw you to the wolves. We take care of our own. But we need to get organized here."

Liam blew out a sigh of relief. He'd been sure he was once and done with Arroyo after this.

"Thank you. I — Just thank you."

"Give us the names of the detectives. Noah, call Charlie Voight. Liam, Charlie's one of our attorneys. He can call the Tampa PD and get information from them. Let them know you aren't battling this alone. And he'll make a case for the return of the laptop. Charlie's plugged into a lot of places and he'll be able to get every bit of information from them."

Liam wasn't going to argue with her about that. The cops might not tell Liam Benedict of Software By Design a whole lot, but Arroyo was a horse of a different color.

"They want everyone on my staff at the office Monday morning at nine for questioning. I got the feeling if I argued about it, they'd haul us all down to the police station to do it."

"Not without an attorney." Taylor was firm on that. "They'll look at the people he knew here before widening their investigation, because nine times out of ten that's where they'll find the answers. If nothing pans out, they'll start to look elsewhere. But let's not just give them carte blanche. Someone will be there to protect your interests."

"Taylor, getting that laptop back is imperative."

"I know and that's at the top of my list. I'll also call his assistant and see if she has anything. If he talked to her or messaged her or anything."

"Assistant?" Liam felt like an idiot for not knowing about this.

"Yes. He doesn't talk about her much because she's his secret weapon. He emails coded critical files to her along with information on the cases he works. I'm hoping he did this with your job."

"Me, too." Liam rubbed his forehead. "That would help solve a lot of problems."

"All right. Let me make some calls and get back to you. And Liam?"

"Yes?"

"I won't tell you to relax because I know that's not possible under the circumstances. But remember, we've got your back on this."

"And it's a pretty broad back," Noah added. "We can do a lot of heavy lifting."

The band of tension squeezing his head eased.

"I need to call his assistant. She's probably going crazy wondering why the cops called her looking for Eric."

"I'll take care of it," Taylor said. "It would probably be better coming from someone she knows."

The pressure eased a little. "Thank you. I wasn't looking forward to that."

"No problem. You've got enough to handle. We'll get back to you as soon as we have more to tell you." Taylor's voice was both efficient and reassuring.

"I don't know what to say except thank you."

When he disconnected the call, he sat there for a long moment, just holding his cell phone. What a damn mess, and just when he was taking a giant step forward. He wondered who he'd pissed off in the universe for this to happen.

He should have asked the cops if this would be released to reporters. He'd hate for his people to read about it before he had a chance to tell them. And he really wanted to tell them in person. He debated about calling one of the detectives and asking, worried they might think he was hiding something, but then he decided leaving it to chance might be worse.

He pulled both cards out of his pocket and dialed the number of the one on top.

"Duarte."

"Detective?" Liam did his best to speak in a reasonable tone. "This is Liam Benedict."

"Mr. Benedict. Did you think of something else to add?"

"I wish. No, in fact I have a favor to ask."

"A favor?" Duarte's voice was neutral, giving away no indication if he'd be receptive or not."

"Yes. I'd like to be able to tell my staff in person about Eric Braun's death. I'd rather they didn't hear it on the news first." He paused, but when Duarte said nothing, he added, "Most of them are enjoying Gasparilla this weekend. If you could keep it out of the news until Monday, I plan to ask them to get to the office at eight-thirty. That gives me half an hour to give them the few details I have and to make sure they know answering your questions is an important part of finding out who did this."

"You sure you don't just want this time so everyone can get their stories straight?" The note of skepticism wasn't hard to miss.

"Not at all. They don't know the man well, but he's been working in our offices for a week so he's not a stranger. That's why I want to do this in person."

Silence hummed across the connection for a long minute.

"Fine, then. We can do that. Just make sure you aren't setting us up with a well-rehearsed story."

Liam gripped the phone in frustration. "That would be hard to do, Detective, since I don't have one to rehearse. And thank you."

After he disconnected, he sent a quick message to Taylor.

Cops will hold off releasing the story until I meet with staff Monday a.m.

It was ten minutes before a reply came back.

Good. If u think one of them is involved it will give you an opportunity to see their reaction.

He rubbed his forehead, trying to ease the tightness pressing against him. *Yeah, Taylor. I do think one of them is involved. I just don't know which one or why. And it will kill me if it's one of them I feel closest to.*

Damn it all, anyway. How did this shit happen?

* * * *

Eight pulled in a deep breath and let it out slowly before getting out of the car and heading into the restaurant. Even the pep talk that lasted all afternoon wasn't enough preparation for this upcoming discussion with Shan. There was just no way around it, however. The news of Eric Braun's death would be out probably before the night was over. And in any event, the danger of him going to Liam with what he'd discovered was no longer a factor. It was to be hoped, since there had to be a bright spot here, Liam would not be finding out what Eric had discovered any time soon. And even if he put another forensic data specialist on it, by the time he or she found what Eric had, Eight would have been paid and be long gone.

As usual, Shan was already there, occupying a booth in a far corner. Eight slid into the seat opposite and motioned for the waiter. Doing this without alcohol wasn't going to be possible. Shan frowned at the order of a double bourbon.

"Are you going to tell me something that will make me unhappy? Is that why you need the liquid courage? You know how I feel about that."

Too bad. Fuck you. You didn't have to stick a knife in someone today. Twice.

"Having this drink is the least of my sins today." Eight lifted the glass when the waitress delivered it and took a healthy swallow. It burned on the way down, but at least the jittery nerves stopped doing their St. Vitus Dance.

Shan frowned. "And what sins would you be talking about?"

Eight leaned forward and in a low voice said, "Today I killed a man. For you."

Shan gave no indication that the news was shocking, other than a slight narrowing of the eyes. "Was this a spur-of-the-moment thing?"

"Of course." Eight gripped the glass. "Do you think I deliberately plan to murder people?"

"I have no idea if you do or not. And what brought on today's unexpected action?"

In short, concise sentences, Eight recited the events of the day, from the moment of arrival at SBD to overhearing Eric on the phone to finding him at Gasparilla and stabbing him.

"And you are positive no one knew it was you doing this?"

Eight gave a short nod. "I had on my Gasparilla clothes and added the head wrap. I looked like everyone else waiting for the parade. Braun was trying to find where the floats lined up so he could grab Benedict. I could not let that happen. *You* could not let that happen."

"I have nothing to do with this." Shan spoke the words in a flat, impersonal voice. "There are no traces back to me. Our meetings have been clandestine and we have had no communications that were traceable. No one even knows of my involvement."

Eight stared. Shan was right. Everything had been handled to leave no trackbacks.

I'm the only one with a neck in the noose.

Fuck.

"I could always drop your name if I get caught."

A muscle ticked in Shan's jaw. "That would be a very bad mistake on your part. Even jail could not protect you from us. Now give me the details of how this disaster happened."

Eight drained the rest of the whiskey in the glass and signaled for another. Then went into a careful explanation of the events that led up to the stabbing.

"And the knife?" Shan asked.

"Back at SBD. I knew Liam would come back there looking for Eric when he couldn't contact him. I made sure I was long gone by then. And yes, I made sure none of my prints were on there. I kept a tissue wrapped around it so I could preserve his prints. Just in case."

"At least you kept your wits about you."

"I also made sure not to wipe all the blood off. I'm sure the cops will come talk to everyone there. They'll see the knife and take it from there."

Shan's lips curved in a malicious smile.

"So. Two birds with one stone. Or one knife, as it were."

"I'm not as stupid as you seem to think." Eight was getting really irritated. "Anyway. By the time this investigation is over and Liam can hire another expert, you should have all the files you need. Have you been able to get in okay? Like the other night?"

"Yes." Shan gave a sharp nod. "We are doing it piecemeal so as not to alert anyone. Your back door is working fine."

"Good. When do I get my money?"

"When the work is complete."

Eight felt a surge of anger. "That's not the arrangement. Half when you know it works, the other half when you have all the files. I want the first half now."

"I will have to speak with my people."

Eight gripped the glass so hard it was a wonder it didn't crack. "I kept my end of the bargain. And I put myself in danger to make sure it didn't get screwed up. Do you want me to put the word out you don't keep your bargains?"

"And exactly who would you tell?" Sarcasm edged Shan's voice.

Eight leaned forward. "Don't forget that I have long tentacles out there on the web. And on the dark net. I don't know who else your 'people' reach out to or what they reach out for, but I can screw it up. So, don't fuck with me."

Shan's face became a mask. "Fine. But don't *you* fuck with *me*, or it won't be pretty."

Eight stared for a moment then slid out of the booth. "Thanks for the drink."

"You have your burner phones. If you run out, buy more. I want regular updates on this situation."

"Fine."

Eight didn't draw a full breath until the restaurant was well in the background.

Fucking Shan. Maybe I'll add another victim to my list. Killing wasn't as hard as I thought.

Chapter Fifteen

Liam wanted more than anything to hide in his townhouse with Sydney over the weekend. Lock away the outside world. Open a bottle of wine. Binge on movies and Chinese food and have stupendous sex. Immerse himself in Sydney and forget about the disasters waiting for him just outside his door. Monday would be soon enough to deal with them.

As usual, however, life got in the way. Sydney had called that morning before he left for Gasparilla to remind him she was flying out for an overnight at her sister's to attend a big family event. She'd be back Sunday night and would call him early Monday morning to check in with him. If not for his Gasparilla obligations, he'd have jumped at her invitation to go with her. Now, when he needed her—make that wanted her—she was in Atlanta.

Damn!

He needed to let everyone on the staff at Software By Design know there would be a key meeting Monday morning at eight-thirty sharp, and it was important for everyone to be there. He discarded the idea of emails. They were all involved in weekend activities, many of them with Gasparilla, and he couldn't be sure they'd even check their email before Monday. Instead he sent a mass text, knowing they were never without their cell phones. Over the next twenty minutes, everyone texted back, with varying responses.

Ok. C u then.

What's up?

Problems?

And finally, from Phil, as expected, *U bringing donuts?*

He replied to each one, telling them he just had some updates to go over before they began the work week. They all knew why Eric had been brought in, so if they thought that was what he would be talking about, well and good. Unfortunately, although it related to Eric, it was far from what they'd be expecting. But he, like the cops, wanted to see their initial reaction. It made him physically ill to think one of his people was at the root of all this, but he'd better find out before anything else happened.

Now, the next twenty-four hours stretched endlessly in front of him, hours filled with nothing but the image of Eric's body and dark thoughts of the Hoffman debacle. He thought about getting drunk, but that wouldn't do much except give him a bad hangover. And if for any reason the cops wanted to contact him, being in an alcoholic daze sure wouldn't keep him on the right side of the ledger. Instead, he decided to go back to the office and see if he could figure out how far Eric had gotten tracing the hack into the Hoffman files. He was sure that was the program the other laptop had been running. The man would not have left the critical project just sitting like that, processing. Not once he found out what the problem was. He wouldn't want anyone's eyes on it but his and Liam's.

He finally discarded his pirate costume, showered and pulled on jeans and a T-shirt. Then he headed for the office, stopping on the way to pick up a fast-food meal. Not that he was hungry, but he hadn't put food in his mouth since breakfast and he didn't want to pass out from lack of it.

Although he entered the building by the rear door, he stopped in the lobby to let the guard know he was there. Just in case anyone came to the building looking for him, he made sure the guard knew to call up to him before getting them into the elevator.

At the SBD offices, he stopped in the break room to fix coffee from the single serving machine before he headed to Eric's workspace. He hadn't had lunch, but food was the last thing he wanted right then. His nerves were stretched so taut he wondered they didn't twang like guitar strings. He was sure he wouldn't be able to digest a bite of food.

He unlocked the door to the room where Eric had been set up then pulled a chair over to the big desk where the laptop sat. After pressing the spacebar to wake the machine up, he typed in the password Eric had given him. At once information began to scroll across the screen.

Liam hit a key to stop the scrolling and began to read the data, one screen at a time. The most skilled hackers could write self-erasing code, fake their web addresses, route their attacks through the devices of innocent victims and make it appear that they were in multiple countries at once. An advanced attack, coordinated over multiple media platforms and using different languages, could be very difficult to trace.

Eric had done a pretty good job so far, eliminating a lot of the fake web address as well as those of innocent victims whose information had been stolen. But he hadn't yet reached the end of the trail. Whoever had hacked into the Hoffman servers was exceptionally skilled and knowledgeable.

Although he hadn't done this for some time, as Liam dived into the slow process it all came back to him. He accepted the fact that he didn't have Eric's level of expertise so it obviously would take him longer. But it occupied his brain and kept him from dwelling every minute on Eric's murder.

He worked at it without letup for three hours, stopping only to fix coffee now and then. And it kept him from checking his cell every few minutes to see if Taylor Cantrell had called back and he'd missed it. As each trail he followed led to yet another dead end, his level of frustration grew. Who the hell were these people that they could create such a complicated system that buried their actual location? He didn't even stop to check his watch until his stomach sent him a message that he'd better get some food or he'd be in even worse shape. He stretched, looked at his watch and realized it was almost nine o'clock.

Okay. Time to stop for the night. He hoped he'd tired out his brain so much that he could fall asleep. If only he could be that lucky. He put the laptop to sleep, making sure the lock code was in place. Turned off all the lights and locked everything up.

He made sure the guard saw him leaving when he headed out to his car. When he exited the building, he took a deep breath of the cool night air, hoping to clear his head of the jumble of thoughts rocketing around inside. But then a different feeling hit him, that same sense of unease that he thought had finally disappeared. He looked around the parking lot, a slow glance, not hurrying. It was impossible for anyone to get in here who didn't belong. During the day, there was a guard who checked visitors. At night, the only way to get in was with a coded card.

Still, that sense of being watched wouldn't go away. He started his car and drove slowly out of the lot, waiting while the security gates slowly opened. When he pulled out into the street, he looked around again. There were more people out because of Gasparilla and even though this was primarily a business section, there were still considerably more cars on the road than usual.

He drove down the street at a somewhat slower than normal pace, but nobody pulled away from the curb to follow him or tried to bump him.

I'm the victim of an overactive imagination and too many thriller novels.

Still, all the way home he watched carefully, taking special notice when he pulled into his garage behind his townhouse. He even made a wide four-block circle to see if anyone was on his tail. Even though nothing popped, the edgy feeling wouldn't go away. He had just walked into his kitchen when his cell rang. He looked at the screen. Taylor Cantrell. At last.

"Sorry it took so long for me to get back to you," she said as soon as he'd answered. "I wanted to make sure I had touched all bases before I called back."

"I understand." *So, what have you got for me?* He wanted to shout the question.

"It took me quite a while to get hold of Nan Dorsey, Eric's assistant. She was out of cell phone range most of the day."

"It can't have been pleasant giving her that news." Liam was just glad he wasn't the one who had to deliver it.

"She's stunned, as you can imagine. I asked her if she had a friend I could call to be with her."

"And did she?"

"Yes, fortunately. Her sister, which is who she spent the day with. They were still together, so I asked to speak with her." Taylor's sigh was audible. "She's taking Nan home with her and will make sure she stays there for a while."

"Thank god for that."

Liam thought about pouring himself a fresh drink but decided against it. Getting drunk wasn't going to help the situation.

"I also had a friend call the chief of detectives at the Tampa Police Department. They've known each other for some time."

"Taylor, I—"

"Just to be clear," she interrupted, "I didn't try to exert any influence. That's a bad habit some people have. But I wanted to get a clear picture of where we were."

Yeah, I'd like the same thing.

"And?"

"As I suspected, they did the autopsy right away but of course won't release a copy of the report. However, I have someone in Tampa who can monitor this. I thought about having legal representation Monday morning when the detectives show up to question you and your staff, but I decided against it."

"You think it would look like someone is guilty and we're just being prepared?" God. Maybe he should have that drink after all.

"Yes. But if the unthinkable does happen, call me at once and we'll get moving."

"Listen, Taylor." How did he say this? "I know you said you didn't want to kill the deal between SBD and Arroyo, but I want you to know if you need to nullify, I understand."

"And I'll tell you again. Nothing you've done changes my mind about this. I certainly don't think you killed Eric."

Liam blew out a breath, relieved at least about that.

"However," Taylor continued, "I hate to say this, but I'm pretty damn sure someone on your staff is in bed with some very bad people, and that's behind all of this."

Nausea bubbled up in his stomach and he swallowed it back.

"I've about decided the same thing, but hell, Taylor. I vetted all these people myself, and some of them I worked with at Winters and Pryce. How would they even become involved with the kind of people who do this?"

"A good question." A pause. "I'd like your permission to do full background checks on all of them. I know you've done your due diligence," she went on before he could say anything. "But I promise you I have resources at my disposal that can find out anything about anyone. When I first took over Arroyo, we had a nasty situation because I didn't have full background reports on key people. I'll never put myself or anyone on my team in that situation again."

"Go ahead," he told her. "Absolutely."

"Good. And I'll keep you in the loop on everything. Telling you not to worry would be like telling you not to breathe so I'll just say this. Keep your shit together. We'll get through this."

He had to smile at that.

"Thanks. I will. And I'll call you right after we're done Monday morning."

"Talk to you then."

Sunday felt as long as a week, but he managed to get through it by working on the trace of the hack. Usually something like this could be accomplished in a couple of days, but this was the most intricate he'd ever encountered. He wondered how long it would take him if someone with Eric's skills and experience hadn't quite cracked it.

He was aware that five countries, of which the United States was one, were considered the world's cyber superpowers. The others were Israel, the United Kingdom, Russia and China. His money was on one of the last two. There was no history — at least yet — for the others to attack this country's cyber networks. So, who on his staff had gotten involved with either of the two possibles? And why? Money of course, but who needed it so badly they'd sell out their country? Just thinking about it made him ill.

By the time he quit for the day, he had worked his way through many more layers. He was close, he just knew it, but he was so tired his eyes were crossing. He closed up and headed home, hoping he could at least get a little sleep.

At last Monday morning arrived. Liam went through the Starbucks drive-through to stoke up on his favorite Café Americano and arrived at the office at a quarter to eight. Rosalie, of course, was already there.

"Something's going on," she said the minute he stepped of the elevator. "You want to give me a heads-up so I can be prepared when everyone else goes off their rocker?"

"How do you know they'll flip?" He gave her a tired smile. "Silly question. You always know everything."

"Well, I don't know this, so how about filling me in?"

She froze in shock when he told her about Eric, and it took her a long moment before she spoke.

"This has to do with the Hoffman debacle, right?"

He nodded and told her about the message Eric had left on his cell.

"I wish to hell I hadn't shut off my phone."

Rosalie shook her head. "You'd never have been able to hear him with all the noise at the start of the parade route, so don't beat yourself up. Let's get set up for the meeting everyone will be here soon." She gestured toward her desk. "I stopped at Tasty Treats and brought goodies for everyone. Maybe with enough sugar in their system, they won't freak for too long."

By the time she had set out everything on the table in the meeting room, people were arriving. By eight o'clock they were all in place around the table, munching on pastries and watching him, much in the same way a mouse stares at a cat getting ready to pounce.

Liam cleared his throat. "I have unfortunate news for you, and believe me, I wish I wasn't telling you this. At the Gasparilla parade site on Saturday, Eric Braun was attacked and stabbed. Twice. Efforts to save him failed. He was pronounced dead late Saturday afternoon at Tampa General."

The room was dead silent. Everyone stared at him, eyes wide with shock, jaws dropping. Teri was the first to speak.

"Do the cops know who did it? Do they have anyone in mind?"

Liam shook his head. "Everything is a dead end so far. He didn't know anyone in town except the people here and at Hoffman. Taylor Cantrell has contacted his assistant in Atlanta but she had no clue who would do this, although the Atlanta PD will be interviewing her. His entire connection here in this city was this firm and all of you."

"Are you accusing us of something?" There was no mistaking the hostility in Phil's voice.

"Not at all." Liam forced himself to portray a calm he was far from feeling and took a swallow of his coffee. "I'm just telling you the police have very little to go on. I'll tell you what I can, because I don't want you to be blindsided. Because we were Eric's connection to Tampa, the police will be here at nine o'clock to talk to everyone."

A bubble of sound erupted, with everyone trying to talk at once. Liam held up a hand.

"Hold, it hold it, hold it. Please. One at a time." He nodded toward Pete Herriot. "You first. At least you raised your hand."

"Thanks." He looked around the table. "I'm speaking for everyone, I think, when I ask again if they think one of us did it."

"At the moment, they have no reason to suspect anyone here. But logic dictates that they start with the only people in town who knew him. And before you say anything else, no, I don't think anyone here is involved."

And I wish to God that was the truth.

"So, what will they ask us?" This came from one of the newer hires, one Liam had been lucky enough to lure away from Harlan Logistics.

"Just how well you knew him. What interaction you had with him here at work. If he said anything that led you to believe he knew people in town or had a problem he was dealing with."

"But—" She looked around at everyone else. "We know nothing."

"Of course. But let's let them do their job so they can move on from us and look for other possibilities."

At fifteen minutes before nine o'clock, Liam broke up the meeting and sent everyone back to his or her workstations. He had just accepted a fresh coffee from Rosalie when the elevator stopped on their floor and the doors slid open. He stepped out to meet Detectives Duarte and Callahan and shook hands with them.

Duarte handed him a folded sheet of paper. "This is a warrant that allows us to search the premises, and to arrest a person if we find anything that deems it necessary. Just a formality, but wanted to cover ourselves in case."

Liam scowled. "In case of what?"

"In case we feel there is something here we need to look for," Callahan told him. "Or something that points a finger at anyone here. Like we said, it's just a formality. If we don't find anything and everyone's in the clear, you have nothing to worry about."

"Then I'm telling you, I have nothing to worry about." But he was bothered by a sudden flutter of unease. What if he was mistaken? What if it was one of his people after all? The thought made him sick.

"Would you like to interview each of my people individually," he asked, "or as a group?"

"One at a time," Duarte answered. "I assume you have a room we can use."

"Of course." He motioned to Rosalie, who had stepped up beside him, and introduced her to the men. "Rosalie will get you settled in the meeting room. If you need coffee or anything, just let her know."

"Thanks, but this isn't a social call." Callahan pulled a folded sheet of paper form his pocket and handed it to Rosalie. "We'll start with Teri LaGrange and take the rest of them in this order."

"Any reason you're starting with her?" Liam asked.

Duarte raised an eyebrow. "Any reason we shouldn't?"

"Nope." He held up his hands, palms outward. "No reason at all. Just asking."

"Okay. Rosalie. Will you get Teri?"

"Of course."

Liam went back to his office. The first thing he did was call Taylor, knowing he should keep her in the loop.

"I wouldn't worry about the warrant," she assured him. "At least not yet."

"Yeah?" Easy for her to say. "When *should* I worry about it?"

"If they decide to arrest anyone. Especially you."

"Me?" He nearly fell out of his chair. "Why me? I had nothing to do with Eric's murder."

"It's never easy to know what they'll think needs further investigation. I know you didn't do it. You know you didn't do it. We'll handle whatever comes up."

"I'll hold you to that."

"I expect you to. Listen, call me as soon as they leave. If I'm out of the office, have my assistant patch you through to me wherever I am."

"Will so. And Taylor? Thanks for everything."

"Like I said, we'll handle whatever comes along."

He knew he should get back to work on the hacking trace but he found himself unable to concentrate. There had to be a reason they'd asked for Teri first. Had they learned something about her that boosted her into the number one interview spot? Teri LaGrange was one of the best coders in the business and had worked for him for six years, first at Winters and Pryce then at Software By Design. Was there something about her he'd missed?

He gave his head a mental shake. No, he trusted Teri, Phil and Sy as much as he trusted himself. That meant doing his own research into the others, even as the cops did their interviews, checking to make sure there was nothing he missed before he hired each of them.

As the morning wore on, he found it increasingly hard to concentrate. About an hour into the interviews, Phil knocked on his door, a tentative look on his face.

Liam leaned back in his chair. "What's up?"

Phil took a few steps into the office. "Since questions are the order of the day, I have one for you."

"Sure, go ahead. Shoot."

"Why did they tell us not to talk to each other or discuss our questions? What they asked us. I mean, human nature would be for us all to compare notes."

"I think they're trying to contain everything as much as possible. They don't have a clue who they're after."

"Well, I probably should not tell you this, but some of us are going out for drinks after work. And you can bet we'll be talking about every bit of this."

Liam smiled, to his own amazement. "What was that you said? I couldn't hear you."

"I said—"

Liam held up a hand. "Can't hear you, sorry."

Phil blinked, then smiled. "Oh. Okay. Gotcha. Thanks. Will they let us know whatever they find?"

"It is to be hoped. Now get out of here before they arrest you for gossiping."

Phil twisted his lips in a half smile and turned away. No one else approached him, so he figured Phil was the advance guard, testing the waters.

The day stretched endlessly as Duarte and Callahan questioned his staff. Some of them were even quizzed a second time. And while they were doing all this, they were also searching the offices. Duarte had told Liam they were looking for something that would fit the wounds as described to them by the medical examiner.

Liam occupied himself with the computer Eric had been using to run a trace on the hackers. He'd seen some complicated setups before, but nothing like this. It almost looked as if it was set to wear anyone out who tried to trace them. But he was determined, just as he was still determined to find who screwed the pooch with the Hoffman software. He planned to talk to Taylor about getting another data forensic analyst in to take over, just as soon as he got these idiots out of his office.

At noon, Liam had Rosalie ordered lunch for everyone. When it arrived, she met them at the front door, carried the food upstairs and let everyone know lunch was set up in the break room. Although she offered refreshments to the two detectives, they assured her their bottles of water and power bars would do them just fine.

Liam did his best to concentrate as time dragged, but his mind did not want to focus. All he could think of was Eric had been murdered and someone at SBD was responsible. Finally, when the day was almost over, the two detectives finally appeared at his office door.

He gave them a tired grin. "Finished with everyone else? You've been at it a long time."

"Just gathering information, like we said," Callahan said as he took one of the chairs facing the desk.

"And have you gathered enough?"

"Almost."

"So, I guess it's my turn into the barrel."

Liam noticed Duarte looking around the office. "Looking for something?"

"I'll know it when I find it," the man told him.

Callahan then took him through his entire day Saturday. Where he was, what he did, who he saw. Who saw him.

As he later told Taylor, at first the questions seemed harmless. Just straight searching for basic information. He gave them as much as he could without breaking client confidentiality. Explained why and how Eric had been hired. Answered some basic questions about office routine and who would have had access to any of the special programs.

Then things took a turn.

"Had you met Eric before this?" Duarte asked.

"No." Liam shook his head. "He was recommended to me by Taylor Cantrell."

"So, it wasn't your decision to hire him."

"No. I mean, yes. Of course, it was. When I told Taylor about the security breach, she said she'd get me the best person. I was pretty damn happy to get him."

"Except he could point the finger at whoever had added some special code to the program. Not that I pretend to know much about it," Callahan added, "but he'd be able to identify who wanted to steal the material from your client."

"Of course." Liam bit back his irritation. "That was the point of hiring him."

"But from what you're telling me, no one had access after it was completed to do this except you," Duarte Pointed out.

"Someone did," Liam pointed out, "and that's what he was supposed to find out."

"Even if it was you?"

"What?" Liam stared at the detective. "It wasn't me. Jesus. My reputation was at stake here. Why would I fuck up my own business?"

"Maybe because you could make a hell of a lot more," Callahan answered, "if you sold it to some foreign spies."

"What?" He nearly fell out of his chair. "Are you fucking kidding me? I would never do that."

Duarte had spotted the knife displayed on his desk.

"This yours?" he asked.

"Yes. It belonged to my grandfather."

Duarte reached in his pocket for a pair of thick plastic gloves and lifted the knife, holding it by the haft and turning it. He pointed to where the haft and blade were joined.

"Hmmm. This looks like it might be blood on here."

Blood? On his knife? Liam was afraid he was going to pass out.

"You have to be wrong. There's no way blood could get on my knife. It's never out of my possession. Always on my desk."

Callahan rose. "We'd better take it with us. And you'd better come along too, Mr. Benedict. We have more questions for you and I'd like to ask them at the precinct."

"The precinct? You're kidding, right?" Liam did his best to keep it together.

"Not even a little," Callahan told him. "Just a friendly conversation, but I think that's a better place for it."

Liam stared at him, beating back the sudden surge of panic. He could just imagine how friendly that would turn out to be. "Fine. But before I leave, I have to call someone."

"You can make your calls from the precinct," Duarte said. "Let's get this done."

Liam shook his head. "Not until I make this call."

The detectives exchanged a look, then both nodded.

"Fine," Duarte told him, but his voice didn't sound too friendly.

Liam turned in his chair so he was facing away from the detectives. He took a moment to get his shit together before he dialed Taylor's cell phone. She'd said to call her directly and he was taking her at her word. He figured after this was over, he'd be lucky if she still wanted to keep him in the Arroyo family. Who wanted a business partner who allowed stuff like this to happen?

She answered at once. "Trouble?"

"You bet." He took a deep breath, let it out and told her what was happening.

She was as calm and unruffled as if he'd just told her he was taking a late lunch. She asked what precinct and he got the information from Callahan.

"Okay." Her voice was even, calm, and reassuring. "Got it. Here's what you do. Go with them. Sit down. Be polite but don't answer one damn question until your attorney gets there. Promise me that."

"I do. Uh, am I arrested?"

"Not yet but they may decide to book you just on what they have. They don't need a lot more for a first appearance."

"Great. Just great." *How the hell did I get into this fix?*

"No, it isn't, but we'll sort it." Her voice was calm and unruffled, as if she was giving him directions to an office. "Go along politely and play stupid."

And that was what he did.

He'd never been in a precinct station before. Never needed to. Everything he knew about them he learned watching television, but he supposed they were pretty much all the same. They marched him into a small room with a table and four chairs, indicating he should sit in one of them. He guessed he should be glad they hadn't handcuffed him.

"Would you like some water?" Callahan asked.

Liam shook his head. "No, thanks. I'm good. What are we doing here?"

"We just thought it would be better to question you away from your office." Duarte dropped into the chair across from him. "No distractions."

"You realize," Callahan said, "you have the best motive and opportunity for this, right?"

Liam stared at him, his stomach knotting. "How do you figure that?"

"Someone made the software for your high value client vulnerable. From what your staff tells me, you had the best opportunity for that."

"But not any reason to. Hell, if I wanted someone else to have it, all I had to do was give them a copy of it."

"But wouldn't that lead back to you?"

He shook his head. "Not if I didn't want it to. This is crazy. Just crazy. I'm the one who hired Eric Braun to trace this."

"Could have been a smokescreen," Duarte pointed out.

"Plus," Callahan added, "you were in the best position to kill him. Already at the parade and dressed in costume so easy to mingle. If the blood on your knife turns out to be Braun's, that's pretty damning evidence."

Liam raked his fingers through his hair. He should have followed Taylor's advice from the minute they brought him into this room. "I think I'd better just shut up.

Duarte studied him with what Liam guessed was supposed to be a friendly expression on his face. "You know, it won't do any harm to tell us your side of the story. I mean, as long as we are just sitting here anyway. It could go a lot easier on you."

"My side of the story?" Liam actually laughed. "Is that kind of like when did you stop beating your wife? I don't have a side of the story because I didn't do anything. And after listening to you, I'm convinced nothing I could say would change your minds. So, I think I'll just shut up."

Callahan sighed. "You know, your attorney's just going to make things more difficult. If you really have nothing to do with Eric's Braun's murder, a short conversation can probably clear it up. If we could get some answers now, things could probably just go away."

Yeah, right. When pigs fly.

"No, thanks. I had nothing to do with the murder, but if it's all the same to you, I think we'll stay away from it. I don't mind discussing the Rays or the Bucs or what the USF football team is doing this year, but that's the limit of my conversational topics."

Since they didn't seem interested in talking sports, the three of them sat pretty much in silence while they waited. He should have done that from the beginning. He was already getting the idea that as soon as his attorney arrived, whoever that was, they planned to book him and go from there.

He did his best not to appear jumpy or nervous, but he couldn't help running everything over in his mind. It literally made him ill to realize someone on his team, someone he put his trust in, had betrayed him. And that person had killed Eric to keep him for passing along that information.

Maybe he should hire his own detective to check out everyone on his team. Dig out their deepest hidden secrets. Maybe find out why they would do what they did. Assuming, of course, he ever got out of this place. He hoped to hell whoever Taylor sent could accomplish that pretty damn fast.

At approximately the moment he was ready to jump out of his skin, a knock sounded and the door opened. No one was more shocked than he was when Sydney Alfiore herself walked in. But then he thought, *of course*. Taylor Cantrell never used anything but top of the line, whether it was people or goods or ideas. And Sydney Alfiore really topped the list.

"Hello, Liam. They treating you okay?"

He nodded. "Although this isn't my idea of a social setting."

"I get that. But you haven't said anything, right?"

"Not a word."

She looked at the two detectives. "Sorry to disappoint you, gentlemen, but my client won't be answering any questions. At least not until I talk to him."

"He'd have been a lot better to answer some questions," Duarte said. "Now we're just going to go ahead, arrest him and book him."

Liam wondered if he had just fallen into the middle of a nightmare.

Sydney just nodded. "Understood. Now, can we have the room, please?"

Chapter Sixteen

Liam could tell at once that Callahan and Duarte were far from happy to see Sydney. He'd make book on the fact that they'd had to deal with her before and it didn't go well on their part. They looked at each other, silently, then nodded and walked out of the room.

Duarte stuck his head back in. "Fifteen minutes," he told them. "You know the drill, counselor."

"I do." She looked at her watch. "And I don't want to waste a minute of our allotted time."

Sydney waited until the door was closed to sit across from Liam. She set her briefcase on the table and leaned closer to him.

"First rule of the day. It's important the police not know we have any kind of personal relationship."

Liam quirked one brow. "Why?"

"Because it taints my representation. I might even get taken off the case and I do not want that to happen. Everything I say and do will be viewed as emotionally biased and we don't want that. At all. We certainly don't want the media to get hold of it, and you can bet they'll be all over this."

Every muscle in Liam's body tightened. "Why? What's the big deal? I'm just a small fish in a big pond."

She shook her head. "Not any longer. You are part of the Arroyo family and that's always big news. Probably one of the main reasons Taylor hired me to represent you."

His mouth turned up in a half-hearted grin. "I hope I can afford your fees."

"Don't worry about it. Arroyo is picking up the tab."

Liam was sure he looked as startled as he felt. "They are?"

"Yes. Again, you are part of Arroyo. That's how the company operates. I swear I don't know how Taylor keeps a finger on every pulse, but she does. Nothing gets by her. Ever."

"I'm surprised she hasn't cut me loose."

"She believes in your innocence." Sydney sat up a little straighter. "Before they made the offer for you to join Arroyo, you as well as your company were vetted six ways from Sunday. She doesn't like surprises. Not being that careful is what got her father killed and now she's pissed that another killing has taken place. But no way does she think it falls on your shoulders."

"Even if whoever the murderer turns out to be someone I hired?"

Sydney nodded. "Even if."

He was still trying to get his head around all that, but he was eternally grateful for it.

"So, what happens now?"

"I spoke to the chief of detectives. Don't freak, but they are going to take you over to the Orient Road jail and book you."

He bolted upright in the chair. "What?"

"Did I not just say don't freak? They have the knife from your desk with blood on it that you can bet will prove to be Eric Braun's and of course your fingerprints will be all over it."

"Because I handle it all the time."

She nodded. "You were also in the general vicinity and dressed like half the crowd. We know what time Eric was killed but they still surmise you could have done it. You would have had time to reach parade central to get on your float with no one the wiser."

"Jesus, Sydney." He scrubbed his face. "Arrested?"

"Again, don't freak, At Orient Road, they'll process you. Here's the hard part. Court is over for the day. I can't get you on the appearance calendar until the morning."

Liam thought he was going to vomit.

"Are you saying I have to stay in jail overnight?"

She leaned forward. "Look at me. We don't have a choice, but I'm going to see if I can get you in a cell by yourself. I'll get you on the calendar first thing and then we'll post bail and get you out of there."

"I suppose Arroyo's taking care of that, too?"

She winked. "Of course."

"Damn!" He nearly came out of his chair. "I can't believe I have to spend the night in jail. And what's happening at Software By Design while I'm being turned into a criminal?"

Sydney took out her tablet and pulled up a screen.

"Okay. I spoke to Rosalie. Whatever you're paying her, you should probably triple it. That woman is pure gold."

"Don't I know it. I think she knows more about the firm than I do."

"Which is a good thing. She's got a handle on what projects are in process and she'll monitor everything. Until you can get back to the office, that is."

"And when will that be?"

"Okay. Let's get into that and some other things now." She swiped the screen and brought up another page of notes. "I'm going to need you for two full days to go over every single thing that happened from the time you got the alarm someone was trying to hack the Hoffman network. You can probably go into the office after that, because this is not going to be a speedy trial. They'll want every screw tightened and every bolt in place before they move forward with an indictment and a trial date."

"Well, that's something." He raked his hand through his hair. "But after you empty my brain I can go into the office?"

She nodded. "But with some caveats."

He frowned. "What does that mean?"

"A number of things, which Taylor and I have discussed." She glanced at her tablet. "We're convinced that the feeling you've had of someone following you, and of the accident, are all related to this. And we don't like how exposed you are in your townhouse."

"So, what does that mean?"

"It means we're going to put you up for the moment in one of the apartments my firm keeps to sequester clients. It has every type of wireless connection you could need. It's swept daily for listening devices, just in case. And it's a totally secure building."

She went down her list. He'd need to give her a list of everything he'd need from his townhouse and someone would fetch it for him. One of Arroyo's experts would check his laptop thoroughly to make sure it hadn't been compromised and bring it to him. Same with his cell phone, but he'd have a separate one to communicate with Sydney.

"Just in case," she told him.

He'd have an armed driver taking him back and forth to his offices, something he objected to vehemently until she pointed out it was better to be irritated than injured or dead.

"I'll bet you still have bruises from that accident. Am I right?"

He nodded, irritated about the whole thing. Some asshole was turning his entire life upside down. When he got out of this and learned who this was, they'd wish they'd never been born.

"What else? I'm out of my home, can hardly run my business, someone is trying to ruin me and I'm being booked for murder. How much worse can it get?"

Sydney put everything away and pushed her briefcase aside.

"I have one more thing, and I'm going to ask you not to show any reaction to this at all."

Dread slithered through him. What in hell could be worse than all this?

"Lay it on me. I'll do my best not to kill someone. Oh, wait. That's a bad joke."

"Yes, and not funny. Okay, here it is. From this moment forward, no one except Taylor can know there has been anything personal between us. Period. We are just two people who know each other, and Arroyo has hired me to represent you. The times we are alone together we will be discussing this case. I'll be taking your statement. Prepping you for trial, if there is one."

For a moment Liam felt like laughing. This could just not be true.

"You're kidding, right?"

She shook her head. "Not even a little. If the prosecutor or the media or even the person who delivers your mail knows about our personal relationship, everything I do will be colored by that. The prosecuting attorney will give interviews that I'm blind to your guilt because of our personal relationship and he'll go after both of us in court. The media will flay us alive. And worse, if it goes to trial, no jury will be able to render an impartial verdict."

"Well, shit." He sat back in his chair, trying to swallow the bitter taste in his mouth. "When I get my hands on whoever this is—"

Sydney held up a hand. "We can discuss that when we're out of here. Right now, I have things to take care of, first among them being to get you booked at once so we can get you in first appearance court tomorrow."

"Will you be there?"

"Of course. Tonight I'm reaching out to Noah, who has access to better experts than I do. We need a team to dig into this, the way I don't think those two detectives will. And I'll confirm bail arrangements with Taylor."

"Jesus, Syd." He closed his eyes for a moment, then opened them. "I feel like I fell down the rabbit hole."

"I get that."

"And I still don't know who screwed with the Hoffman software." He sat up straight. "Shit! I have to finish running that trace."

He explained to her what was going on at SBD.

"The room is locked where the laptop is?"

"Yes. Only Rosalie and I have key cards for it. Eric had one, but the cops probably have it with his stuff."

"When I get you out of here, we'll send someone to fetch it. For now, just concentrate on staying calm."

"I'll do my best."

While I'm locked up in jail for the night.

At that moment, there was a knock on the door and Callahan walked into the room.

"Time's up, Miss Alfiore. We need to take your client to Orient Road booking."

Liam's stomach cramped at the words, but Sydney looked unruffled.

"Good." She rose from her chair. "The sooner the better. I'm going to see about getting him on the head of the list for tomorrow morning's first appearance calendar."

"The prosecutor's planning to ask for high bail," he warned her.

"No problem." She smiled at them. "We've got it covered." Then she held out her hand for him to shake. "See you this time tomorrow, Liam. Don't worry. I've got it under control."

By the time they were through with the routine, Liam felt as if he'd been run over twice. He managed to blank his mind while they put him through the booking process and keep it that way while they took his personal possessions and his belt. Then they led him to a cell. Thank god Sydney had managed to get him one alone or he really would have lost his mind.

Somehow, he managed to choke down a little of the terrible dinner they brought him and nap on and off during the night, despite the noises from the other prisoners and a growing feeling of claustrophobia. Not to mention the fact he wanted a long, hot shower. By the time the morning rolled around, his personal discipline was seriously shattering.

When they brought him into court for his appearance, he breathed his first sigh of relief when he saw Sydney waiting for him. Everything about her shouted 'professional high-priced attorney', from the well-tailored suit to the carefully upswept French braid to her makeup still impeccable this late in the day. She whispered a few words of encouragement, told him not to say anything except 'Not guilty' and handled everything from there on with a minimum of fuss. The prosecutor looked ready to do battle, sure that when he asked for one million dollars bail, Liam would end up back in his cell. At least Liam got a little bit of pleasure at the shocked look on the prosecutor's face when Sydney told them she was prepared to guarantee that amount.

Finally, he was processed out and Sydney led him out of the building to the garage where her car was parked. His eyes opened wider when he saw a Diamond Silver Mercedes Maybach. It comforted him to have an attorney representing him who could afford a six-figure car. People didn't fork over that kind of money in legal fees to someone who didn't produce for them.

He did his best to relax in the ultra-comfortable seat as they followed the exit signs down to the cashier and the exit. Sydney just waved a key card at the exit bar.

"I'm driving you to the condo," she told him as they pulled out onto the street. "Jim Vega, your driver and bodyguard, is waiting for us there."

Liam heard the word 'bodyguard' and flinched, hating that he was in a situation that required one. But Sydney said it so naturally Liam realized this was probably routine for her.

"Bodyguard? Really?"

"For your safety. I'm not taking any chances with my favorite client."

"Favorite? Does that mean the no consorting rule is off the table?"

She sighed. "Sadly, no. We'll just have to make up for lost time when this is over."

"Which I sure hope is pretty damn soon. What happens next?"

"Now the prosecuting attorney will go to the grand journey, convince them he has enough evidence to charge you and you'll be formally arraigned."

Liam thought he might throw up.

"Arraigned? Evidence? What in hell could he possibly have?"

"I think they're banking a whole lot on that dagger you keep on your desk. They tested the blood and it is Eric Braun's. Plus, it fits the wounds in his body and yours are the only fingerprints on it."

"Fuck." He rubbed his temples. "I keep hoping this is a bad dream and any minute I'll wake up."

"Would be nice, but that probably isn't going to happen. That means we all have a lot of work to do."

He frowned. "All who? Who else is working on this?"

She chuckled. "You mean besides my associate and others in my office?"

He blew out a breath. "Yeah. Sorry, Syd. I'm just..." He held up his hands in a helpless gesture. "So, then what? Jail again?" He scrubbed his hands over his face, as if he could wash away the whole situation. "Have you ever been inside that jail, Sydney?"

"Too many times. But there won't be any cell," she assured him. "They'll continue your bail and we'll get to come back here and begin plotting your defense."

"My defense." He snorted. "All I have is I didn't do it."

"I believe you." She rested her hand on his arm. "That means we have to find out who did."

"Oh, right. Just that easy, right? The cops are convinced it was me so they aren't going to be looking elsewhere."

"No, not that easy. But we have a plan of action." She maneuvered the car through the snarl of downtown Tampa traffic. "Reinforcements have arrived."

"Such as?"

"Noah Cantrell arrives this morning. As soon as he gets here, he'll be on his way to Graham and Associates, the top security and investigative firm he and Taylor put together. He plans to rip apart the lives of every person who works for you."

"Jesus, Syd." He sat up straighter. "Is that necessary?"

She slid a quick glance at him. "You're kidding, right? Think about it this way—everything revolves around Software By Design. Eric obviously found something and the wrong person learned about it. That's why he's dead. So, if it isn't you, it has to be one of them."

He swallowed the sudden taste of bile. "I think that's what upsets me the most. That and the fact whoever this is doesn't mind seeing me go to prison."

"Right. Whenever you start to feel sorry for them, keep that thought in mind."

Sydney turned at a traffic light and drove over the bridge to Harbor Island.

"I'm going to do my damnedest to make sure that happens."

"Pretty fancy digs here," Liam commented. They had stopped to go through the security that blocked off part of Harbor Island not open to the general public.

"Triple security," she told him. "The partners chose to buy the condo here because you need codes for the gate, the parking and the building itself. We don't want anyone getting access to you that isn't on the approved list."

And that's when it hit home that it wasn't just his business that was in danger, but his life. Who in the hell was doing this way and why?

He hadn't paid lot of attention as they drove through this part of Harbor Island but now he realized they were at an underground garage. Sydney slipped her coded card into the reader and the electronic arm swung up to admit them.

"Couldn't someone just slide in under the arm?"

"Not hardly. It's rigged to set off a siren if that happens. Okay, here we are."

They had pulled into a slot against the wall in the garage. He rubbed his face, trying to wake up his brain and his body.

A man in a dark T-shirt and jeans, wearing a shoulder harness with a handgun, was leaning against the wall by what Liam assumed was the elevator. When Sydney pulled into her parking space he pushed away from the wall and came forward.

"Liam Benedict," she said, "meet Jim Vega. He'll be glued to you until this is over. Jim, were you able to get what we needed?"

The man nodded and turned to Liam. "All the things from your townhouse are upstairs in the room you'll be sleeping in. I also picked up your laptop along with some other things. Rosalie gave me some software at your office that Eric Braun was doing his best to parse, and I've got the laptop he was using. Your more-than-able assistant made me swear in blood I wouldn't turn either of the computers on or take them anyplace but here." He grinned at Liam. "I'll bet that woman's the one who really runs the business."

"Sometimes I think so," he admitted.

"Let's go on upstairs." Sydney punched the button to open the elevator door. "Liam, I'm pretty sure you'll be comfortable here."

As they stepped into the elevator, Liam was thinking the same thing. Except it wasn't home, there was still someone on his ass and he had a murder charge hanging over his head.

He noticed that Sydney used a key card in a slot in the panel containing the floor number buttons.

"How does an average person get up to an apartment here?" he asked. "Or park their vehicle?"

"Parking for visitors and delivery people is out in front. A guard in the lobby checks their credentials and phones up to the resident to make sure it's okay."

"Hmmm," was all he could think of to say.

Jim Vega kept respectfully quiet as the elevator zipped them up to the fourteenth floor in a silent glide. The doors opened with a soft *whoosh!* and Liam stepped out into a thickly carpeted hallway. Sydney led the parade down the hall to a heavy door with a discreet number by the knob and knocked twice. Then she opened it with the same coded key card and ushered Liam inside.

He stood in the foyer for a moment and blinked. There was nothing shabby about his townhouse, which had cost him in the high six figures, but as he looked around he understood what people meant by understated luxury. Everything quietly spoke of unlimited resources, including the million-dollar view of the Hillsborough River and beyond it the city of Tampa.

Now that they were safely away from the jail and the hearing, he had a desperate need to pull her into his arms and breathe her in. Two things stopped him. He remembered what she'd told him earlier about their personal relationship plus the presence of Jim Vega. It took every bit of his self-discipline just to stand there next to her and not lose himself in her. But when she turned and smiled at him, well, he knew that was just for him and he absorbed like water to a thirsty man.

She drew him into the living room. "I imagine you'd like to shower and change."

No shit!

"Yeah, the hotter the better."

"Let me show you your bedroom with the en suite bath. I took the liberty of putting all your things away for you. Hope that was okay."

He managed a tired smile. "More than. Show me the way."

The bedroom here was as large his own at home, tastefully furnished even down to the big wall-mounted television."

"In case you want to watch in bed," she teased.

He wanted to tell her there were other things he wanted to do in bed, preferably with her, but he had to respect the situation. Intellectually he knew she was right. But physically? He hoped this damn thing was over sooner rather than later. He closed the door after her when she left the room and headed into the bathroom, stripping off his clothes as he went. The water was hot and he stood under it for a long time, relishing its heat and the steady pounding of the spray. He had no idea how long he stood there, and he wondered if any stretch of time would be enough to wash away the stink and miasma of the Orient Road jail.

Well, if anyone could get him out of this, it would be Sydney. God, if he could just touch her in more than a casual way.

Forget it.

Stripped, he adjusted the water in the shower and stepped beneath the rain shower spray. He thought it probably should be ice cold, as hard as he was just from riding in the car with Sydney and knowing she was just steps away. Of course, he'd discovered just being in the same room with her could make him hard as a railroad spike. And being deprived of anything smacking of a personal relationship was putting a real strain on him. Yeah, he knew it was the smart thing to do, but fuck! It was just killing him.

Soaping up his right hand, he braced himself against the shower wall with his other hand and slowly began to stroke his throbbing cock.

Sydney was standing in the shower with him. He had just spent a long time teasing and tormenting her, bringing her to the edge of completion then forcing her to pull back. By the time he pinched her clit, hard, she was panting and her pulse was beating hard at the hollow of her throat. He'd discovered it was one if his favorite things to do, although with Sydney he'd discovered their relationship seemed to knock down any self-imposed boundaries they put up. Each time they were together, they pushed each other harder.

Tonight, he had made her wait a long time, until he knew her control was fraying. The pinch of her clit was his signal to her that he was going to tumble her over the edge. Kneeling between her luscious thighs, he squeezed her clit even harder and thrust two fingers deep inside her cunt.

Jesus!

She was soaked, her juices flowing so hard the scent of her musk surrounded them. She was so slick he was able to add a third finger to the first two, and he began that steady in-and-out rhythm that drove her to the peak. Harder and faster, pinching and tugging at her clit. She moaned, delicious little sounds that drifted from her mouth as he fucked her with his fingers and made his cock swell with need.

He felt the first flutters of her orgasm in the walls of her slick channel, pressing against his fingers, and he increased the speed of his thrusts.

"Come for me," he urged her. "Come right now. Hard!"

As if his words tripped a hidden switch, the walls of her pussy clamped down on his fingers like a vise and began milking them. Grabbing them, as her walls spasmed again and again. She twisted her body, thrusting into his hands, tiny moans and cries streaming from her lips.

Then, at last, the spasms subsided, her body relaxed and the breathless sounds quieted. He eased his fingers from her and lifting his hand, licked each of his fingers with careful deliberation. Then he bent forward and placed his mouth on hers, slipping his tongue inside to share the traces of her flavor with her.

They stood there, limp, for a long moment, Sydney with a tiny smile curving her lips as her heart rate and breathing returned to normal.

He brushed another kiss over her mouth. "Let's take a shower. I can't wait to get my hands all over your slick body."

Her laugh was soft and sexy. Of course, Liam thought everything about Sydney Alfiore was sexy.

"I think it's time for me to get my hands on your body." She nudged him. "Come on."

The water was soft and warm as it sluiced over their bodies. Liam reached for the bottle of body wash but Sydney took it from his fingers, smiling and shaking her head.

"Let me."

She poured some in the palm of one hand, rubbed her hands together to create a sudsy lather and began to stroke the foam over his body. The touch of her hands was magical. Erotic. Exciting, as they followed every contour of his body until every speck of skin was covered with the scented foam. Sliding one hand between his thighs, she cupped his balls in her palm and began a gentle squeezing motion.

Holy shit!

His cock, already swollen and needy from all the touching and licking of her body he'd done and from watching her epic climax, became painfully hard and an ache consumed his balls. He started to take the bottle to lather up his own hands, but she took it from him and put it back on the little built-in shelf.

"Uh-uh. This one's all mine."

She closed her slim fingers around his raging hard-on and began to stroke him with a slow, gentle rhythm. Liam propped himself up with one hand against the wall and closed his eyes, giving himself over to the magic of her fingers and the ribbons of heat and hunger unwinding and curling through his body.

Up and down her fingers worked his shaft, her other hand cradling and fondling his balls in a matching rhythm. His body was one big ache as the orgasm began to grow deep within him. Up and down she moved her hand, fingers working their magic between his thigh.

"Feel good?" she asked in a low voice.

"Fucking damn good," he growled. "But I want to be inside you."

"Next time," she promised. "This time I want to see you spill all over my hand."

His words were like a trigger, his body responding by rocking back and forth into her grip. The muscles low in his back tightened and his balls tingled as the orgasm began its climb from low in his system.

Then it was there, exploding, his cock jerking as it pulsed over and over again, until he was completely drained. Her fingers squeezed his shaft in a slow, rhythmic motion, milking the last drop from him.

"Don't let go," he murmured as he waited for his breathing to even out.

"Never," she promised.

"Come here." He reached out with his other arm to tug her closer to him, shocked when all he touched was air. He opened his eyes and –

Fuck!

It had all been a dream. And instead of Sydney's slim fingers, it was his own thick ones wrapped around his cock. Traces of cum still adhered to the skin of his hand even as droplets of water ran over it. His body felt as depleted as if he'd had real sex, not solo sex, and the image of a naked, water-drenched Sydney was stuck in his brain.

He sure as hell hoped this whole thing got reconciled soon and the real killer found, so he and Sydney could get on with their lives. Then he remembered that Eric was dead and he, Liam, was about to be arraigned for the murder. He tucked the memories of his fantasy in a corner of his brain, in a place where he could pull them out if he needed them.

Then he shut off the shower and went to get dressed, hoping his freedom wasn't about to be shot down.

Sydney was waiting for him at the dining room table. She and Vega were already holding mugs of coffee and one filled with the steaming liquid sat by an empty seat.

"Yours," Sydney acknowledged. "And help yourself to something to eat."

Liam lowered himself into the chair, lifted the mug and inhaled the fragrant steam before taking a reviving swallow. He was almost afraid to look at Sydney after his hand job in the shower but he managed to pull himself together. He plucked a flaky pastry from the plate in the center of the table, took a bite and tried not to moan with pleasure.

"Okay," he said at last. "I'm ready for whatever you need."

"Good." She placed a small recorder on the table between them. "I've asked Jim to sit in with us. He knows the drill and the more he understands the situation, the better he'll be able to prevent anything from happening to you."

Liam didn't want to ask her what that would be.

Sydney refilled her mug and topped off Liam's.

"Drink it. It will keep you going." She sipped the hot liquid. "Just to let you know, Noah has just landed. He texted me to let me know he's here and off on his mission."

"I know he's great and all that. He'd have to be to run that company with Taylor. But exactly what kind of mission is this? What can he do?"

"Let me give you a little background. Noah Cantrell started with Arroyo as Josiah Gaines' personal bodyguard. He worked his way up to chief then vice president of security for headquarters. Now he's the head man for security for the entire conglomerate. He created an agency that's based here but now has operatives all over the world. Part of what they do is train security agents for other companies that need it, so every unit of Arroyo is always well-protected."

"Bodyguards," he pointed out.

"That's only part of it. They have staff trained in every form of detection and investigation. Even as we speak, Noah himself has arrived in Tampa and is meeting with the top guys at the agency."

Liam's brows rose to his hairline. "And why is he doing this for me?"

Sydney leaned forward. "You're an important part of the company, Liam. Taylor has plans to help you expand so eventually you can write your special programs for every unit of Arroyo. You know that, right?"

He nodded, slightly dazed. "I guess I'm still trying to absorb the whole thing."

"He and Taylor believe, as do I, that whatever is going on has its genesis right here, with Software By Design. He'll be assigning men to dig into this entire situation. Among other things that means turning the lives of your staff inside out. Because, Liam? I'm sorry to say this, but it has to be one of them. There's just no other answer. No one else could have gotten into the software to do anything to it."

"Yeah, I know." And didn't that just suck. "But why? I pay them very well, they have a lot of creative freedom, and they know big bonuses are coming."

Sydney shrugged. "Many reasons. A financial hole that the bonuses won't fill. A weakness that someone's discovered and is using it for pressure. Could be any number of things."

"You know how hard that is for me to accept?"

"I do. And I'm sorry it's come to this. But your life — your future — is at stake here so we're turning over every rock."

"What do you look for in a situation like this?"

"Easiest case? Someone who's in a huge financial jam. All right." She pulled over both her tablet and her miniature recorder that she had sitting on the table. "We're going to go back to square one here. Then I'm going to walk you through what to expect this afternoon and what our schedule will be after that."

His mouth curved in a rueful grin. "Good thing we've got a lot of coffee."

By eleven o'clock, his brain was fried and he felt as if he'd been 'rode hard and put away wet'. If he was this dragged out already, how was he going to withstand a trial, assuming there was one?

Sydney leaned back in her chair and rolled her head to relax her neck.

"Why don't you take a shower? Then we'll have some lunch and give you a chance to get yourself together before we leave for the courthouse and the arraignment."

"The courthouse," he repeated. "The arraignment. Yeah. Right." He scraped his hand over his chin. "This ought to be a lot of fun."

"This will be fine," she assured him. "You won't have to do much except enter your plea. We'll ask that bail be continued and the judge will set a date for trial."

"I've heard it can take weeks before a case comes to trial. Will they continue bail for all that time?"

Sydney nodded. "I promise you, today is just a formality. I already have people looking into everything. And Noah Cantrell is pulling out all the stops. He's putting a full team on this. Don't you worry. It's going to be just fine."

Fine. Right. But it's my ass in jail if it isn't.

"I'll hold you to that."

"Fine. Now let's hear it all from the beginning. Right back to the night you told me you thought someone was following you. Maybe even trying to kill you. And don't leave out a single thing."

Liam took one more swallow of coffee and set the mug down. He rolled his head, trying to loosen the tension gripping him, and thought back to the beginning of all this. And what a shitshow it was turning out to be.

Chapter Seventeen

Eight was caught between clashing feelings of anger and fear. How had life become so complicated? And why had the solution to a gigantic problem seemed so simple at first and now had become so fucking complicated?

Shit, shit, shit.

Now that asshole, Shan, was sitting once again across a table in a restaurant looking pissed beyond belief at the news about Eric. As if there'd been a choice. Who needed this crap?

I do, because I've been so fucking stupid.

When Shan finally spoke, it was in an uninflected tone all the deadlier because of that. "I hear what you are saying but I still cannot believe you were so stupid. What did you think you were doing?"

Through clenched teeth, Eight said, "I was getting rid of someone who could blow the whistle on me and screw up this whole deal."

"And you didn't think to call me? That's what your burner phones are for."

Ah, yes, the infamous burner phones, with only one number programmed into them, and blanked so it could not be seen.

"I had no idea where you were," Eight pointed out.

"I did not have to be the one to handle it. We have had people in the area all the time."

"Oh, yeah." Eight snorted. A derisive sound. "Like the idiot who pushed him into a gigantic traffic accident. That was real smart."

"We were looking for opportunities to incapacitate him so you would have free rein with the software."

"And how well did that work out for you?" Eight swallowed the rest of the liquor in the rocks glass and signaled the waiter for another. "Besides, it wasn't necessary. I flipped the program without him being any the wiser."

Shan leaned forward, dark eyes blazing with rage. "If you are so fucking smart, how is it you did not know Benedict had put a digital tripwire in the program to signal him when someone was trying to hack in?"

What? What the hell? When had he done that? Oh, hell. Oh, fucking hell.

Fear raced through Eight's blood and not even fiddling with the rocks glass could hide that. Not when the hands holding it were shaking so badly.

"How do you know that?"

Shan sneered. "Because I have very clever people working for me who knew exactly what had happened because they've used the same thing before."

Eight just sat there, staring across the table. "I was just…

"Don't make excuses. It's bad enough that you took this on yourself, to kill this way. But to use Benedict's knife and put it back for the police to find? Stupid, stupid, stupid."

"I knew they'd come to the office," Eight protested. "I wanted to throw suspicion on him."

"So now we have the police all over everything. Did you not think it would be better to use your brains, divorce yourself from this and let us clean up the mess?"

Eight shrugged. "I thought I could take care of it myself. And by the way, all the clues point toward Liam Benedict. By the time they figure out it's not him, I will have my money from you and be long gone. Right?" When Shan said nothing, Eight leaned forward and repeated, "Right?"

For an unending moment Shan said nothing. Nausea surged in Eight's throat. What the fuck?

"Right?"

Shan stared into the damn teacup, taking a long time before answering.

"We do not yet have all the drawings and specs of the design. We must be sure that what you have directed us to really works."

"Wait just a damn minute." Eight wanted to strangle the other person. "Our arrangement was half on delivery of the software, the other half when the design was tested. What the fuck is going on here? I've got my offshore accounts all set up. You can't weasel out of this. It's my ass on the line and I need to get the hell out of here as soon as possible."

For a long moment, Shan said nothing. When the answer came at last, Eight was torn between committing murder and running like hell.

"This has not gone as smoothly as you promised." Each word fell like a heavy stone in water. "We did not bargain for all these problems. Now we must make sure we have all the files and that no one has tracked them back to us. Then we must verify that they are the correct drawings."

"But that could take months!" *Shit, shit, shit.* "I have to be long gone by then."

"If you must leave the area, as long as I have your new address and phone number, the deal will still be consummated."

"Leave the area?" Eight sat back, stunned. "With what? I need that money."

"And we need to know that you kept your part of the bargain and nothing will trace back to us."

Eight wanted to yell and scream. Beat the walls. Beat the shit out of the weasel across the table. This was not the way it was supposed to go.

Fuck. Just fuck.

"Fine." Deep breath. "But time is running out on my end. How long do you think your so-called verification will take?"

Shan shrugged. "Not long. We want to have a working model up before Hoffman. I will call you in one week."

Eight forced an outward calm. "Fine. You'd better hope I'm not arrested by then."

The look in Shan's eyes was positively lethal. "If that should happen, I can assure you, death would be your most beneficial option."

Eight struggled to stay composed walking through the parking lot to the waiting vehicle. This had turned into a disaster. A true, fucking disaster. Getting this finished was now at the top of the priority list. No, getting it finished and staying alive was the goal.

Then disappearing off the face of the earth.

* * * *

As Noah Cantrell headed down the multilane highway from the airport to Tampa's West Shore district, he had a sixth sense that someone was on his tail. No real reason except that little tickle that always signaled him something wasn't quite kosher. Being half Comanche, he'd discovered, had great benefits in situations like this.

He had no reason to believe anyone even knew he was arriving in Tampa. He hadn't exactly advertised it and he knew Liam had just learned about it. But too many broken eggs, as his mother used to say, made for a mess, not an omelet. As far as he was aware, only Rosalie at SBD knew about his trip, but she could have been overheard on the phone. Any number of things could have happened to light someone's fuse. In this screwed-up situation anything was possible.

It had to be the same people who'd caused Liam's accident, the people obviously woven somehow into this clusterfuck. He decided to do a little zigging and zagging to see what he could shake loose. And sure enough, there it was, an innocuous gray car keeping up with him, although doing its best not to be obvious.

All right, he thought. But two can play at this game. He wanted a look at the license plate, so he pulled abruptly onto the shoulder and got out as if checking his front tire. Sure enough, the gray sedan zipped past him, even moving one lane over. But Noah had taken out his cell phone and as the car went by, from his bent position he snapped three quick shots.

He climbed back into the car and headed back toward Kennedy Boulevard. He was pretty sure whoever was driving wouldn't be stupid enough to be waiting for him where SR 60 hit Kennedy. He might have called someone else to take his place, but then again. Maybe not. Whatever. He didn't really care. He had a license plate to trace and that was a start.

Let them follow him to Charley Graham's office and worry if he was onto them. Or soon would be.

The entire floor of the office building was occupied by a company with the innocuous name of Graham & Associates. To the unknowing it could be a law firm, an insurance agency, a financial firm or any of a number of other entities. In reality it was a high-powered confidential investigations firm, wholly owned by Arroyo. Noah had put it together shortly after he and Taylor were married and he became vice president of security for the entire conglomerate.

It was based in Tampa because the man research had identified as the best person to head the agency lived in that city. And John Martino had concurred. Taylor saw no reason to uproot him and his family. Noah had scoped out the best place to locate the offices and Noah had led the team, with Charley Graham, to recruit the very best people. There was very little the agency didn't have the resources to do.

Jolene Moore, the receptionist, greeted him as he got off the elevator. Noah had always been impressed by the fact that she looked like she should be presiding at a board meeting, could score one hundred percent on the gun range and knew at least six ways to kill someone without a gun. Charley told him when he hired her she had many skills that bubbled beneath the surface. When he asked the man why she was wasted as a receptionist, Charley just grinned at him.

"Jolene vets every single person who steps off that elevator," he said. "She has a sixth sense about people and is my first line of defense."

Noah nodded at her now. "Good to see you again, Jolene."

"Good afternoon, Mr. Cantrell. I'll let Mr. Graham know you're here, but he said to go right on down to his office."

"Thanks, Jolene."

Charley was already out from behind his desk with his hand outstretched to greet Noah when he reached the office.

"Not that we aren't always glad to see you," he told Noah, "but it must be pretty damn important for you to hotfoot here from San Antonio and tell me to get four of my top agents together."

"It is." Noah shook the man's hand. "Is everyone here?"

"They are. Let me have Jolene buzz them and send them down to the conference room."

"While we're waiting, I'm texting you a license plate number. Can you get someone on it ASAP to see who it's registered to?"

"Sure. Someone on your tail?"

Noah nodded. "I'm sure they thought they were invisible. They were damn good at it."

Charley laughed. "But not good enough to fool you. Okay, let me pass this along to someone in the IT unit."

In less than five minutes, seven agents were seated at the conference room table with Noah and Charley, and

Jolene had set a carafe of coffee and a platter of pastries in the middle, with cups, plates and napkins.

"Thanks for this." Charley nodded to her and winked at Noah. "Jolene thinks it's part of her assigned duties to make sure we're always caffeinated and have enough sugar in our bodies to keep going for hours."

"A woman of many talents," Noah acknowledged.

"And more added every day. Okay, ladies and gentlemen, let's get our coffee mugs filled so Noah can lay out for us what's brought him hotfooting to Tampa."

"Let me start by saying I cannot stress enough the confidentiality of what we discuss here. We have a high-level defense contractor working on a top-secret project for the DoD. Whatever we discuss here never leaves this room."

Charley nodded. "Understood. And that goes for all of us."

In concise, clear sentences, Noah laid out the situation for them. He started with the reputation of Software By Design and why Taylor wanted to bring it into the Arroyo fold and worked his way up to the Hoffman project, the unexpected problems, the death of Eric Braun and Liam's arrest.

"First thing we need to do," Charley told him, "is dig into every inch of the lives of the people who work for him. Only someone who knows how to write code could have messed with the software and probably put a back door in there."

Noah nodded and looked across the table at Sarah Gaffney. When Charley had hired her, he'd told Noah that there was none better in her area. If it had to do with programming, tracing, digging around in files or whatever, there was no one better.

"Eric was also running a trace on the hack." He explained what SBD has set up in the Hoffman system to trap any hacks and trace them back. "It's complicated, the way the hackers are set up, and bouncing all over the place."

"Sometimes they set it up so there are more than a hundred bounces," Sarah told him. "If you get me the laptop, I can set it up here and continue running the trace."

"I'll do that." Noah made a note in his cell phone. "Liam had tried to pick up where Eric left off, and while he's well qualified in many areas, he's no forensic specialist, which is one of the reasons he hired Eric Braun. Anyway, I don't think his mind's truly focused on that right now, no matter what he says."

"What about the back door in the Hoffman software? You said that was Eric's primary focus. Did he find out who did it?"

Noah nodded. "He left a note on Liam's voice mail when he couldn't reach him. That's what he was doing at the Gasparilla parade. Looking for Liam."

"Okay, get me that too, please." She turned to her boss. "Charley? I know another forensic data specialist. I can call him if you want. He can find whatever Eric Braun did. If he's free, we can get him on the next plane. But he's expensive."

It was Noah who answered. "Call him. If he's free, I'll send the Arroyo plane for him. And whatever he costs, it's worth it. And we'll get him to tell us how to protect against this in the future."

"Good, Sarah," Charley told her. "Call him right away."

She hurried from the room.

"Let me arrange to get those laptops," Noah told the others, while he punched in a number. "Yeah, Syd? When are you leaving for the courthouse? Uh-huh. And when will you be back? I want to send someone to pick up those laptops. We're getting another forensic data specialist and Charley, here, has an ace that can keep backtracking that hack. Uh-huh. Okay. Call this number when you leave the courthouse and ask for Charley. Good luck today."

"When can we pick them up?" Charley asked.

"They're on their way to the courthouse now. She'll call the minute they are finished and arrange for one of your people to meet her and pick them up."

"Okay. I might just do the pickup myself."

Then Noah outlined for the group the rest of what he needed.

"Basically, every last detail of the lives of every employee at Software By Design. I not only want their complete histories, including the things that never make it into their resumes. I also want each of them followed. Charley, you've got enough people you can pull in to do that, right?"

Charley nodded. "I'll get on it as soon as we're done here. Just get me their files."

"I'll have Rosalie from SBD send them over." Noah chuckled. "I told Liam I think she really runs that place, not him."

At that moment Charley's phone buzzed and he looked at the screen.

"Damn. Noah. You guys are playing hardball with some dangerous folks here."

Noah frowned. "What do you mean?"

"The plate on that car comes back as registered to Far Eastern Tourism." He gave a derisive snort. "On the surface, the head of the firm is a member of the Chinese Board of Tourism. They arrange tours from this country to China and vice versa. But you can put your mind to work on all the under the counter things they can do under the guise of tourism, everything from spying to drug smuggling."

Noah frowned. "Nobody I'd want to have cocktails with, for damn sure. You think they're involved in this mess at Software By Design?"

"I'd bet on it." Charley nodded. "This kind of stuff is right up their alley. Like I said, their real business is spying for the Chinese government. But what could Liam's firm have that would make them do this? And screw with Liam?"

Noah was silent for a moment. "This is only to be shared as necessary. That's an absolute. Hoffman Contractors does business with the Department of Defense. They currently are working on the design for a state-of-the-art drone that can make itself invisible to radar and any other tracking devices. It can do surveillance without being spotted or deliver a variety of payloads. It's a versatile little bugger and a key part of our arsenal. If they can steal the design and produce it before we can, we're facing a whole pot of trouble."

Charley stared at him. "How the fuck did the Chinese even get wind of this? Never mind. Forget I said that. I understand they can find out anything from anyone anywhere."

"The question is," Noah told him, "how did they know who to target at SBD? Someone obviously has a weakness they dug out and used as leverage. Something that didn't show up on any of Liam's background checks of his people. We need to know what it is."

"Or maybe," Charley said in a thoughtful tone, "they created the weakness, fed it, until that person had nowhere to turn except to do what they asked.

"Sounds about right to me."

A knock sounded on the door and Jolene entered with a thick pile of papers in her hands.

"From Rosalie," she told them. "Everything she has on everyone who works there. She emailed me the files and I printed it all out."

"Excellent." Charley took the files and looked around the table. "Then this is where we start. Let's divide this stuff up and get on it. Whatever you can find online, track that first. But by the end of the day, at their quitting time, I need one of you on each staffer at SBD. I want to know where they go, who they see, what they do. And as always, be invisible."

"We'll wear our invisible cloaks," Sandra Harlan joked.

"Do that. Time is short here. Liam's arraignment is this afternoon. Sydney will get bail continued but they will probably move quickly on this. We have to move faster."

Half an hour later Noah was on the phone with Sydney delivering his update, focusing on the information about the Chinese involvement.

"I know this whole thing is a setup," he told her. "We just have to find out who has their ass in a sling and could be pressured to do something like this. From what Liam had told us, he swears by every one of them. Especially those who came over from Winters and Pryce with him."

"As long as Charley's people are on it," she said, "we've got the best. What's your role in the game plan?"

"I have a quick errand to do for Taylor. Then I'm going back to Charley's offices to work with the people digging into the background of SBD staff. I know they'll do a great job, but time is short and two sets of eyes are better than one."

"Agreed. I'm taking Liam to the courthouse after lunch for the arraignment, then bringing him back here. He wants to go to his office but I think we'll wait on that until tomorrow. Call me if you get anything, no matter how small it is."

"Will do."

Noah disconnected the call and pressed the button for Taylor's cell.

"Where do we stand?" she asked at once.

"Charley's on it," he answered, "and has his best people assigned to it. But as soon as I take care of your little errand, I'm going back there to work with his research people. Somewhere in their personal histories is the answer to all this. I feel it in my bones."

"And your bones don't lie," she chuckled. "Touch base with me after you see John, and we'll catch up again at the end of the day."

Noah disconnected and headed for John Martino's office. Charley Graham's people might find out every detail of a subject's life, but no one could find hidden money better than Martino. He had saved Arroyo's bacon when Taylor's father died and left controlling interest in the conglomerate to her, and helped both them and their friends in many other situations. If an SBD employee was getting money for screwing up the software for Hoffman, Martin would find its source and where it was hiding.

He had a feeling they were closing in on the truth. He just hoped it happened before Liam had to go to trial.

As he pulled out of the parking lot, he checked both his rearview and side view mirrors. Nothing popped out at him but he would be making sure today that every one of his senses was on high alert.

Chapter Eighteen

Shan was on a secure long-distance call to their boss in Beijing.

"This is turning into a disaster of epic proportions," Chen Wang said in his annoyingly harsh voice."

"Yes? Tell me about it. I never bargained for a mess like this."

"Are you telling me this is beyond your capabilities?" Wang's tone was laced with censure. Everyone knew that tone of voice meant trouble for anyone within a hundred yards. Maybe even a hundred miles.

Bastard!

When this was over, Shan was taking everything and disappearing somewhere. Anyplace where Wang did not have tentacles. She hesitated to tell him about this latest wrinkle, promising herself to take care of it first. But how?

Because of the nature of this situation, they had photos of all the key players in the game, easy to identify them if necessary. She had been excited when one of her people, dropping someone off at the private terminal at Tampa International Airport, had spotted Noah arriving on the Arroyo plane. But what the hell was Noah Cantrell doing back in Tampa?

"I am well in control of the situation," Shan assured the man. "I have my finger on everything, and my heel on the neck of our code specialist. My people who are hacking the system are working at a steady pace and will have the breakthrough in the next twenty-four hours."

"And Benedict? You tell me his conviction is all but assured, but I don't believe that's true. I have seen situations like this before. Too many things can happen before the final verdict."

Shan nodded, even though no one was there to see. "He is being arraigned as we speak."

"That does not assure a conviction," Wang pointed out. "A good attorney — which we know he has — can muddy the waters, so to speak. It might serve us better to eliminate him. Yes, that is what we must do. What *you* must do."

Shan jerked upright in the chair.

What the fuck?

"You want me to kill Liam Benedict? Are you out of your fucking minds?"

"Not in the least."

Shan felt perspiration popping out. "Wang, this is too high profile to do something like that. Everyone in the world has eyes on him and this."

"I don't care." Anger edged Wang's voice. "I believe this is our best answer. We have wasted too much time already. His death will cause everyone to re-examine everything. Perhaps then you can arrange for the appropriate person to whisper in Hoffman's ear that they should start all over with the security software. And have our pet code writer handle the whole thing."

"And if he chooses to hire a different firm?"

"I trust you will not let that happen. Otherwise it would be your body the police find. We do not tolerate failure."

"I will do my best." *Or hide someplace you'll never find me.*

Silence hummed across the connection.

God, Shan hated that silence. People had been killed if that silence lasted too long.

"I want your assurance on this," Wang ordered.

"It will be taken care of. In fact, as soon as we hang up I will be on the way to meet with our prized pigeon."

"I want a report the moment you have made the arrangements," Wang snapped. "And the results had better be what I want to hear."

Shan had been flipping a pencil back and forth during the conversation. Now, a muscle reflex caused it to snap in half.

If only it was Wang's neck.

"Of course. Count on it."

"I do. If you want to continue living, you'll make sure what you have to tell me is positive."

When the call ended, Shan resisted the urge to slam the cell phone down on the desk. How had everything gotten so fucked up? It wasn't supposed to be this complex. The tip that Hoffman Industries had a contract for a super-secret new type of drone. The news that Software By Design was creating an impenetrable wall of code around it. Seeking out the coder known as Eight. Seducing Eight into more and more gambling losses, then draping the noose and pulling it tight. Getting the back door inserted in the code.

It had all seemed so fucking simple. A few minutes to tweak, and Shan's people could electronically walk through that back door and steal all the design plans.

Then it had blown up in their faces. All because they had not credited that fucking Liam Benedict with the brains he apparently had.

Well, it wouldn't be Shan that went down the tubes on this. If it all fell apart, Eight and Liam Benedict would be going down first. Count on it.

Shan pulled a burner phone from a back pocket and, fingers flying, texted Eight. No asking this time. No suggesting. Just a terse message.

Meet at usual restaurant. Eight o'clock. Do not be late.

* * * *

Liam walked out of the Thirteenth Judicial District Courthouse in downtown Tampa, feeling as if he needed a shower. Or maybe a drink. Maybe even both. Sydney had been fantastic, mentally propping him up while they waited their turn in front of the judge. The actual appearance took less than five minutes. It was the waiting that got to him, and the knowledge there was a slim chance the judge would decide to deny bail. Syd had assured him that would not happen but after the past few days, he wasn't sure she could guarantee him anything.

He took off his sport jacket, yanked the tie from around his neck where it had begun to feel like a noose and just stood for a moment letting the sun warm him.

He sensed rather than saw Sydney come up to stand beside him.

"Feeling better now that we got that over?"

He snorted. "I'll feel better when they get the real killer and I'm out of this totally."

"We're working on it."

Liam looked around for the bodyguard, who'd driven them to the courthouse.

"Where's Vega?"

"He'll be back any second. I sent him to the condo to fetch your two laptops."

"What?" Liam tensed. "Why did you do that? I need to go back to the condo and work on them. Both of them. We are far from solving the problems."

"Liam." Sydney rested a hand on his arm. "You are in no mental shape to do anything. Please believe me. Charley Graham is meeting us here in a few to take possession of them. He—"

"What the hell, Sydney?" Someone else was getting their hands on those laptops?

"You are in no mental shape to work on either the backtrace or digging into the Hoffman security software for the glitch. Charley Graham gave Noah the name of another forensic data analyst and he is on the Arroyo plane as we speak."

"And the backtrace? Which is taking way more time than it should, by the way."

"Charley has a super expert in his office who is taking that over. Noah assured me no matter how many times whoever wrote it pinged it off multiple locations, this woman can track down the point of origination."

"And what am I supposed to do? Sit and twiddle my thumbs?" He shook his head. "Not happening."

"I understand. Look at me a minute."

He turned his head and caught his breath at the sight of her. She was the image of the consummate professional, in her gray suit, silk blouse, five-inch heels and her hair ruthlessly pulled into a twist at the back of her head. There was a fierce light in her gorgeous blue-almost-violet eyes that made him damn glad she was on his side.

Despite his situation, he found himself smiling. "Yes, ma'am?"

Her full lips curved in a tiny grin. "You don't want to work on things that intricate when your brain is only at half power. When you're distracted. And besides, you hired outside expertise to do this to begin with. Keep with that program."

"And what do I do with my time?"

"Tomorrow you can go back to the office," she told him. "Vega will drive you back and forth and be a quiet shadow while you're there."

"Swell. A babysitter."

"A man who is going to protect you from whoever wants to hurt or kill you."

Liam swallowed back another retort. "And today?"

"Today Vega is taking you back to the condo. There is a full workout room on the top floor. Use it to work off your aggression and your anger. It works." She winked. "Trust me. I know."

"And after that? Where will you be?"

"At the office working on the details of your case and coordinating with Charley Graham's people to put them together. To see if we can find out who is doing this." She smiled again. "Please. Just let's get through today. Tomorrow you can get back to your office. I know you have clients who need to speak to you."

"Oh, yeah. Clients." He made a rude noise. "As if anyone wants to do business with me while this is hanging over my head."

"You may be surprised. Oh, here's Vega. And right behind him, Charley Graham himself."

Liam glanced at the curb, saw Vega pull up in the black SUV Sydney had told him the man would be driving. An identical vehicle pulled in right behind it. The man who hopped out with a smooth, athletic grace was at least six feet four, with broad shoulders, thick blond hair and a muscular body encased in khakis and a navy T-shirt. Vega pulled two laptops out of his vehicle and both he and the other man walked over to where Sydney and Liam stood.

Sydney shook hands with the blond. "Thanks for helping us with this, Charley."

He dipped his head. "Noah asks and we oblige." Then he grinned. "For you, too!"

"Liam, shake hands with Charley Graham. He and his people are going to find out who's creating this mess so we can save your bacon. Jim and Charley used to work for the same agency. Then we stole Jim and Arroyo tapped Charley to head their high voltage security and investigative agency."

The men smiled and bumped fists.

"I take it those are for me?" Charley nodded at the laptops.

"They are." Jim handed them over.

Charley looked at Liam. "I swear to you these will be in good hands. We have someone as good as Eric Braun if not better on the plane here as we speak. And my tech expert, Sarah Gaffney, is second to none as someone who can trace the origination of the hack. We'll get you taken care of."

"Sydney vouches for you, and that's good enough for me."

Charley looked at Sydney again. "I hope to have an update for you by tomorrow morning. No one's sleeping until we get to the source of this."

"Thank you, from both of us."

In what seemed like seconds, Charley was gone with the laptops, Sydney headed for her car and Liam was in the back SUV with Jim Vega heading back to the condo. Maybe, if he took a nap, when he woke up he'd discover this whole thing had just been a bad dream.

* * * *

Eight hoped never to see this damn restaurant ever again. Ever. And wondered how easy it would be to commit murder. Shan, already there and sitting in a back booth, would certainly be a good target on which to practice.

How the fucking hell did I get into this, anyway?

"What's with the command performance? I thought with Liam out of the way things were progressing nicely."

Shan simply sat there with narrowed eyes. "We do not have all the files yet. We believe your boss, or Eric Braun, did something to the Hoffman server to deliberately prevent us from downloading more than two files at a time."

Eight frowned. "How many are there supposed to be?"

"It takes at least a dozen with all the schematics for a project like this. And the longer we have to keep going into that server, the easier it will be for someone to detect us."

"I thought your people were experts at this."

"A smart mouth will not serve you well here," Shan snapped. "Perhaps if you had been better prepared for your boss to screw up what you'd done with the software, you wouldn't have to worry about it."

Rage sizzled through Eight's body, even as she grabbed the filled mug the waitress had set down on the table.

"I *was* prepared. But he's never done anything like this before. Ever."

Coffee. Yes, coffee. Anything to make my brain function better and my anger get under control.

"Well, it matters little now. Do you know that Arroyo has put a high-ticket investigative and security agency on this? I looked them up. They have experts on everything, including computers. My sources tell me they have a female expert who is better than everyone at SBD except your boss." Shan leaned forward. "You know what that means, right?"

A sick feeling wriggled its way through Eight's body and up into the throat.

"They'll be able to finally trace the source of the hack."

Shan nodded and sat back.

"Even more than that, it means we're screwed. I have discussed this with my people back in Beijing. Everything is taking way too long for this. We need to scrub it and start from square one."

"Oh, yeah?" Eight took another gulp of coffee. "And exactly how do you propose to do that? Liam will never go for that. Especially if he's got outside help again."

"Very simply." Shan stared across the table at eight. "We're going to kill Liam Benedict."

Eight's body was suddenly consumed in a wave of ice cold air.

"K-kill? Did you say kill Liam?"

Shan nodded. "My people and I have discussed this and see it as the only solution. Once he is out of the way, we will arrange for the proper person to convince Robert Hoffman to start from scratch with his software and that you are the appropriate person to handle it."

Eight felt the stabbing pain of a sudden headache.

"That's crazy! Why would they even consider me?"

"You can do anything if the right person is chosen. That's what we will do."

"But..."

"No buts. This is an order that came down from the top."

Eight wondered if they'd fallen down the rabbit hole.

"But you said you'd figured out a way around this. That you were into the Hoffman system and slowly extracting the schematics files."

Shan nodded. "But not fast enough. For whatever reason, the new setup on their server only allows access to one or two files at a time."

Eight was suddenly consumed with a sick feeling. What if Liam and his now-dead expert had loaded a ghost program onto the Hoffman server? What if it took a hacker not to the real files but to dummy files? Files that looked enough like the real thing to convince whoever stole them until it was time to make the project actually work. Was that what happened here? If so, Eight was already deader than Liam would be.

Fuck, fuck, fuck.

"Are you listening?" Shan tapped a fist on the table. "We have to act right now. Take him out of the picture."

"And exactly how do you propose we do that?" Eight asked.

"We have the solution. Take this and put it in your pocket." A tiny vial appeared beneath Shan's palm. When Eight hesitated, Shan hissed, "Now, you fool. Take it."

With obvious reluctance Eight palmed the little vial and slipped it into a jeans pocket.

"Very good." Shan nodded. "A little of this in his coffee and he's done."

Eight didn't know whether to scream or throw up. "How the hell am I supposed to do that? Rosalie always brings him his coffee. Or he gets it himself."

"Quit being such a whiny idiot. Go to his office, tell him you know all of this will be over soon. They'll find Eric's killer. The office will settle back into it's routine. And, oh, by the way. You were getting a cup of coffee for yourself and thought you would fix one for him, too."

Eight didn't want to mention the fact she never brought Liam coffee, or that killing someone had not been part of the plan. This trap had snapped shut because gambling had a siren's lure, which was irresistible. It would not be far-fetched to say the future looked very bleak. And when Liam Benedict died, they would look first at Eight, who brought him the damned cup of coffee.

Which she pointed out to Shan.

"Then be inventive. I don't fucking care. Just remember, it's your life or his."

Sadly, there weren't a lot of choices here.

"Fine. And now I have to get out of here."

"I want this done quickly," Shan reiterated. "The moment he is dead, we will be putting part two of the plan into place."

"I'm telling you," Eight objected, "they won't even consider me to write the replacement software for Hoffman. They'll want a hotshot like Liam or Eric Braun to do it."

"Leave it to us. Go back to work. I have a feeling your boss may not be in the office today, so be prepared to make your move tomorrow."

Eight slid out of the booth and walked as casually as possible out to the parking lot. The little vial was burning a hole in the pocket where it rested.

I wonder, if I ran away, would they find me?

Probably, and hack me to little pieces.

Fuck, fuck, fuck.

Chapter Nineteen

"How about another cold drink?"

Sydney stood at the refrigerator, looking at Liam.

He sighed. "Sure. Why not? If I'm good, can I have a double bourbon?"

He looked so defeated Sydney wanted to forget about the rule she set down and put her arms around him, kiss him hard then take him into the bedroom and soothe him with her body.

The pizza she'd ordered for dinner, in an attempt to tease his appetite, was barely touched. He'd picked at his food until she'd finally given up and cleared it away.

When she arrived at the condo about six from the office, he was sitting in the living room, the big screen television on but muted, Liam staring at the screen but not really seeing anything. Vega told her he'd put himself through a punishing workout in the gym and even slept for a couple of hours. Understandable, since she was sure he'd hardly closed his eyes during his night in jail.

She had brought home with her a list of questions she and her associate had prepared after going over every note on the case to date. Some of it covered territory they'd already gone over but sometimes on the second or third round, a nugget that had been hiding could be discovered.

Some of the questions were based on information in the SBD personnel files, others on information dug up by the people at Charley Graham's shop. She was trying to fill in as many blanks as she could, hoping to identify which of them could be the one she was looking for. It had to be someone from SBD who had done all of this. No one else would have access to the software to monkey with it. And certainly no one else would have been able to grab the dagger from Liam's desk then return it.

Now, after two hours of going at it hard and heavy, she could see he really needed a break. It was hard seeing him look so defeated. Liam had gone from a high at the sudden explosion of success for Software By Design and the excitement of becoming part of Arroyo to the frightening threat he could lose it all. She wanted to kill whoever was behind this.

She hoped Noah would have something to tell her soon. He had texted her to tell her the Graham agents were on their assigned targets and would report in if anything the least out of the ordinary occurred. Maybe they'd get lucky and someone would do something that gave them away. A long shot but it could happen. He had also told her the new forensic data analyst was hard at work, and she wondered how long it would take him to find what Eric had discovered.

Damn! If only Eric had been able to share that information with someone. Of course, he'd never expected to be killed, either.

Stop it, Sydney. You'll drive yourself crazy. Focus. Liam needs you to focus.

And that's what she was doing. No one, except probably Liam, wanted this to be over more than she did. She wanted the two of them to be able to get back to their growing relationship. He was the only man who had ever touched her emotionally as well as physically. The only one she could see herself building a life with. And all indications were he felt the same way. That made it even more imperative that she clear his name and get him out of this mess so they could get on with their lives.

She had just settled herself back at the table when her cell phone rang. She looked at the screen.

Noah.

"Cross your fingers, Liam. If Noah's calling, we may have something here." She hit Answer. "Got anything?"

"Maybe the jackpot." Noah's usual stoic tone of voice was edged with a trace of excitement.

"Damn it, don't keep me in suspense." She gripped her phone. "Let's have it."

"I've got the data about the license plate on the car that was following me."

"Yes, yes. Far Eastern Tourism." She did her best to curb her impatience. "So, what's happened?"

"It's a known fact—or at least a strong supposition— that the Chinese integrate agents into businesses in this county. They open something, staff it and operate behind a dark curtain with the business as a cover."

Sydney felt excitement course through her. Would this really be the break they needed? She hardly dared hope.

"The license plate belongs to just such a business. And guess where we found it again."

"Come on, Noah. You're killing me here."

"Okay." He paused. "I just heard from the Graham agent shadowing Teri LaGrange. He followed her to a restaurant where she hooked up with an Asian woman."

"And?"

"And the car following me was parked in the restaurant lot. It belongs to a so-called Chinese travel and tourism agency here."

Sydney wanted to jump up and down and scream. This was it! "We've got the connection."

"Yes," Noah agreed. "We do. Our operative got a picture with his camera watch of the woman Teri met, sent it to the office to have it run through facial recognition software and just got his answer back."

"And?"

"Her name is Chow Shan. She is a member of the Chinese Tourism Board and the head of the office here in Tampa. Two things. One, a friend of Charley's in the CIA let us know they are definitely a cover for covert ops like spying. And two, Liam's top dog in coding, Teri LaGrange, met with Chow Shan tonight for half an hour. And from the body language, it looked like they'd met several times before."

Sydney felt a chill race over her body. "This is going to kill Liam, you know. To find out an employee he trusted has betrayed him like this."

"No kidding. One of the things we have to find out is where the hole was in the vetting process."

"How long were they together?" She hoped her voice didn't show the shock she felt.

"About half an hour. Our shadow says when LaGrange walked out, she looked angry."

Sydney glanced over at Liam, who was staring at her with an intent look.

"Noah, I have to say. Coupled with the other thing we learned today, this doesn't make me feel very good. Where's our subject now?"

"Our agent thinks she's on her way home. At least, she's driving in that direction." He was silent for a moment. "But, Sydney? This doesn't feel good to me. Not one bit. And you've got the unenviable job of telling Liam."

She swallowed a sigh. "I understand. I promised him he could go back to the office tomorrow, but I'll have Vega glued to his side from the moment he leaves here in the morning."

"And while he is in his office, too. Taylor and I want him protected every single minute. Who knows what these people will do now that their plan did not go the way they wanted."

"Of course. Call if you get any more information tonight."

"I will," Noah agreed. "Right now I'm headed back to Graham's office. I called him and he's meeting his hot techie gal there. We're going to find out everything we can about Shan, that agency and anything connected with it. I'm calling Taylor as soon as I hang up to give her an update." He gave a short, humorless laugh. "To say she'll be unhappy is the understatement of the year."

"Check back later, okay?"

"Will do."

She disconnected the call and sat for a moment, gathering her thoughts.

"I know it's bad," Liam said, his voice taut with anxiety, "so you might as well just let me have it."

"I don't really know any other way to tell you than straight out. Teri LaGrange is the one who sabotaged the Hoffman project and killed Eric Braun."

Liam just stared at her, every bit of color drained from his face. For a moment, she was afraid he'd pass out. She nodded at Vega who was half watching television in the living room. He looked at Liam, then back at her, worry plain in his eyes.

"What's up?"

She gave him the information, watching the wash of pain on his face as he heard it for the second time.

"I can't believe it." Liam shook his head. "I *won't* believe it. It just seems so impossible."

"Liam." Sydney reached over and touched his hand. "You have to believe it. Our operative took pictures."

"Damn it, Syd." He smacked his fist on the table hard enough to make their glasses jump. "She worked with me at Winters and Pryce. She's been one of my stars at SBD."

"And I'm sure the one who fucked up the software program. If it hadn't been for your secret tricky little alarm, they would have hacked the Hoffman server and gotten the plans for the drone. That would have been a huge national disaster."

Liam rubbed his face as if trying to wipe everything away. "Is he sure? This person following her?"

"It's a she and yes. She said Teri went home from the office, spent some time there then took off for the restaurant where she hooked up with Shan. And it was very obvious that this was not the first meeting. The question now is how many times they met and why LaGrange is involved with Chinese spies."

"Fuck." He shook his head. "You think I can coax some of that bourbon out of you? I could sure use a shot right now."

"I think you deserve it. Jim, will you do the honors?"

Vega nodded. "How about a double?"

"Sure. He's not going anywhere tonight."

"You know," Vega said as he fetched glasses, ice and the booze, "that accident you had Liam, plus those near misses before, all that make sense now."

Liam frowned. "How do you figure?"

"They didn't want you dead. Too messy and too many questions. But they must have figured if they got you sidelined, Teri would be the one to step up and take over."

"Not one of the others?" Sydney asked.

"No, Jim's right," Liam told her. "Teri's been my number one person from the very beginning. There has to be something we missed in the vetting process, and I wish to hell we knew how and what it is."

"Trust the people at Graham and Associates to do their job. They are hard at work on it as we speak."

Her cell rang just as she finished speaking. Noah again.

"Anything?" she asked, skipping the greeting.

"We're working on it. I wanted to let you know Taylor's on the way. We decided to give our pilot a rest so she chartered a ride from a friend. She'll be here close to midnight and checking into the DaCosta Waterside."

"She's dropping everything to come here? Now?"

"This is a big deal to her," Noah pointed out. "A foreign agent tries to fuck with one of her people. They have no idea the wrath they've unleashed. I'll be working late here at Charley's, with his team, but breakfast in the suite at eight-thirty in the morning. See you then, unless I call you back tonight with some unearthed nugget."

Sydney just stared at the telephone after Noah hung up.

"Well!"

"What?" Liam took a healthy swallow of his drink. "If it's more bad news, I'm not sure I want to hear it."

"Not bad at all. Taylor Cantrell is on her way here. Breakfast in her suite tomorrow morning at eight-thirty."

Liam's eyes widened. "Here? She's coming here? For this?"

"Actually, I guess I'm not all that surprised. If foreign agents can screw with one of her companies, they could theoretically get to all of them. Show of force and strength here."

They were silent for a long moment.

"All right." Liam drained his glass and set it down. "No more pity party here. Let's get back to the questions. It's time I pulled up my big guy shorts and dug into this with you. Pull out your questions again. Where were we?"

Sydney swallowed a smile and noticed Vega hiding a grin as she pulled her tablet in front of her again and swiped to another page.

Chapter Twenty

Despite the fact that he'd slept very little, Liam was wide awake and alert at seven-thirty the next morning. By eight he was showered and shaved, dressed for the day and drinking coffee with Vega in the kitchen while they waited for Sydney.

"Glad to see you look like you've got your shit together today," Vega commented. "Be a shame to let those assholes get you down."

"Yeah, I'm done feeling sorry for myself. Your biggest problem today might be keeping me from murdering that traitorous little shit when I get to the office."

"She'll be in today?"

"Oh, yeah. We're just waiting for Charley Graham's people to finish scouring her life to find all her dirty little secrets before we confront her."

"You aren't contacting the cops?"

"We will," Sydney answered as she walked into the kitchen. "Just as soon as we've dotted all the i's and crossed all the t's. I want to be able to go to the prosecutor with proof that will force him to drop the charge against Liam without a big argument. Noah texted a while ago that they worked through the night but it was worth it."

"Sounds good to me." Vega rinsed out his mug and set it in the dishwasher. "Syd, you taking your own vehicle today or are we riding as a group?"

"We'll go together. After we're finished with our breakfast meeting you can drop me at my office before you take Liam to SBD. If I have to go anywhere, I can Uber. Let's move it."

When Liam walked into the Cantrells' suite it was déjà vu all over again, as they said. For a moment he was back at the dinner that had set all this in motion.

"Nice to see you again, Liam." Taylor Cantrell held out her hand.

"I wish the circumstances were different," he told her in a wry voice.

"Yes, well, my husband might have some news on that front, too. Noah?" She raised her voice a bit to call him.

"Right here."

Liam was impressed that a man who had probably had no sleep was so alert and well put together. But then, Noah Cantrell was no ordinary man. In fact, there was nothing ordinary at all about either Cantrell.

"I had them set up breakfast as a buffet." Taylor gestured to the sideboard along one wall. "I wasn't sure what everyone wanted."

"Lots of coffee," Noah told her and squeezed her shoulder. "It was a long night."

"Okay." Sydney looked across the table at Noah when they were all seated. "I can't wait any longer. Give."

"Here's the highlights. Then I'll go into details." She fortified herself with a swallow of coffee. "All our research has turned up the information that Teri LaGrange has a bad gambling habit. An addiction, as a matter of fact."

Liam looked at him. "How'd you find that out?"

"Doing a lot of digging. Details to follow, but it seems she was well-known at the Hard Rock Café. And people talk when enough money flows."

"Chinese money," Taylor added. "It seems Teri was targeted. Word of the Hoffman drone leaked out and Teri was identified as a weak link. Someone they could manipulate and threaten."

Liam swallowed a bit of sweet roll and chased it with coffee. "How'd they do that?"

"Followed her to clock her habits. Identified her as a gambler with a budding addiction, and fed that addiction."

"They waited until she had a big night at Hard Rock," Noah continued, "to entice her into a private big stakes game. Then, very carefully, when they'd extended thousands and thousands of dollars—even hundreds of thousands—to her in credit, they dropped the noose and tightened it."

"Pay up or you're finished," Sydney guessed.

Taylor nodded. "You've got it. And to tie it up neatly, Dean Michaels, the forensic data analyst Charley found for us, cracked the code in the Hoffman program, too."

"And?"

"And he discovered that Teri had gone into the program between the time you signed off on it and the time it was delivered to Hoffman and put in a back door for the Chinese to use. But she wasn't counting on you being smarter than everyone. Liam, his exact words were, 'That Liam's a fucking genius.' Apparently, none of your staff, Liam, knows that when you assigned each of them to a work station, you coded the computers so any work they do can be tracked back to the person who did it."

Everyone turned to stare at him.

Then Sydney smiled at him. "Of course, you did. My associates digging up information to help put your defense together said in the industry you're known as an innovator and security freak. Which is why this whole thing was such a shock to everyone."

"He finished that at four-thirty this morning," Noah added. "And, to add a little spice to the recipe, had a program running on the other laptop while he was doing that. We found the original source of the hack."

Liam's jaw dropped. "This guy must be something."

"Something expensive," Noah grunted.

"But worth every damn penny," Taylor put in. She looked at Liam. "And not one damn word about the cost of anything. If word got out that one of our companies could be infiltrated and virtually destroyed, all the others would be vulnerable. This will send a strong message when word gets out."

Sydney looked at her watch. "What's the plan for today? I need to get to my office."

"Charley still has his people following everyone on the SBD staff," Noah answered, "at least until we can put a pin in this. He's got Dean writing up a report as well as the agent shadowing Teri. She'll be posing as a new client when you get to your office, Liam, so she'll have an excuse to be inside until we can wrap this up."

"When do you think that will be?" Sydney asked.

"Sometime today. As soon as we've got it all in writing, you'll have it to take to the prosecutor."

"But they've still got the dagger with my fingerprints on it," Liam pointed out, "as well as Eric's blood."

"But what they don't have is proof that you were somewhere else when Eric was stabbed."

Liam frowned. "How'd you do that?"

"With a lot of money to pay a lot of people. They tracked down every reporter, photographer, newshound, whatever, who was taking pictures for publicity at the parade. We found three of your float time-stamped over a thirty-minute period, covering the time when Eric was stabbed."

For the first time since this had happened, Liam felt he could draw a full breath.

"Then I really need to get to my office." Sydney put her napkin down and stood up. "Noah, can you have Charlie fax everything over to my office?"

"We'll do better than that, I'll have him send an agent to hand deliver it."

"Excellent."

Liam looked around at everyone. "I don't know how I'll ever be able to thank all of you. I'm… I just…" He couldn't seem to find the right words.

"It's not over yet," Noah pointed out. "You've got to get to your office and act like nothing's different until Sydney has the package together, gets it to the prosecutor, and he has the cops arrest Teri."

"Can they make the murder charge stick?"

"That's what we're working on. Okay, get going. And keep your eyes peeled. The Chinese are mighty unhappy about this, if what our agent observed at the restaurant last night is any indication. Keep Vega close to you, and Charley's agent when she shows up."

Liam was still digesting it all when they arrived at his office. In the elevator he put on his best worried look, which, when he thought of all the things that could go wrong, wasn't so far off.

"Oh, Liam." Rosalie rushed to him and gave him a big hug. "Everyone is stunned that the police would think you did this. But you've got the best lawyer in the southeast."

"Don't I know it. Listen, I have an expert offsite running those two laptops. If he calls at any time, put him right through. His name is Dean Carmichael."

"Absolutely," she assured him. "Anything else?"

"Yes. My luck is not all bad. I have a new client coming to see the place today. Before she talks business, she wants to see what kind of setup I have. Her name is Mary Sirota."

"I'll call down to the guard and tell him she's expected. Also the parking lot."

"Thanks. And, Rosalie? Thanks for everything."

"We'll get through this," she assured him.

The most difficult thing he had to do was his usual morning walk around, checking on what each of his coders was doing and where they were with their assigned projects. It was especially difficult for him when he stopped at Teri's work station. He couldn't afford to give anything away, so he made his stop as quick as possible.

"Liam?" She swiveled in her chair to look at him. "Rosalie told me you wanted me on the Sanchez project today. That one's pretty simple and won't take me any time at all."

Don't give her anything sensitive to work on, Noah had told him.

"Maybe so." He made his tone as even as possible. "But it's still important and I want it done right. That's why I wanted you on it."

She studied his face, as if not quite trusting what he said. Then she shrugged.

"Okay. Thanks. I think. I'll come let you know when I'm done."

He wanted to tell her that wasn't necessary but he didn't want to get into an argument with her so he just nodded.

Vega shadowed him the entire time, and while his employees looked at him strangely, no one asked who the guy was and Liam made no introductions. Still, his stomach was roiling and he was sure his blood pressure was at a peak when he finished.

By the time he got back to his office, Mary Sirota had just arrived. He took her into his office and closed the door so they could have some privacy.

"I'd like you to show me around the place," she told Liam. "That way I can assess Teri without her knowing why."

"No problem."

"I don't trust her. She's a slimy little sleaze and capable of anything."

Liam shrugged. "What can she do? Especially with you and Vega here. She can't get to any of the secure programs. I took care of that."

"What's she doing now?"

"Basic coding. I didn't want to give her anything sensitive to work on."

"Good move. Okay, show me what you've got. I want to see my target in her workplace."

But Teri wasn't at her desk when they stopped at her cubicle. Figuring she might be in the break room, he headed there with Mary on his heels. When they walked in, Teri was standing at the counter, two cups of coffee in front of her, stirring one of them.

She turned when she heard them and smiled. "Oh, Liam. I was just coming to your office. I fixed a cup of coffee for you."

He lifted an eyebrow. "Rosalie usually fixes it. You don't have to take time for that."

"Oh! No problem. I can fix one for your guest, too."

But as she turned to grab another cup, she tried to slide one hand into her jeans pocket. In a flash, Mary Sirota reached out to Teri, grabbed her wrist and yanked the hand out. As she did, a tiny vial fell to the floor.

"Don't touch that," Mary snapped to Liam. "Get me a paper towel."

As she reached to take it from him, Teri, who had been trying to pull her arm away, yanked Mary's arm down, kicked her in the stomach and shoved her, hard. Mary lost her grip as she doubled over and Teri ran down the hall, just out of Liam's reach. The whole thing had taken mere seconds.

"Are you okay?" he asked Mary.

"Yes." She sucked in a breath and waved toward the hallway. "Go. Don't let her get away. I want to get this vial."

Liam ran after Teri, shouting, "Stop her. Someone. Anyone."

People stuck their heads out of their offices and cubicles. "What's going on?" someone shouted. "What's happening?"

Liam just blew past them to the entrance.

"Rosalie!" Liam hollered over his shoulder as he, too, shoved the stairway door aside. "Call down to the guard and tell him to stop Teri. Right now."

He took the stairs down two at a time, realized Mary had caught up and was right on his heels. They burst into the lobby and saw the guard looking for Teri.

"I got Rosalie's call," he told Liam, "but she didn't come this way. Check the back and the parking lot.

"I've got this," Liam told him as he and Mary raced for the exit.

Then all hell broke loose, so fast it was almost a blur. They reached the parking lot in time to be nearly sideswiped as Teri barreled toward the exit gate, heading nonstop for the automatic security arm. Mary pulled out her gun, took aim and shot out the rear tires, but the car still kept moving.

As she and Liam raced closer to it, another car, a silver sedan that had apparently been sitting at the curb, hopped the sidewalk, blocking Teri. The passenger side window rolled down and the driver aimed at Teri's car, fired six shots into it then sped away. To Liam, those shots sounded like a cannon going off, loud and explosive, filling the air. They were punctuated with the sound of glass shattering and a scream.

As the car accelerated and pulled into traffic, it sideswiped another vehicle, nearly rear-ended a second one and chased a third up onto the sidewalk before maneuvering into traffic.

Later, Liam would realize with shock that the whole thing took just seconds. At the moment, he only concentrated on one thing — seeing how badly hurt Teri was. He wanted her alive so she could be arrested. He reached her car before Mary did and tried to yank open the door, but it was locked.

"Move away," Mary ordered. She used the butt of her gun to smash the passenger window, then reached in to pop the locks.

"Shit, shit, shit," Liam cursed as he yanked open the driver's door. Teri was leaning back against the seat, her side and her shoulder oozing blood.

Mary was right beside him. "Liam, I am so fucking sorry. I—"

"Call nine-one-one," he snapped. "Tell them to hurry. She's alive, but barely. I'm not letting her die before I get some answers and she gets a lot of years in prison."

Don't you die on me, you traitor. I want you to pay for everything you did.

He yanked off his shirt and held it to the wound in her side. Mary handed him her jacket, which he used on Teri's shoulder. His ears still rang from the sound of the gunshots, and his hands shook as he did his best to stanch the flow of blood from the wounds. He breathed a sigh of relief when he finally heard the sirens and she was still breathing.

More sirens shrieked and two squad cars pulled up right on the heels of the ambulance. The EMTs nudged Liam out of the way as they went to work with efficiency on Teri. The deputies in the patrol cars had piled up onto the sidewalk and into the parking lot.

When Liam glanced to his right, he saw most of his staff had hurried out of the building, drawn as much by the chase down the hallway as the shots in the parking lot. As he pulled out his handkerchief to wipe the blood from his hands, he saw two of the cops were talking to Mary. He saw one of them ask for her gun, which she turned over without an argument. He was sure this wasn't the first time she'd been in a situation like this.

"Want to tell us what happened here?" one of the other cops asked Liam.

"I'll do the best I can. It just all happened so fast."

He took a deep breath and let it out slowly, trying to pull his thoughts together. He was having trouble sorting the whole thing out in his own mind. He finally managed to tell them, in terse sentences, what had happened. They took his name and Mary's and one of them went to call it in.

"Does this woman work for you?" A deputy who identified himself as Robert Mason pointed at Mary.

"She was doing some work for us," Liam explained. "Listen, this whole thing happened so fast."

"It always does." He looked from one to the other. "Okay, give me your names. And, ma'am? I'll need to see a license for this gun."

The deputy, who told them his name was Derek Boone, wrote down the information from the license, then focused on Liam.

"Any idea what happened here? What started the whole thing? And who is the woman in the car?"

"One of my employees. She was—

"Hold on, Boone." Another cop, who had been talking on his radio, jogged over to them. The nameplate on his pocket identified him as Rod Fenton. "Put a pin in it. This is the guy who's accused of murder."

"And free on bail," Liam pointed out, and looked at Mary.

She pulled out her cell phone. "Let me make a call, officers, and I think I can get you that information."

"Wait." Boone held up a hand. "Who are you calling?"

"Radio in and tell them I'm calling Charley Graham. I believe he's well-known in the department."

While Boone passed along the information, Mary turned away so she could speak privately. Then he handed her phone to the deputy. "Here you go."

They both waited while the deputy took the call. His attitude changed from slightly belligerent to respectful. Then he gave the phone back to Mary.

"Okay." He nodded. "We'll wait right here for you until the gentleman gets here."

Liam just stared, then shook his head. It was getting better and better to have friends in high places.

"We're going to need to question all those people in the parking lot. I'm guessing they work here?"

Liam nodded. "For me."

"Then you could help us by telling them to be cooperative."

His staff had more questions for him than the cops did for them, but he just told them to give them whatever they knew. He did take Rosalie aside and brief her. She was already on the phone, calling someone to repair the security arm.

Finally, the police were satisfied they gotten everything they could from everyone — which amounted to very little because they knew almost nothing. Charley Graham had arrived to make nice with the cops and wind things up at the building.

And Liam was free to head for the hospital with Mary Sirota right behind him.

* * * *

When they reached the hospital, Noah was already there, waiting for them at the Emergency entrance.

Of course, he is, Liam thought. *I shouldn't be surprised at anything anymore.*

"She's in surgery," he told them. "Your quick action helped, Liam. Probably saved her life. She'll be out of surgery in a couple of hours or so. The cops are sending someone to guard her as soon as she's moved to Recovery."

Liam dropped into one of the waiting room chairs. "One of my programmers told me Teri called herself Eight. I asked why and she said because the woman always found herself behind the eightball in life's game of pool. How sad is that?"

Noah shrugged. "I like to think people can make their own luck. We all, at some time or other, are in desperate situations. It's how we handle it that counts."

Liam wondered what dark episode on Noah's life had made him make that statement, but he wasn't about to ask.

"I'm not going to ask how you pulled all the strings you did," he said instead. "I'm just incredibly grateful. But how did you make everything happen and so fast? I mean, calling off the patrol car deputies, moving everything so fast."

Noah smiled, but it was a particularly lethal grin. "My wife can do anything."

"Apparently."

Then all humor left Noah's face. "We got the vial and had it tested. A few drops of that in your coffee and we'd be attending your funeral instead of sitting in this waiting room."

Liam felt all the color leach from his skin. "She wanted to kill me."

Noah nodded. "My guess is the Chinese figured killing you would disrupt things enough at SBD, someone else would take over for the moment and they could still get their shot at the Hoffman drone."

"Jesus!" Liam rubbed his face with both hands as if he could erase this whole thing.

"Yeah. And Shan was waiting outside with orders to either get confirmation from Teri that the deed was done or kill her if it wasn't."

"I feel like this nightmare will never go away."

"It will," Noah assured him. "We're working on that now."

"Any word on Teri yet?" Mary Sirota hurried into the waiting from. "Sorry, I was just giving my report to Charley. Plus, he got someone over here to take delivery of that vial Teri LaGrange was trying to empty into your coffee."

Liam shook his head. "This whole thing feels like it's an unending nightmare. Did the description of the killer's car go out on the radio? Did anyone spot it?"

"Charley was able to get information from a lieutenant on the police he's good friends with," Noah answered. "The car was found about two miles from SBD offices." He made a rude noise. "Empty, of course. The cops wiped it down for fingerprints. I don't think they'll find any but I think we all know who was driving."

"So now what?"

"Now Charley and Sydney put their heads together to prepare your case to take to the prosecutor and get the charges against you dropped."

"Even though they don't have another suspect?"

"That's not our problem. All we have to do is present sufficient information that proves you couldn't have done it. And we have that."

"I'm not sure I even know how to thank you." Liam rubbed his face as if trying to erase everything that had happened.

"Just keep doing what you're doing," Noah told him. "That's thanks enough."

"I'll just be glad when this nightmare is finally over."

"Soon," Noah assured him. Even as he spoke, his cell phone jittered in his pocket. "I need to step outside to take this. Just hang in there, Liam. I'm seeing the finish line."

Mary Sirota touched his arm and looked at him with eyes filled with sympathy.

"I know how devastating this has been for you, but both Charley Graham and the Cantrells are working to wrap up all the loose ends. Meanwhile, let me get you a cup of coffee."

He accepted the filled Styrofoam cup from her more out of courtesy than anything else, just because she was being so nice. He wandered over to the window, staring at the parking lot below and wondering how the hell everything got so fucked up on a day so filled with sunshine.

Someone touched his elbow and he nearly sloshed the coffee turning around, almost spilling it on Noah.

"Oh, hey. Sorry."

"No problem. Sorry I startled you. But I do have some good news for you."

Liam cocked a brow. "Yeah? I could sure use some."

"Taylor's been busy. She called a friend in DC and gave him the details on our Chinese friend. The Tampa Police Department has a BOLO — Be On the Look Out — for her and they've received permission to send someone to stake out the tourist agency office. When she's caught, she'll be arrested, charged, arraigned and deported. The proper authorities are all set."

"I'd like to see her tried and convicted, and imprisoned here, for what she did but I'll take whatever I can get. Tell Taylor a big thank you."

"I will. I also gave Charley Graham the go ahead to finish thoroughly investigating and vetting the rest of your staff. Just in case. You don't want another Teri popping up." He held up his hand. "And no thanks. You've done that enough already. Let's get this charge against you dismissed and then we'll all celebrate."

Liam had no words for this. But he knew he owed a big thank you to John Martino, who had put him on Arroyo's radar to begin with.

Epilogue

Liam reached up to the ledge of the hot tub and picked up his glass of wine. He took a sip, letting the crisp flavor roll around on his tongue. He could hardly believe that a month ago he'd been under indictment for murder, one of his top clients had been ready to throw him to the wolves and a woman he'd thought of as his most trusted code writer had been helping the Chinese steal secret plans for a hush-hush drone. Now here he was, in a villa in the Caribbean, finally alone with Sydney and looking forward to the rest of his life.

If she'd just get off the damn phone.

He chuckled. He supposed it was something he'd have to get used to, if they made a life together. Which was exactly what he wanted and what this trip was about.

He closed his eyes, took another sip of wine and let the sun beat down on his face. The warm water of the hot tub gently caressed his naked skin, beating gently against his very hard cock. Where the hell was Sydney?

This whole naked-in-the-hot-tub was no good without her. In a minute he'd have to get out and go look for her, walking naked through the house, a condition he was unexpectedly getting used to.

Shan had been arrested at the tourism office, but not without a lot of yelling and screaming. She had been put through the booking process and formally charged, then released into the company of a Chinese official who had been sent to fetch her. Liam didn't know if the woman had been sent back to China or if she was dead and her body had been disposed of. He just wanted her out of their country, although for all the damage she'd done he hoped back in China, she'd be subjected to a long, unpleasant imprisonment.

The prosecutor had dropped the charges against him, although Sydney had told him the man obviously would rather have prosecuted Liam than deal with the Chinese situation. Sydney had also made sure the media covered it. After all, she'd told him, they should give as much attention to his exoneration as they had to his arrest.

Software By Design was once again operating smoothly, although he knew his staff would remember all this for a long time. After reading the reports from Graham and Associates, he had promoted Phil to the position of senior programmer and devised a different system for how he processed programs once they were written and beta tested. He had also had a long, intense discussion with each of his people on the seriousness of what had just happened, and how it affected the reputation of SBD and its ability to get the high-ticket clients. He was pleased with the results of those meetings. He and Taylor had huddled for several hours on how SBD should proceed going forward to take advantage of its position with Arroyo.

He'd had a long meeting with Robert Hoffman that Taylor had insisted on participating in. Afterwards, he'd thought how nice it was to have that kind of clout. However she'd done it, she'd gotten the DoD off their backs and Liam had written an entirely new security program for the Hoffman server.

All in all, he was feeling very good about things. He'd feel a lot better if Sydney finished her damn phone call and got her very delectable ass back in the hot tub.

He set his wineglass back on the deck, stretched out his arms along the rim and leaned back, letting the sun drench him.

"I'd say that's the picture of a very contented man." Sydney's musical voice was like a caress.

"I'd be a lot more contented if the love of my life was naked and in this hot tub with me," he answered without opening his eyes.

"Is that so? Well, maybe we can arrange that."

The water moved as she eased herself into it and shifted around until she was not only facing him but straddling him, her legs wrapped around his waist. He could feel the naked flesh of her sweet, sweet pussy — freshly waxed — as it pressed against his skin. His cock, already demanding attention, bumped its length against her.

"Somebody's anxious to come out and play," she teased, sliding back and forth.

Liam cupped her ass with his palms and squeezed the firm flesh.

"He's more than ready to. But first tell me about your phone call. Another hotshot client who can't wait for you to return?"

"Not this time. The word is out. Sydney's off-limits until the end of the week."

"Damn good thing, too."

He gave her ass another squeeze then slid his hands up along her sides until he reached her breasts. He gave each nipple a gentle pinch. Then another one, not so gentle.

She tilted her head back. "Hmmm. Wonder if I can extend this time off one more week."

Liam laughed. "Not that I wouldn't like it, but I think both of us have things we need to get back to." Then he sobered. "I'll never be able to thank you enough for taking care of everything so I *would* have something to get back to."

"You were innocent," she reminded him. "Truly innocent. That put me ahead of the game to begin with."

"So, what was the call?"

"Well, smart ass." She paused and rubbed her center against him again, groaning as he continued to torment her nipples. "Remember we discussed about where we were going to live?"

He'd never forget it. That discussion had taken place in his bedroom after he'd made her come three straight times before finally sliding into her and giving them both an explosive orgasm that he thought he could still feel. It had been two weeks after the case against him was dropped, two weeks in which they'd stolen every free moment to be together. It might have been fast and furious, and exacerbated by the high-voltage situation that surrounded them. But they had both agreed they had found something very exceptional. That their feelings for each other weren't temporary or based solely on sex.

"I love you, Syd. I've never told it to another woman and I don't expect I ever will."

"Ditto." She'd kissed him then, and given his bottom lip a gentle bite. "God! Who'd have thought something this great would come out of that disaster."

And that meant they needed to move in together.

The question was where.

"Uh-huh. You pointed out that while my townhouse was great, it didn't really provide for a lot of privacy, being right on the street the way it was."

"And that my condo was wonderful but we really needed a bigger one."

He nodded. "Go on."

"That was my assistant. Everyone else knows not to call me upon pain of death. Anyway, I put her on the hunt and there's a condo in my building that would be perfect for us that is about to come on the market. It's exactly what we want."

She gave him all the details. Liam believed he could live with Sydney in a jungle hut but he knew getting a new place was high on their list.

"Let's do it. Our places will sell very fast so we won't have to worry about that."

"I love a man who makes up his mind in a hurry."

He brushed his lips against hers. "Good, because I love you, Syd. I want everyone to know you're mine."

"Ditto." She nipped his lower lip.

"I can't wait until we're living together," he told her. "Permanently."

She lifted an eyebrow. "Permanently?"

"Uh-huh. I want to marry you, Syd. I want everyone to know you're mine and I'm yours."

A look of vulnerability suddenly filled her eyes. "Are you sure, Liam? Because we can live together a long time while we make sure."

"I'm sure. I was sure five minutes after I met you." He ran his tongue over her lips. "What about you?"

She smiled. "I'm sure, too."

"I think we should seal the deal. Don't you?"

When she nodded he slid a hand between them so he could reach her cunt, sliding his fingers between the soft lips and rubbing the tender flesh. Each time be brushed her clit, she sucked in a breath, so he did it over and over again. She rode his hand, clinging to his shoulders and moving her hips back and forth.

Liam wasn't sure how long he could hold on, as badly as he wanted and needed her right now. But he wanted to make sure he gave her every bit of pleasure he could first. When her movements intensified, he pinched her clit hard, before sliding two fingers deep inside her core.

"Oh, god!" She pushed down on his hand.

Liam cupped her head with his free hand and pulled her close for a kiss while he continued to drive his fingers into her again and again. He nipped her bottom lip before soothing it with his tongue and thrusting that tongue inside her.

Damn, but she tasted good. His cock was sending him urgent messages, but he told it to behave. He wasn't finished with this. He increased the pace of his hand, adding a third finger, stretching her and reaching deep inside her. She moved her hips, riding that hand, letting her tongue duel with his. Her sexy little sounds made him even harder.

Then he felt it, the first little flutters in the walls of her pussy, first stronger, then harder. He increased the pace of his hand even more, stretching his thumb to reach her clit. Then, there it was, her body shattering, her inner walls gripping his fingers with the power of a vise. He felt the strength of her spasm clear through his arm. He stroked her with his fingers until the last of the little tremors faded away. She dropped her head onto his shoulder and let out a long shuddering breath.

"You always make me feel so good," she murmured.

"How about this?"

She was so wrung-out she was pliant in his arms as he turned them both and moved so her core was directly aligned with one of the jets. Then he punched the button for the highest speed, the stream of water now forcefully pulsing right on her clit.

"Oh, god, Liam. Oh, god."

She tried to squeeze her thighs together, but he pushed them farther apart and tilted her body for maximum effect. It didn't take long until she began to move in his grasp, moaning as the water punished her soft, tender flesh. The second orgasm hit her with sudden force, and she shuddered in his grasp as the walls of her pussy spasmed.

The orgasm had barely subsided before he lifted her out of the hot tub then hauled himself up on the deck to join her. In seconds she was under him on the big double lounger, he'd rolled on a condom and, lifting her legs over his shoulders to open her wider, he drove into her with one hard, fast thrust.

Liam had to close his eyes and hold his breath to keep from coming right then and there, but he wanted to feel her squeeze around his cock. Reaching for his control, he began that slow glide and thrust, in and out, now slower, now faster.

He had to clench his teeth to hang on to his control. His cock was so swollen, his balls ached so much he was afraid they'd explode. Then he felt it, the first of the little spasms in her inner walls. Bracing himself on one arm, he slipped the other hand between them to find her clit, massaging it with quick yet gentle strokes. Her breath came in short, quick pants as her body responded to the friction, the thrust of his cock filling her completely.

The orgasm hit them simultaneously, ripping their bodies and shaking them with the force of a hurricane. His cock throbbed and pulsed inside her as her inner walls grabbed and milked him. He had no idea how long it went on, only that they seemed to be caught up in a hurricane.

Then it subsided, like the waves in a storm rolling back from the beach, leaving them limp and spent. Liam had no idea how much time had passed while their breathing returned to normal and their heartbeats settled into an even rhythm. Liam took her mouth in a slow, soft kiss, caressing it with his tongue, drinking from her with a kind of desperation. Then, still joined, he smiled at her.

"So. When are we going to do this?"

She lifted an eyebrow. "Do what? I thought we were already doing it."

"Get married."

"Wow." Sydney just stared at him. "In a hurry, are you?"

"Uh-huh." He brushed a kiss over her lips. "I want everyone in the world to know how I feel about you. I want you to be my wife."

She was silent for so long, studying his face and his eyes, he wondered if she'd changed her mind in the last few minutes. Then she smiled, a little upturn of the lips.

"As soon as you want to."

"As soon as I want to? I want all the words, Sydney Alfiore, soon to be Sydney Benedict. I hope."

Now the grin was wider, warmer. "Yes, I'll marry you, Liam Benedict, just as fast as we can arrange it."

"The sooner the better?"

"As soon as we get back, if you want."

He grinned. "I definitely want." Then he sobered. "This whole episode nearly destroyed me, Syd, but it taught me one thing. When you have something good, hold on to it with both hands."

"We'll hold on to each other.,"

And for the first time since the alarm had gone off on his watch, Liam Benedict felt at peace.

Want to see more from this author? Here's a taster for you to enjoy!

Corporate Heat: Masquerade
Desiree Holt

Excerpt

The night was hot and muggy, typical of Florida any time of the year but especially in the summer. The force of it hit Craig Wainwright as he emerged from the air-conditioned office building into the sticky heat that surrounded him. He was glad that he'd learned years ago to dress for comfort, favoring lightweight slacks, and soft collar shirts with the Elite Marketing logo on as opposed to more formal ties and button-downs.

He'd hoped that because he worked late, the oppressive heat of the day would have faded, but no such luck. Just something else to add to his itchy mood, one that had plagued him for more than a week. He had some decisions to make — very unpleasant ones that he wasn't looking forward to. He definitely didn't want to have the talk he planned with Lindsey, but it couldn't be helped.

Making Lindsey Califaro executive vice-president of Elite was one of the smartest things he'd ever done. It allowed him to pursue side projects without worrying about the agency's operation. But he hadn't been fair to her, and that day of reckoning was coming far too soon. The headache he'd been fighting all evening was a sign that he couldn't put this off any longer. He had called her tonight and asked her to meet him early for coffee at the office. Maybe he'd stop and pick up some of those French breakfast rolls she loved so much. Something to put her in a good mood.

How the hell had he gotten himself in this fix, anyway?

He was glad his car had the ability to start remotely, letting the air-conditioning kick in and cool the air before he had to climb into the vehicle. Hitting his key fob, he unlocked his car, to slide in behind the steering wheel and press the button to engage the motor. Modern science was wonderful, providing every possible creature comfort imaginable. And Craig was all about comfort.

As he pulled out of the parking garage and headed toward Las Olas Boulevard and home, his thoughts shifted in another direction. The pressure from the other Elite activities was getting to him. He wasn't sure how much more he could take. It forced him into a crazy schedule and the pressure of dealing with it was affecting him physically. In the past few weeks he'd developed a tendency toward blinding headaches. A checkup with his doctor revealed exactly what he thought—they were cause by tension. Now he had a small bottle of little blue pills that could attack the pain the moment he took them. He'd popped one during his last half hour at work, just to take the edge off.

Too bad they aren't the other *little blue pills.*

He smiled at the thought. Maybe he'd get a prescription for those, too. Not that he thought he really needed them. He was positive his problems in the bedroom had the same cause as his headaches. What he really needed was to take two weeks off and spend it with Natalia, his wife, straightening out their lives. He had never dreamed the situation would escalate the way it had. He wanted to go back to the way things had been *before*, even if it meant shrinking his income. He had certainly accumulated enough to spare.

Yeah. Fat chance.

He sighed and turned on the radio, searching for one of his programmed stations. *Ah. There.* Soft instrumental music. That would help him relax. He was wound up as tight as a drum and he wanted to ease up before he got home. Maybe he'd take a little detour. The major thoroughfares were fairly empty this time of night. Yes, that was it. He'd take a drive on I-95. Maybe he could put off the inevitable a little while longer.

Changing direction, he entered the highway, turned up the radio a little and rolled down the windows. A soft breeze blew through the car. Maybe it would soothe him even more. The pill hadn't done as much as usual. In fact, his headache seemed to be getting worse. The familiar band tightened around his skull, shooting pain into his eyes. And now a sharp stab in his chest had been added.

Can't breathe. Can't breathe.

Maybe he should pull over onto the verge. There wasn't much traffic this time of night. He could sit there for a few minutes until the worst of the pain subsided. He turned on his signal and began to ease toward the right. As he did so, a car behind him was suddenly on his bumper, bright lights flooding his vehicle and exacerbating his pain.

What the hell?

"Hey, buddy. Back the fuck off."

As if he'd heard him, the driver did just that, but the moment Craig began to ease to the right again, there he was, practically kissing his rear bumper. Thank god there were so few cars about at the moment.about. He didn't want to crash into any of them. Suddenly the driver behind him began flashing his lights from bright to regular to bright. On, off, on, off. It only exacerbated the pain in Craig's head and chest, which were becoming intolerable. He'd have to pull off and figure out how to deal with the idiot behind him.

Without signaling, he cut across two lanes and headed for the shoulder. At that moment, the pain spiked and he thought his body would explode. He tried to maintain control of his car, but the pain stole his breath and shut down his brain. He barely even felt the impact of the crash as he hit the barricade wall.

And then he felt nothing.

* * * *

The ringing of her cell phone woke Lindsey Califaro from a deep sleep. She looked at the clock. *Midnight.* Who on earth was calling her at this hour? The phone chimed again and she checked the readout, eyes widening. *Wainwright.* What the hell? Why would Craig call her from the landline at his house?

"Lose your cell phone, boss?" she asked. "And by the way, did you check the time?"

"Lindsey?" The words came out in a rush. "Oh, thank god. This is Natalia."

Natalia? Why would she be calling? Where's Craig? Has he asked his wife to call because he's busy? At midnight?

"Yes, Natalia. What's going on?" She pushed her hair out of her eyes and tucked it behind her ears.

"Oh, Lindsey. I need your help. The most awful thing has happened. Craig's dead."

Shocked reverberated through her body and for one second she thought her heat had stopped beating.

"Craig's dead?" Even repeating the words did not make sense. When she'd left him at the office he'd been fine. Distracted and tense, but no more so than usual.

She tried to remember her last conversation with the man tonight. Had there been a problem she'd failed to catch?

"Dead?" She must be hearing things. "Did you say he was dead? But when I left him earlier tonight he seemed fine. What happened?"

Maybe those headaches he'd been complaining about were worse than she'd thought.

"An accident on I-94." Natalia's voice was shaky. A one-car accident. What was he doing there? He was supposed to be on his way home. To me."

A good question. Something was very, very wrong here.

"The police were just here." Natalia's voice sounded less than steady, unusual for her. "Lindsey, they wanted to take me to identify the body. I-I don't think I can do that by myself, and they insisted I come down there now. Could you please go with me?"

Her voice broke a little. Lindsey wasn't used to hearing the woman in an emotional state.

"Are you sure you wouldn't rather call one of your friends?"

"No. No, you're the person I want." Her voice dropped. "Please do this for me. If it is Craig, he'd want it to be you with me."

"Of course." As she spoke she was pulling clothes out of drawers and her closet. "I'll be on my way in just a few. Hang tough, Natalia. We'll get through this."

Hang tough. What kind of advice is that to give to a brand-new widow?

It was strange to hear Natalia Wainwright so unsettled. The woman could be the poster child for self-control. Smart, beautiful and rich, it was her money that had funded Elite Marketing and her connections that had brought them to the attention of the vast international conglomerate, Arroyo. Lindsey had joined the firm three years earlier and immediately been given specific accounts to handle that kept her more than busy

All the lights were on in the Wainwrights' huge home in Idylwyld, the very exclusive community where they lived. Natalia must have been watching for her, because the gate at the foot of the driveway swung open before Lindsey could touch the control box. She had barely pulled up to the front of the house when the door opened and Natalia hurried out, purse in hand.

"Thank you for coming." She drew in a breath and let it out slowly. "I think I'm still in a state of shock. Craig was such a careful driver. I cannot imagine how this happened."

Lindsey glanced at the woman as she settled herself in the passenger seat. Dressed impeccably in black slacks and a black silk blouse, she wore no makeup and her hair was pulled back in a tight ponytail. Not her usual look. A good indication of her state of mind that she hadn't taken the time to primp and fuss.

"We'll find out everything," Lindsey assured her. "Okay? Just take a deep breath."

"I keep hoping this is just a big mistake." Natalia had a death grip on her purse. "That you'll take a look at…whoever this is and we'll see it's the wrong man."

"Unfortunately," Lindsey said, "they wouldn't make the notification unless they were pretty sure. They could at least match his driver's license photo."

"Of course, of course. You're right." Hands clasped tightly in her lap, she was silent for the rest of the ride.

Lindsey had little in common with Natalia Wainwright and neither of them seemed to have much to say to each other. There wasn't much talking at the morgue, either. She recognized Craig's body right away. Beside her, Natalia just stared for a long time before giving a sharp nod of her head and turning away.

"Can you tell me what happened?" Natalia asked the cop who'd met them at the morgue.door.

"I wish I could. Someone saw the wreck and called it in. It looks like for whatever reason he ran full tilt into the retaining wall."

Natalia's eyes widened. "Deliberately?"

"I can't say, ma'am. There are still a lot of details to sort out. Someone will be in touch with you."

"What about…the body?"

"As soon as they finish the autopsy, they'll release it to you."

"A-autopsy?"

The cop nodded. "To determine if the accident was alcohol or drug-related."

Natalia's face paled, but she just nodded. Lindsey waited as the woman signed whatever papers they needed then walked in tight-lipped silence to the car. The drive back to the house was as long and uncomfortable as the one on the way in.

"Thank you again for this." Natalia climbed out of the car, her face expressionless.

"If you'd like some help with the funerals arrangements…" Lindsey began.

"The funeral. Yes, yes, of course. Thank you. I'll let you know when they tell me I can move forward with it." She started to close the door, then turned back. "I suppose we'll have to meet to discuss Elite, also. After I've figured out how to deal with this nightmare, of course."

"Elite. Of course. Just let me know. I'll make myself available."

"Thank you. Right now, I'm still trying to make sense out of tonight."

Lindsey wasn't sure if she should just drive off or not.

"Would you like me to call someone to be with you? I'm not sure you should be alone right now."

Natalia shook her head. "No. Thank you, but…no. I think I need to be by myself right now and try to figure out how this happened. But again, thank you."

"Of course."

Lindsey watched the woman until she walked into the house and closed the front door. She sat for a moment, rubbing her forehead, wondering if she'd imagined the entire thing.

Well, that was totally weird. I still don't know why she called me instead of a friend. And what was that about Elite? Has she forgotten it's not an independent corporation any longer?

When she was far enough away from Idylwyld, she tapped the controls on her steering wheel. It was close to two o'clock in the morning, but she was sure Taylor Cantrell would not want her to wait until morning to call.

"Siri, call Taylor Cantrell."

She had all the Arroyo numbers programmed into her cell, and that included Taylor's personal phone, which she'd insisted Lindsey have access to. She wasn't surprised when the woman herself picked up on the second ring.

Does she ever sleep?

"Hello, Lindsey. It must be pretty damn important for you to call me this late at night."

"I'd say it is." She blew out a breath. "I have some very bad news. Craig Wainwright died in a one-car accident tonight."

There was silence for one second. Two.

"Was he drunk?"

"Absolutely not. He would never drink and drive. He was a maniac about it. In fact, he was working late at the office, still wrapped up in something when I went home."

Now she heard the murmur of voices, soft in the background.

"I've had some questions about Elite lately," Taylor said when she came back to the conversation. "And about Craig himself. Who made the identification?"

"His wife. She called me after the police notified her and asked me to go with her. It was definitely him, unfortunately."

"How is Natalia doing?"

Lindsey thought for a moment. "Hard to say. She's always been a very controlled person, and I could tell she was doing her best to hold on to her emotions."

"All right. Give me a minute." More talking in the background. "We'll be arriving at the Fort Lauderdale airport in the morning. We'll have transportation so no need to pick us up, but I would like you to meet us at the office. The employees have to be notified and you and Noah and I need to have a closed-door meeting."

Lindsey made a turn, heading toward the area where she lived.

"I have to ask. Am I in some kind of trouble?"

"Far from it. In fact, you're probably going to be our most important person in the days to come. Get some sleep. We'll see you there at seven."

Lindsey disconnected and checked the time. It as already close to two a.m. She'd have to sleep fast at this rate. She wondered if the Cantrells ever slept. And what it was they wanted to discuss just with her.

She had a feeling in the pit of her stomach the coming days were going to be anything but fun.

About the Author

A multi-published, award winning, Amazon and USA Today best-selling author, Desiree Holt has produced more than 200 titles and won many awards. She has received an EPIC E-Book Award, the Holt Medallion and many others including Author After Dark's Author of the Year. She has been featured on CBS Sunday Morning and in The Village Voice, The Daily Beast, USA Today, The Wall Street Journal, The London Daily Mail. She lives in Florida with her cats who insist they help her write her books, and is addicted to football.

Desiree loves to hear from readers. You can find her contact information, website details and author profile page at http://www.totallybound.com.

www.ingramcontent.com/pod-product-compliance
Lightning Source LLC
Chambersburg PA
CBHW030919260626
47169CB00002B/326